# pest Wounds

## McIntyre series, book 3

*ovel*

don Brown

Published by
Strident Publishing Ltd
22 Strathwhillan Drive
The Orchard
Hairmyres
East Kilbride
G75 8GT

Tel: +44 (0)1355 220588
info@stridentpublishing.co.uk
www.stridentpublishing.co.uk

First published by Strident Publishing, 2017
Text © Gordon Brown, 2017
Cover art & design by Andrew Forteath
Typeset in Plantin by Andrew Forteath
www.andrewforteath.co.uk

A catalogue record for this book is available from the British Library.

ISBN 978-1-910829-18-9

Printed by Bell & Bain

Books by Gordon Brown:

*The Craig McIntyre series*
*Darkest Thoughts* – book 1
*Furthest Reaches* – book 2
*Deepest Wounds* – book 3

*Falling*
*59 Minutes*

# Chapter 1

There's a time to die and a time to live. It's my time to die. The rope around my neck is tight. Air is already at a premium. I'm drawing short breaths. Asphyxiation is not a good way to go. Lack of oxygen and an excess of $CO_2$ demands that the body breathes.

The rope draws taut around my throat. Rough hemp. Scraping skin as I twist my head. The fan above me beats out the rhythm of a failing heart. The blindfold I'm wearing lets no light in.

My feet are numb. Up on my tiptoes I sway. The rope keeps me vertical. My neck is taking the strain every time I over-balance. My hands are tied behind my back.

The room is cold. The winter outside has come inside. To add to the chill, the fan blows an iced wind onto my head. The nearby door, open to the outside world, lets freezing rain splash on me. My naked body shivers.

A gust and the chair wobbles. My feet dance. My neck strains. The radio in the room tells me that for $199 down and nothing to pay for six months I can own a new waterbed.

I chew on the gag. The gasoline in my mouth is bitter. The gasoline on my body is leaking more heat from my skin as it evaporates.

The door to the outside cracks back on its hinges, as more wind is funneled into the room. My toes, slick with fluid, slide on the chair. I brace my neck and pull myself upright. My throat is closing. I gag. I slip and slide. Gain some purchase but the rope is a little tighter. A slip knot. A choker.

A howl from a beast outside echoes around the room, like a warning from Hades. Distant. I lift myself a quarter of an inch higher. Enough to ease the thick necklace. I draw in air. Cold sustenance pours down my throat. My life, measured in two half-full lungs. Ill-inflated balloons – crumpled plastic bags in my chest. I hold the air. Maxing the oxygen exchange. Sucking the last molecule.

My ribs start to hurt. Aching. The air inside me is heating up. My body wants to spit it out and drag in the fresh stuff. The primeval in my head is taking over. I exhale. Air sprays between my teeth. My toes fold. The rope grabs.

I search for anger. Defiance. A last throw of the dice when the game is already over. But my vocal chords are neutered. A dribble of spit leaks between my lips.

My feet slip again. The rope grips, my toes losing contact with the chair as my airway slams shut. Blind panic kicks in. I thrash around. My world lights up. Flashes of brilliance as rods and cones fire. No last thoughts. No lifetime in a heartbeat. No last minute calm. Just sheer fear.

My feet scrabble for the chair. A toenail clicks on the surface. I try to focus. To slow down. I search for the wood beneath me – my feet slashing. Inside my head there's nothing but a scream. And the scream is all I can hear. All I can do. All that I am.

Then I'm down. Falling. I slam into the chair and bounce off it. I roll across the floor. The rope is still tight but I can breathe. I suck. Suck hard. Hauling at the air. My throat is a raw pipe. I roll onto my side. A quarter of a breath. I try to inhale and exhale at the same time. I choke as more air rushes in. My heart is a tap dancer in full flow.

'Had enough?'

I ignore the voice.

The screaming in my head has stopped. I bite another chunk of air from the room and chew.

'Enough?'

I cough up bile. Then drink in more of the breathable stuff.

'I said, have you had enough?'

The voice is a few feet away. Not threatening. Not really a hard question. More a gentle enquiry. Quiet, assured – like asking if you want another beer midway through a Friday night in the pub.

As my breathing eases, my head goes looking for the past. Why am I here? What the hell is going on?

'I'm stopping this. This isn't helping.'

I agree with the voice. This isn't helping at all. In what way could this help anyone? But the statement suggests that help was the desired end game. I want to nod. I also want to enjoy the next breath. The breath wins.

'Craig. This is as extreme as it gets. No more.'

The blindfold is ripped from my head. I close my eyes as the light blinds me and, then, after a few seconds, I open them slowly, adjusting to the re-introduction of vision. Blinking. Squinting. Focusing. The man above me steps away. A door shuts, stopping the cold breeze.

'This is just fucking stupid.'

I agree again. But stupid is the wrong word. It implies that I'm a co-conspirator. Part of this. It implies that help and stupidity are not mutually exclusive. That one led to the other. Unintended but causal.

Hands work behind me to free the bonds.

'Can you get up?'

I'm cold as death, the floor is slick with gasoline. My muscles are fatigued – burnt out from trying to keep me upright. I shake my head.

'Lie there for a moment. I'm not up for lifting your naked corpse. Friends or not.'

Friends. What kind of friend would subject someone to this?

'Here.'

A coat lands on me.

'Curl up in that. I'll start the shower. Once I've cleaned up in here I'll get the fire going.'

I lie. Shivering. My breathing shallow. Normalizing. Thoughts swirling. I find the past. And it dawns on me.

I asked for this to be done to me.

*

Charlie pours me a glass of JD and Coke. Not cola, the real thing. Two lumps of ice. More JD than Coke. The perfect serve. I'm showered. Dressed in jeans and a sweat top – the word *Really?* writ large on my chest. Sneakers and sport socks wrap my feet. I'm hugging a fresh blanket. The fire in the grate is building to a peak. The smell of gasoline still lingers but Charlie has been thorough. The smell is in my nose – the room has been scrubbed clean.

Charlie sits across from me. A bodybuilder of old. Medals to show for it. Thick in the chest. Bald on top. With my lack of hair, together we're two eggs. His T-shirt is too tight. More fat than muscle in places where there used to be more muscle than fat.

'I nearly died.' My voice is hoarse.

'No you didn't. I had you the whole time.'

'You let me swing.'

'You told me to go for it. All the way, you said. Don't hold back.'

'And you enjoyed it.'

He laughs. 'Can't deny it. Watching you dance naked has always been a fantasy of mine.'

'Was I good?'

'I've seen better.'

I laugh. Sore. 'Zip though?'

'You tell me.'

'Nothing. I can't tell if that's good or bad.'

'Got to be good.'

I sip at the drink. 'If the curse is lifted, I agree.'

'Do you think it is?'

I know it's not. 'No. Bottled but not gone.'

Chalrie points at the table. 'That was out there. I've seen you let it loose with far less.'

My name is Craig McIntyre and I'm a freak of nature. I bring out the worst in people. I act as a catalyst for violence in others. I may be the by-product of some fucked-up experiment by a secret US organisation. I'm a weapon. Designed as an assassin. I affect people who know each other. Under stress I release the evil in them. Buried history pulled to the surface. In simple terms, you can put me in a room and someone will probably kill someone else.

How does it work? I've no idea. Am I really an experiment? I'm not sure. Paranormal? Supernatural? Who knows. Well, someone does. Just not me. Nor Charlie.

I've been through hell over the years. Been responsible for the deaths of hundreds. I'm a wanted man. In the main by a senator – Tampoline. An evil bastard. I'm valuable merchandise to him. He heads up an agency. Some deep-cover black-ops shit. We've clashed twice. I've got away from him twice. Whatever it is that I can do he wants it – he wants it with sugar on.

And he wants it bad enough to be on my tail. He's running for president. I know things he doesn't want given the oxygen of publicity. So I'm a man on the run. I have two friends: Charlie, a bar tender from Los Angeles, and Martyn, another one of Tampoline's 'most wanted'. He too has a screwed-up superpower. I bring out the bad. Martyn can put people to sleep. Marvel will never turn us into caped wonders but at least I'm not alone.

Such is the life of Craig McIntyre.

'Penny for your thoughts?' Charlie is leaning on the arm of the chair.

'My JD is dry.' I throw the last of the drink down my throat.

Charlie shakes his head. 'You ask me to near kill you and

now I'm your slave.'

I hold our my glass. 'Comes with the territory. You've bound yourself to me for life. The alternative is that I report you for attempted murder.'

'That's nice. Try and help a friend and what do you get?' He pauses and then looks me in the eye. 'Seriously, what we just did is as extreme as it gets. And nothing happened?'

'Nada. But it's still there. Buried in my head. I can feel it. Curled up tight.'

'Did you keep it locked up?'

'Maybe. But at the end all I was doing was trying to survive.'

'I thought it was stress that brought your shit out.'

'So did I.'

We were trying to release my inner demon. To push the envelope. To see where it got us. It was a dumb attempt. I need two in the room as a minimum but I thought I knew enough about what I can to do to sense if it wanted out of the box. I think I've learned the sum total of nothing. In the process I got a hell of a lot closer to death than I intended.

Beyond the door the night begs to get in. Charlie found this place after my first tangle with Tampoline. Charlie used to own a bar in LA. Michael's. An Irish bar. If you were blind.

'Do you miss the bar?' I take the new JD from him.

'Yes. Thanks for fucking it up for me.'

'Hey. You could have cut me loose anytime.'

'And the last I'd have seen of you would have been in an open casket.'

'You think open's the way to go.'

'With *your* face I'd go for the lead-lined lid – nailed down.'

'Gold handles?'

'Brass.'

'Figures.'

The chat is light. It's my way of escaping the obvious. I'm not full of options. I have a pocketful that I've examined on more occasions than makes sense. Each one a sticky candy, rejected and re-wrapped – but not discarded. Any option is good but none, so far, have tasted right. All have been tough chews with little going for them. I want ones that taste better. Chocolate-coated normal. Easy to digest. A treat to look forward to.

A few in my pocket have a nice flavour but turn sour if you munch on them long enough. Most have the flavour of sweat. Hard graft to stay ahead of the chasing pack. Candy for a runner. I want candy for a lazy bastard. It turns out that, in my local shop, that flavor's out of stock. Charlie's worried. He knows what trails in behind me. He also knows the resources that Tampoline has. But he never stops being there.. He just keeps giving.

The fact that he killed my wife might have something to do with his loyalty to me.

# Chapter 3

The bed is like Goldilocks' second choice – too soft. Sleep is far away. I stare at the ceiling. My throat hurts. I reach over to grab another bottle of water. The third in an hour. I'll be pissing like a racehorse soon. Charlie has left the question of 'what next' alone. I haven't. It dances around my head. A naughty child that won't sit down. One that keeps asking the same dumb thing. *What do I do?* And each time I give the same dumb answer. *I don't know.*

I hear a snap from beyond the window. In this neck of the woods noises from outside don't scare me. We're wrapped in the sticks, where wild things roam free. City folk like me know nothing of the dark out here. But I do know that the animals don't consider it an invasion of our privacy if they come up to this house. Yesterday a young doe lay not five yards from the back door. Catching the sun. Two days ago a rat the size of a bread bin tried to sneak in the cat flap. This is where the wild meets the tame.

The noise repeats. A sharp snap. Twig on stone? Claw on concrete? Tooth on bone? I envisage a bear chewing on our leftovers. Except that Charlie has seen to that. All waste is wrapped tight. Held in the garage until he can get to the dump. Leaving food around is rolling out the red carpet to the zoo.

A cough. My breathing stops. The cough is from outside. Not Charlie. His snore is still good to go.

Shit.

I'm still clothed. It's been an age since I last stripped to go to bed. Born to run, as Bruce would say. I slide my feet over the edge of the mattress. My boots are sitting ready. Laces undone. Easy to slide on.

I lift the handgun sitting next to my boots, before sliding

it under my trouser belt. The drapes in here are solid. Heavy duty. Built to keep heat in. I move in the pitch black and slide my hands near my thighs – ready to push up. I listen intently.

Nothing.

I slowly ease myself from the springs beneath. They uncoil with a hiss. Air filling voids. I turn to the door.

We have a plan for this. Charlie insisted on it. I pull my cell from my pocket. A cheap pre-paid model with no calls made or received. It's searching for a network. When it finds it I'll press the number three. Short dial. Charlie's phone should be under his pillow – on vibrate. I keep my hand over the screen. Shading the light. But I can see that it's not connecting. There is a signal around here. It just goes walkabout every so often.

Finally a bar appears on the phone. I press *3*. It rings to an answering machine. I kill it before it tells me to leave a message. *Come on Charlie; we've rehearsed this a dozen times.*

I grab the door handle. Listening. More coughs. Not the sign of a professional. Or maybe we have a professional on a bad day. Or someone out for a walk. Unlikely – we're twenty miles from the nearest town and two miles down a dirt track from the nearest road.

The night holds no new sounds.

I hit *3* again. Charlie's bedroom is at the other end of the house. Plan A is for him to check the rear – me the front.

I'm on my way to do my bit. He, on the other hand, is sleeping – the phone kicks to answer machine again. I check the corridor. Clear. I keep my part of the bargain and start for the main room. I hit redial again.

The room still holds some heat. The fire has a faint glow. Dying embers. I concentrate on the job at hand, keeping away from the windows, backing along the rear wall. I pass by the fire. The heat plays on my legs.

The shadow from the fire casts me on the far wall. I press the cell yet again. It rings. Then a text.

*Fuck off.*

At a rough guess I would say Charlie was on my side now.

Time for an evening stroll. Whoever is outside isn't Tampoline-backed. His crew don't fuck around. They lack subtlety. Mike Tyson in *Swan Lake*. If it was Tampoline's goons I would, by now, be breathing gas while staring at a gunsmiths' wet dream of hardware.

There are two doors to this house. The one I'm next to and the one in the kitchen. I reach for the door's handle, breathe and ease the ancient Colt from my waistband. At least I know it works. I test fired it the day Charlie handed me it. It's old-school but a bullet is a bullet. It's not accurate beyond ten yards. I don't care. It looks good, it goes bang and if you are inside the kill zone it will ruin your suit.

I depress *3* again. As soon as it connects I'm out of the door. If all is well Charlie should be doing the same. We figured a long time ago that sitting tight was a one-way ticket.

It connects. I run.

# Chapter 4

My feet hit the concrete slabs that guard the door. I put my head down and sprint. No looking around. No fancy shooting from the hip. I only care that ahead of me is clear. I have a destination in mind.

I leap the small dry-stone wall that surrounds the house. Beyond the wall the land slopes away. I roll with the fall. At the bottom of the slope I swing the gun back the way I came. No one is there. I start to run to my left. Away from the cough.

Charlie came up with this plan. *Look Craig, if they want us dead we won't get time to react. If they want us alive, staying in the house is a bad idea. Surprise them. Get the fuck out. Take our chances outside. It's the only way.*

I argued over this. Even suggested digging a tunnel. Charlie laughed. *I'm not letting you watch The Great Escape again.*

I keep low. Charlie might just have been right. This is working so far. No gunshots. No shouts. No black suits rappelling from choppers. Our rendezvous point is an old elm, a hundred yards out. The cloud above keeps the light to a minimum. The tree is a ghost, materializing as I run.

I grab bark, dropping to the earth. Charlie is already there. He puts his finger to his lips, pointing to the house. A small light is bobbing towards the front door. It stops. Then it's gone. Charlie leans in. Old Spice fills my nose. So '70s.

He whispers. 'They've gone inside.'

I shake my head. 'Not *they*. Just one person so far. Do you think there'll be others?'

'Maybe, but this is no grab team. Strictly amateur.'

I agree. No one uses a flashlight to scour a building. It gives a few feet of light while you can be seen a mile away. Night vision goggles or just good old-fashioned groping are better.

I whisper through the aftershave again. 'Give it five. Then we go back.'

He nods.

I'm thinking burglar. Not agency. The sticks are a good place to turn over houses. No one nearby to see you. But, whoever it is, they're taking a risk. We have an SUV parked outside. A good sign that the house is occupied. Druggie? Smash and grab?

It used to be jewelry, TVs, DVDs. Hit the main room. Be quiet and…bingo. But our TV is nailed to the wall. It also weighs one-forty. Our DVD cost thirty dollars. My collection of Fabergé eggs is at the cleaners.

Nowadays it's mobiles, tablets, laptops, games machines, cash and – still in the top five – good old jewelry. But people keep that stuff in the bedroom. To get at that you need an empty house. The SUV says *occupied*.

From where we are the land either side of the house forms a ridge. Anyone walking will be silhouetted against the night. Pros would know that but I'm sure we are Little League here, not Yankee Stadium.

Charlie taps my shoulder. He signals. We climb back up the slope. At the dry-stone wall we wait. Listen. Watch. The near window brightens and fades. The flashlight at work.

Cough.

Feet away. We both freeze. We hear the strike of a match. A flare, just over the wall, lights up the immediate area. It's followed by the suck and chuck of a cigarette. A small cloud drifts inches from our noses. The smoker is so close I could reach over and touch their hair.

I was wrong on Little League. We're pitching to my grandmother with a beach ball. Smoking is for afters. Now I know there's at least a duo in the vicinity. What I don't know is if they're triplets?

We hold.

How we got so close without being heard is hard to fathom. Unless, off course, our unwanted guest is plugged into an iPod. I listen for the distant buzz of a disco classic. Nothing. We're not yet in *Dumb and Dumber* territory. But we're close.

I'm guessing that two is the charm. Maybe a car somewhere. It's miles to hike up here. I turn to Charlie and point over the wall. I draw my hand across my throat. He nods.

There's no easy way to subdue someone. All the fancy talk of silently taking them out is usually bollocks. There are two ways to win at this game. Fear or blunt-force trauma. The latter is simple. Remove one rock from the dry-stone wall. Lean over. Let rock meet bone. Simple but unpredictable. Skulls are hard little bastards. Miss a little and your victim cries out. Game over if there are others.

I take option one. Fear.

The man is right below me. I place the barrel of the Colt at the base of his neck. 'Move or make any noise, and I shoot.'

No fancy talk. No threats of blowing his brain to mush. It might sound cool to tell him that you will turn his perfectly-formed head into a firework if he doesn't play like a good little boy, but in situations like this you want no dubiety. Clarity is all. 'Nod if you understand?'

He nods.

Good.

Charlie climbs over the wall. He levels his gun at the vic. I lift mine clear, crossing the wall to join him.

I bend down but keep out of range of a flying fist or head-butt. 'How many of you are there? Don't speak, just nod. Two?'

He nods.

'Are you armed?'

He nods.

'Give me the gun. Slowly.'

He points to the left. A shotgun is lying on the ground. Out of reach. We are closer to *Dumb and Dumber* than I thought. I grab it and break it. It's a side by side. I eject the two cartridges before placing the weapon on the other side of the wall.

I lean down again. 'Ok, when I give the signal you're going to call for your friend. Nice and loud. Friendly. As if you've found Cameron Diaz willing to play a threesome. Do you understand?'

He nods.

I turn. 'Charlie. To the door. I'll cover this one. You welcome his pal when he comes out.'

I feel calm. In control. No sign of the inner monster wanting to get out. This is almost fun. I check myself; that's just when things go tits up.

A small wave of my hand. The signal for Charlie to move. I focus my gun on the man beside me. Every word so far has been at a whisper. 'Ok, when I signal, you shout.'

I step to the left, keeping my gun trained. I can now see both Charlie and the man. Charlie's waiting by the front door.

I step back from the world for a few seconds. Make some space. I take in the sky. Clear. Starbright. Cold air slides down my throat. The man shuffles. He's nervous. I would be. I hold a breath. Let it warm in my lungs. I stream the hot return into the night. A trail rises and spreads. My head comes up with a memory. Half a memory anyway.

Iraq. First time we went in. On watch. South of the real trouble so there was little to keep me awake. Save the cold. Two in the morning. I was deep frozen. My lightweight gear designed for summer. My sergeant had ripped me a new one about my clothing an hour earlier. But he hadn't let me get changed. That was the punishment with two dark hours to go.

I couldn't even go for a walk. My watch was on the perimeter. Out of sight. Looking for enemy. We might have been away from the main nonsense but only two days earlier an IED had taken out three of my colleagues. A week previously a sniper had body-bagged a guy I had signed up with.

Twenty-four seven you were a target. The rent per calendar month in Iraq was fear. Everybody paid. How much was up to you. If you were clever you paid a little too much. If you were dumb you tried to shortchange. Simple really. Fear was a good thing. In the right dose. It kept you alert. When it faded – that was the time to worry.

Only you didn't worry. You just felt good. Then shit happened. The boys out there didn't give a monkey's about you. They just needed a chance. Their country and all that. We weren't liberators. Invaders. So they waited. Waited for you to drop your guard. Waited for you to stop doing the basics. And the basics were there to save your skin.

The basics at this time of night are simple. Cigarettes. Out. Movement. Out. Noise. Out. Break wind but only silent killers are allowed. That night the sergeant made it clear, in sign language, that I was useless. I hadn't heard him approach. I was a rookie. A lot of us were.

Back then, unlike tonight, I couldn't see my breath. Unlike tonight, I didn't know where the enemy were. Unlike tonight I was scared. Tonight I'm not. I should be, but there's only so long you can run and keep fear next to you. It will eat you. Turn on your soul. Depression will become the norm – go ask some of my former army colleagues. I have a handle on it. I have to. Fear can turn to anger. And the monster inside me eats anger for breakfast. Feeding it is a bad idea. Anyway, it's after midnight. Everyone knows you don't feed gremlins after midnight.

The man shuffles again.

I lean forward. 'Now.'

I signal Charlie as I move but the man plays dumb. I tap him lightly on the ankle. A bruise-inducing tap. Enough to get him back on the page. 'Now.'

'Help.' He sounds like a Furbie with crap batteries.

I lean in again. 'Much louder.'

'Help!' Better.

I swing towards the door, keeping the gun on Furbie. Nothing happens. But nothing is the usual. Time plays with your head in situations like this. Ring a doorbell and you'll wait thirty seconds before trying again. That's a long time when you're primed for action.

I wait. If we reach a minute and there's no sign of Furbie's friend then we'll try again.

At forty-five seconds the door cracks. Charlie doesn't move. A head appears. Amateur night. Charlie waits. He knows what to do. If you grab someone's head you're most likely to pull the door shut on yourself.

The Head can't see Charlie. He's too close into the wall, hidden. I'm lined up between the tree and the door.

The Head opens the door and steps out. Charlie moves. Takes the man down, dropping on top of him. Forces the Head's hands up his back. Knee in the small of the back, gun playing with the guy's ear. He whispers something to him before letting him go. The man plays possum. Charlie kicks him. He's encouraged to join his friend. The new boy squeals. 'Look...'

I slap him. 'Quiet.'

I'm still thinking that three in a bed might be on. Charlie vanishes for a once around. He spent a lot longer in the army than me. Special forces? Maybe. I sat the wrong side of a bar from him for a year. He won't talk about it. He could have been a stripper at the local Wal-Mart for all he has ever said. But he did let slip that he spent time in the same institution I was shipped off to when they sent me home. That and his intimate knowledge of how to hurt people give me reason to suspect.

I kneel. Checking out the two invaders. The light is poor. Furbie is thin. He sports a short moustache, making him look like a '30s spiv. His friend is carrying a few pounds round his belt. His bloated face shows his season ticket at Burger King should really be handed back.

I keep my distance. 'Hold hands.'

They don't move. I stand. Sighing. I play football with Furbie. He grabs his friend's hand.

'Both hands.' I add.

They oblige.

Nice. As long as they keep on holding I'm not in for any surprises.

I kneel again. 'Are there any more of you?'

Furbie shakes his head.

I shake mine. 'Now, you wouldn't lie to me?'

I lift the barrel of the gun a little.

Another shake. This time from Chubby. I'm still not a believer.

★

Ten minutes tick by before Charlie returns. 'Their car is just up the track. Two sports bags. Two sleeping bags.'

I look at them both. 'Well at least you can tell the truth.'

My voice sounds loud after the silence. 'So who are you? Why are you here and who sent you? You can either tell me of your own free will or we can find ways of subverting your belief that you can tough it out. So what do you fancy? Talk or pain?'

Chubby speaks first. 'We were doing the place over, trying to see if there was anything worth stealing.'

'That's it. Burglary.'

'Yes.'

I rub my nose. My kick takes Chubby high on the thigh. 'Look I gave you the options. Let's not play dumb.'

'But...'

The second kick is in the same place. 'Let me try this for you. You aren't casual housebreakers out on the prowl. We're a country mile from civilization. You would need to know this house is here. And, if you did, you would know it's empty at this time of year. So what's to steal? But of course you knew it was occupied. Otherwise why come? An out-of-season rental will hold nothing of value. So you had to know someone was here. But you're not locals. Accent is all wrong. Also, locals wouldn't set out into the wild in brogues.'

They both look at their feet.

I press on. 'It's midwinter and your jackets are better suited to a chilly Florida night. And this isn't anywhere near Florida. You're not professionals. Anything but. You entered a house that was clearly occupied. Dumb. You didn't see us leave, even though there were two of you. God alone knows how your buddy here missed me running out of the door. But he did. And pros don't smoke at night. Nor do they sit next to a wall. Nor do they use flashlights inside a house.'

I lean in a little. 'Now this all confuses me. You're too dumb to be anything but opportunistic thieves but...' I rub my nose. 'But what's with the sleeping bags. Housebreakers don't need sleeping bags. In, out and away – is the order of the day. Well, from your smell, I'd say you've been out here a few days. Maybe hiding out in the car. Waiting. Maybe hoping we'd jump ship. But again, why? So all in all it begs the question – why are you here?'

'Could we go inside? It's cold out here.' Furbie is shivering.

'No, not yet. Tell me what's going down. Then you'll get the reward of a nice warm house round your shoulders.'

Chubby sighs but says nothing. This is painful. I raise my foot.

Furbie cowers and speaks. 'Tell him.'

Chubby looks at him as if shit has just squeezed out of his mouth.

I nod. 'Your friend is giving good advice. Talk and this can all be over.'

I want to go in. It's not just Furbie who's cold.

Chubby chews over the options. If he were hard enough he would stall. Hold out for a chance to take us. But he's not hard. He's also not going to get a chance.

He speaks. 'The internet.'

Not what I had expected. Although I'm not sure anything would be what I expected.

He continues. 'Both of you are on the internet.'

I shake my head. 'Nope. Don't think so. My Facebook page has been deleted and I can't think there's a website for strangers living in the wild. Although you never know.'

'Dark Web.'

It's like pulling teeth. 'I've heard of it…'

'There's a site and it's offering a hundred grand if the two of you are spotted.'

Charlie steps in. 'Dark Web?'

Furbie gets mouthy. 'It's like the internet only you can't track people's online habits. It's hidden and connected through many back doors.'

He almost smiles as he says this. We may have a geek on our hands.

'Who is offering the hundred grand? What do they want us for?' Charlie is playing the interrogator as well.

Chubby shrugs. 'I don't know. That's not the way it works. The site is well protected. Customers post up their most wanted and if we post a recent picture of you both, we get part of the cash. We put up an address and we get some more cash. And once they get a hold of you we get payment in full.'

The wonders of the modern age. The cold is getting to me. 'Both of you up and in. I'm still not clear on any on this but I'm also freezing my butt of here.'

# Chapter 5

The warmth is welcome. I urge our guests to take a seat. To keep holding hands. I close the door before checking the drapes. I still want to be sure there aren't more unwelcome guests. The dark beats me. If there's someone else out there I can't see them.

I snap a crick in my neck. Then drop a sigh. A deep, heartfelt gust of hot wind that carries a feeling words can't do justice to. A sense of resignation mixed with tiredness, topped up with aggravation.

Life on the run is more *Butch Cassidy and the Sundance Kid* than *Thelma and Louise*. I draw a breath back. It slides over my teeth and hits my tongue. I focus on the change in temperature as my mouth cools. The air cushions the back of my throat, pushing on my upper palate. I open the bottom of my ribcage – an age-old actor's trick – pushing my lungs to the limit. Stretching the lining. Straining muscle and bone. Hold. Count to ten. Don't let go. Count ten more. Loosen the shoulders. Rotate them in their sockets. Snapping sinew on bone. Head back. Count five more. And breathe out. Long. Deflating. Chilling.

I look up. The others are fixated on me. Who cares? It works for me. I double up on the exercise, taking in our new housemates between the counts. Furbie is leaning forward – elbows on knees. Chubby is trying to feign indifference. It isn't working. His breath is short, shallow and speedy. The fat, under his chin, is red as blood flushes his face.

I think about parking my weapon. These two look less of a threat than a pet hamster. Vicious bastards though, hamsters. I keep the gun in hand. No point in taking chances.

I lose one more breath. 'Charlie, coffee, very strong, very black and very sweet.'

'Yes, darling. Would you like me to massage your dick at the same time?'

'Would you, dear? It's been such a long time.'

Furbie and Chubby don't like the humor. They both look like they've swallowed a brick. Charlie heads to the kitchen. I can't be bothered with any more questions. Not yet. Let them sweat. See if their story changes.

Silence is a great interrogation tool. Underrated. People's heads are wonderful at screwing them over. Let someone's head stew long enough and they'll come up with a far stronger bag of consequences than I can ever dream up. These guys know they aren't getting a hundred grand to grass up their aunt. For that much money, someone wants us bad. Maybe to kill us. And that means we're dangerous. Furbie and Chubby will be thinking that over – and hard.

I slump into the chair next to the fire. The coals in the grate are gray, still warm from last night. I poke around. Some embers glow red. I throw on two logs. A few minutes later smoke rises.

Charlie comes back with two coffees. His manners with guests are appalling. I mainline the caffeine, empting the mug in two swallows. I wait for the kick.

Time for a little more Q & A. 'Ok, from the top. Let's take a trip through your fairytale again.'

They look at each other. Chubby's breathing has me a little worried. Hyperventilation lies that way. We're so deep in amateur world that I'm stunned they found us. In fact… I put my hand up as Chubby opens up to repeat the story from outside.

'Let's make it simple. How did you find us? Assuming we are who you think we are.'

'Karen Thornton,' Chubby offers in between breaths.

'Who?'

'She told us.'

'And who is Karen Thornton?'

'Lives on Caliber Street. Married to John.'

'And...'

'Her old man is Teddy.'

Charlie steps forward. 'Son, you have two minutes to start making sense or I'm going to stick your head in the fire.'

The flames are catching nicely.

Chubby gulps. 'That's how we know who you are. She told us.'

I sigh. Deeply. 'Look, I have no idea who Karen Thornton is. And whoever she is, I've no idea how she would know who we are. So let's get this shit in some sort of a decent pile. Start from the beginning.'

'I'll do it.' Furbie places his hand over Chubby's mouth. 'We are cyber bounty hunters.'

My dumb look encourages him to elucidate.

'We're able to track the people who use BitTorrent.'

My confused face helps some more.

Furbie fires on. 'It's a tool that allows you to download stuff without being traced. Film, music – worse. Only it's not untraceable if you know what you're doing. We track big-time players. We also work on cyber bullying. You know, trolls. We hire our services out for a fee.'

I play with the fire. 'And part of this service includes finding people?'

'All of our services include finding people. It's what we do. We find the bad guys and we get paid to do it.'

'Well you look the part.'

Furbie rubs at the lightweight jerkin. 'Yeah, well we don't usually leave the office. We do most of it online. Only when we've got an address do we sometimes have to check it. Most times not. But for you two it was a different game. We got a gig to find you. Anonymous, but that's not unusual. The fee was good but they wanted physical evidence.'

I'm intrigued. I've been off the grid for months. No internet.

'I'm not on the Web.'

'You've got a cell.'

'And? You're not the NSA. So how do you track a cell? And, more specifically, how do you know what cell to track? Pre-paid cells can't be easy.'

Charlie sips at his coffee. His face is a question mark. 'Look, let's rewind a touch. Trolls, BitTorrent, bounty hunters. Forget the cell for a moment. Enlighten me as to what language you're conversing in.'

Furbie's face brightens. He likes this stuff. Even with a gun in the room he wants to talk shop. 'Simple really. We live in a digital world. Communication is always on. Web, social media, phones, TV, radio...the list goes on. The air is full of ones and zeros and if it's not in the air, it's in the wires and cables. A never-ending avalanche. But with all the instant gratification comes the dark side. And we're the dark-side police.'

Charlie still looks confused.

Furbie steps it up a gear. 'Take the Web. You use it to shop, find what's on at the movies – maybe order a pizza. But there's as much communication outside the everyday Web as on it. A whole subculture. Only it's not really a subculture anymore. It's mainstream. And you can traffic what you like because it's not on Google's radar. And that's just the start. Peer-to-peer communication with encryption is now ten-a-penny stuff. You can even rig your mobile to work where Verizon don't shine. Make and receive calls through Wi-Fi or local networks. TV that has no watershed. Shows even Fox won't show. Direct satellite feeds. Some state-sponsored, some private. Satellites are getting smaller and are now in private hands. All unregulated.'

Furbie pauses to look at Chubby, who is still finding it hard to inhale and exhale at anything less than warp speed.

Furbie's on a roll though. 'Then there's the legit world – Twitter, Facebook – social media. Even there the bad guys haunt you. They post the nastier side of life. They cause distress. Lies or truths – as long as it causes grief, they don't care. Across all of this there is a new breed of hero riding the digital plains, six shooter at the ready, holding out for justice – dispensing it where others fear to tread.'

This guy is wired. His mouth is a steam piston.

He rattles on. 'We hold sway in this new world. Digital is our territory. Remember *The Matrix*? Keanu? A man plugged in to a made-up world? Then he escapes and finds a new reality? Well this is the new reality and it's here, right now. Data, servers, devices, connections... Want to know how much your dentist is worth? It's out there. Want to know you neighbor's bank balance? Out there. Want to know who is humping who? Out there. All of it. All for the want of a little time, knowledge and technical gear. Or money. Money can buy the lot. A hundred thousand is buying you. It's old-style bounty done in a new way.'

I've had enough. 'Ok, Lone Ranger. On this ride across the desert, how did you find us? Cell you said?'

Furbie grins. 'Craig McIntyre, ex US military. 1st Infantry Division, 4th Brigade, 2nd Battalion, 16th Infantry Regiment. Spent a few months in Iraq in 2003 – in Ramadi before being sent home on the Permanent Disability Retirement List. And your friend, Charlie Linton, also ex-military. Owned Michael's – an Irish bar in LA. Bugged out when the going got tough for you. He had a relationship with Tina. The relationship is kind of dead now you're both on the road.'

Charlie flares.

I put my hand up to calm him. 'Go on.'

'The Tropicana Terror a few years back. The TT. All those people going wild, killing each other. Rumor is you were there. So was a senator named Tampoline. And some black-ops guy called Lendl. He's dead now. Tampoline lost his sight and manhood and blames you. He's a big cheese – running for president.'

'Cell phone?' I add.

'Easy. We've been at this game for years. You build up a hell of a network in our world. Lots of friends. People you've helped. Especially on cyber bullying. It's a crap thing to happen to you and once we sort it out we have friends for life. And we sort it out. You might think you're some sort of star in the cyber bullying world. Wait 'til you meet us. We can wreck your life. Cyber bullies don't last long with us on their tail.'

He is so juiced I could run a George Foreman off him.

'So, step one, we put out photos of the two of you in the right places – seed the digital and wait. It always works. Someone has always seen someone and you two were spotted three months ago, less than thirty miles from here, by a lady named Karen Thornton. She works at Jesse's in Chinook. You two bought a pair of prepaids from her fair hand.'

'We did, but for cash.'

'Makes no odds. You bought Sprint and we know guys who know guys. They did us a favor. They checked all prepaid cells in the area that fired up within the time window that Karen gave us.'

'We made no calls.'

'You didn't have to. All you had to do was switch the phones on.'

I wince.

Furbie is frinning. 'So, we had your number. Next we hacked your phone and the rest was easy.'

Charlie smiles. 'That easy.'

Furbie shakes his head. 'Not really. We've been at this for a long time. I just make it sound easy.'

I stir a few more embers. 'So why not hand us in? Collect the hundred grand?'

Chubby seems to have finally taken control of the air entering his lungs. His face has lost the red hue but he still lets Furbie do the talking. 'We needed to send photos. It's part of the conditions. We need recent photos. I suppose a hundred grand draws a lot of chancers. Payment by instalments is the norm in our game.'

I shake my head. 'That's what telephoto lenses are for. Why come into the house?'

Chubby's breath speeds up again. Furbie drops quiet. I wait. Chubby splutters.

Furbie gives. 'It was Sandy's idea.'

Sandy/Chubby looks surprised at the use of his name. 'Was it hell. It was your idea.'

'Whose idea to do what?' I keep my focus on Furbie.

More silence. I wait.

'A hundred grand.' Furbie again. 'Why would you be worth a hundred grand? We get ten tops for this kind of work. We got curious.'

'So you broke in looking for what? Our hidden stash? Diamonds?'

Silence.

'Well?'

Furbie looks at the floor. 'You can't blame us. There had to be a good reason for a hundred k.'

I stop stirring. 'And you thought we would sleep through a break-in?'

More silence.

I point at Furbie and Chubby. 'Given the genius twins found us, I'm surprised the Marines are not here.'

'It ain't that easy.' Furbie sounds like a ten-year-old pleading his innocence after being caught snogging his cousin. 'Your boy Tampoline might have the might of the US behind him but what does that count for? The Unabomber hid out in the sticks for eighteen years. In the Noughties we let the 9/11 nutters in without a blink. Ok, the authorities got smarter – got on top of it all. For a while. Then Edward Snowden did us all a favour and let the world know where the art of surveillance was at with the good guys. So all the bad guys got smart as well, which means we need to up our game. And so it goes on.'

'Sounds like you guys have something to offer the Feds,' I point out.

'Not really. They're suspicious of people like us. They don't share. Don't trust us. When they do ask us, it's got more caveats than a hedge fund. You two took a lot of effort and time. And in our world time is always against us. We're never the only ones out there.'

I close my eyes. That's what was bugging me. Not a third person. Others. Others like these two. If *they*'ve been able to track us, who else can? Who else *is*?

I open my eyes. 'Will there be others?'

Chubby finds his voice. 'You can guarantee it. A hundred k is a lot of cash. There'll be *lots* of others.'

'But not as quick as you?'

Furbie shrugs. 'We got lucky with Karen. But we would have found you even without her. It might have taken a little longer but someone would have seen you. And then it's just a clock ticking.'

'How long have we got?'

Furbie throws his hands up, causing me to grip the gun more tightly. 'Ten minutes, a month – who knows. But it'll go down.' He pauses. Then: 'So what happens now?'

I shake my head. 'That's a good question. And not one that I'm going to answer while I need some sleep.'

Charlie's eyebrows go north. 'Sleep?'

'I think better after a night's kip. These two somewhat inter-rupted it. Get the duct tape. We'll make them comfortable for a few hours.'

Charlie looks like he's going to argue, then changes his mind.

I call after him as he heads for the kitchen. 'Kill your cell.' I power mine down as I say it. 'You two as well.' They don't move.

I level the gun at Furbie. 'Who would hear the shot?'

Phones fly put of pockets. I smash them with the shotgun butt. 'Any more wizardry in the car? And remember, if you lie I'll go look and come back to take your kneecaps off.'

'A couple of iPads and a laptop. All switched off.'

'GPS?'

'No.'

'Carrier pigeons?'

My joke misses. Charlie returns with the tape. He pushes both of the geeks onto the floor. Back to back, he binds them at the wrists and around the waist. He finishes off with their ankles.

Furbie moans. 'What if we need to pee?'

I lower the gun. 'It's not my carpet. Feel free.'

# Chapter 6

Sleep is not on the horizon. Furbie and Chubby have tossed a grenade into the mix. I always assumed we would be on the run from the agency for the foreseeable future. At least until I could figure a way to end this nonsense. But that plan relied on me staying one step ahead of Tampoline.

In the beginning that had me scared. Me *vs* the US of A. But lately it has been easier than I thought. Furbie and Chubby have changed that. Tampoline, or whoever posted the reward, has recruited the might of the world's geeks to his side. And that's more worrying. Geeks don't play by normal rules. They don't know there *are* rules. They see it all as a game. That makes them dangerous.

Hacktivists do it for the thrill. Denial of service attacks, WikiLeaks, shut down a bank, screw over a transport network... Just because you can. Or just because you think you have the moral high ground to occupy.

I get up to make another coffee. Halfway through making it I have a dumb idea. I can hear Charlie snoring as I walk the five yards between kitchen and living room. Furbie and Chubby are still awake.

I kick Furbie. 'I need some information. It might help your cause if you're straight with me. Killing the two of you is still the easiest way to move on.'

'Can I have coffee?'

I tip some into his mouth. He swallows. Chubby just watches.

I sit next to Furbie. 'If you had to drop out completely how would you do it?'

'What, off the grid?'

'Yes.'

'It's not easy. For a start I'd get out of the US. You two are way too hot. But – and this is good news – you're not wanted for anything on a legit level. At least nothing that makes sense. You're not flagged as terrorists and you're on none of the official lists. We checked. That makes you odd. It also means that outside of the States you'd be harder to find.'

'Why?'

'If you were high profile it would be a different game. But the fact you're on the Dark Web means they're trying to keep it under wraps. No official trail. That makes it harder to call in favors from foreign friends.'

'And you think Tampoline might be behind this?'

'It's possible.'

'So we need to get outside the US.'

'That would be my number one goal.'

'Where?'

'It makes no odds.'

'Ok. Let's talk about how much you really know about Charlie and me?'

'That's easy. My top pocket. The one with the zipper. There's a flash drive. Plug it in. The password is C*99(3.'

I get a pen and write the password down. I pull the flash drive out of his pocket. 'Now what do I do for a laptop?'

'Ours are in the car.'

I'm in for a stroll. 'Keys?'

'It's not locked.'

'Is the laptop hidden?'

'Under the mat on the passenger side.'

'Password for that?'

He tells me.

'What will you do with us both?' Chubby's breathing is calmer.

'Not sure.'

Fifteen minutes later I'm installed in a car that needs

de-fumigated. The floor is awash with discarded food and wrappers. Pringles seem to be the diet of choice. Empty cans of Red Bull testify to the long haul of a stake out. The back seat is filled with clothing. It smells well used. I keep the window down, cranking up the engine, flicking the heater to full.

The laptop is a scruffy machine. I've never heard of the make but it fires up with speed. I tap in the password. Pushing in the flash drive I open the passenger window a bit more. The smell is growing as the heat kicks in. A cold breeze chills my head. The heater burns my feet.

The flash drive has one file. I click on it. I discover that some-one has been writing our biographies. A word doc for me, the same for Charlie.

I scan mine. Short but with a little depth. A series of copies of records. My stint in the army. My time in Hatch Roll as a patient. My job in Iraq with Steeltrap Security. Even a reference to my screw-up, when a state official and a prostitute died on my watch. A vague reference to the TT, annotated with my name and a question mark next to it. A picture of Lorraine. Another clip from a newspaper over the kidnap of Tampoline when he was in Stamford, Connecticut. My name, up there in lights, with Martyn's. No other reference to Martyn though. I wonder where he is? We went through hell with Tampoline.

Charlie's biog is shorter. He's not the target. I am. It tells me nothing new. There are two more files. The first is a scan of an old paper document. The scan is poor or the source material is faded. It looks like it was typed on a typewriter. There's not much of it. Some words are blacked out. Redacted? I zoom in a little to read it.

Subject: Dynamite.
Date: ████████

MI: Coded DNA. Full issue on all counts. Positive
on ████████ samples. Genetic pattern consistent.
Connection with subject aura highly likely. Highest
correlation with ████████ and ████████
Replication possible but technology not available.
Maybe ████████ years. Recommend annual revisit as
tech unfolds.

Highest priority.
Signed: ████████

Alfred

 

I reread it but have no idea what it is or what it has to do with me.

Try as I might, the other file won't open.

I shut down the laptop and pocket the drive. I leave the windows open. Engine running. Given there's less than a quarter of a tank left, the car will be dry by the morning.

It'll be light soon. I hurry to get back out of the cold. As I re-enter the house the duct-tape couple look at me.

I shrug. 'The copy of an old document. What has that to do with anything?'

'Why should I tell you?' Brave pills for Furbie. A last stand?

I pick up the gun. He backs down. 'Ok, so I'll tell you. It was on your file from the institution. I think it was a mistake. I don't think it was meant to be there. Your main file was easy to get.

The other file is locked solid. Even I couldn't crack it. That old document was in an appendix. I lifted it but it's nonsense.'

'Where did you get those files?'

'An agency hard drive somewhere in Washington.'

'Really.'

'Easy. If you know where to look and what you are doing.' He smiles.

I want to kick him. 'Why would that old document be on my file?'

'You tell me.'

Charlie's standing in the door.

I stretch, pointing to the door. Charlie walks.

Once outside we start to circle the house. We don't speak. Just thoughts. The sun is graying the sky. My soul is draped in the same colour. I turn the note over in my head but draw a blank. 'Charlie. You know what I can do. You've seen it. What do you think? Nurture or nature?'

'Craig, my bet's always been on Tampoline.'

'Nurture then. Go on.'

'What you have is an ability that the military would die for. You can turn people into killers, just by being in the same room as them. I should know. I killed your wife.'

The words from his mouth are a shock. They take me back to the prison cell. Charlie and my wife thrown together. Me strapped down. Watching. Tampoline winding me up. Setting me off. Releasing the beast. Charlie rising into the air. Lorraine's hair in his hand. And then down. Her head smashing into the metal of the bed. Finally, Charlie looking down as if trying to figure where he has left his car keys.

But it was me who caused her death. Not Charlie. Me who killed Lorraine. Charlie was the tool. Me the unwilling tradesman. No control. Just the ability to open the door to the darkness in someone's heart. To uncage the primeval.

I found out that, a few years earlier, Lorraine had rejected Charlie's advances. A single moment in time. A moment when he laid his love out, only to watch her stand on it. Driving a heel into his future. Charlie packaged that moment in cotton wool. Unwrapping it on lonely nights. Love and rejection, for playing out in the quiet moments. Then I pulled it from its safe place. Gave it life. Energy. Somehow I modified it. From embarrassment. From a misreading of the situation. I took it and injected it with anger. Full force. Rage in the machine. He could take no other route. Once out, he killed. Then the anger faded like a flash flood. And he was left standing over my dead wife.

Charlie knows what I can do better than anyone. He has been touched by the palms of the devil.

Did I want my wife dead? There lies a journey I don't want to take. I do what I do without understanding. Without control. That way I can live with my affliction. Control would mean responsibility. And how could I be responsible for my wife's death?

My thoughts hang in the cold.

'What's it like?' I turn to him. 'What happened when I let loose on you?'

'We've been here before.'

'Just tell me.'

'I don't remember.'

'Don't, or won't? Life was good, Charlie. Before all this, life was good. I thought the army was my destiny. But I was wrong.'

'Maybe that's when it happened.'

'What?'

'Whatever it is that is wrong with you. Perhaps you're an army experiment gone wrong.'

'Or gone right.'

'True. As assassins go, you have the golden touch. No weapons. No need. Just a little history between your targets. Stress you out and bang – someone dies.'

I change tack. 'What about the note or the file that was locked? Isn't that proof?'

'Note? Locked file?'

I tell him.

He touches my arm. 'Can I see it?'

'It's in the house.'

He vanishes, returning with the laptop.

Charlie sits on the wall to read the files. The glow on his face lights up wrinkles. Charlie has ten years on me but has aged twenty since we went on the run.

He closes the laptop. 'And this was on your file?'

'So our bounty hunters say.'

Charlie opens the laptop once more. I watch his smoke-gray eyes flick back and forth.

'Well?' I'm beginning to get cold.

'I can't get access to the locked file but the other file is a scan is of something old. It predates your spell in the army. So the question is why is it on your file? You have to give the army credit. Their administration is thorough. Sometimes a bit haphazard, but thorough. If this was on your file then it's there for good reason.'

I stare at the water-thin sun emerging from behind the hills.

Charlie shuffles his feet. 'Tell me what you don't see when you read this?'

'What I don't see? The blanked out bits. That's what I don't see.'

'Yeah I get that, but what else? What else is missing?'

I read it again. It still makes no sense. 'What am I looking for?'

'Relevance.'

'Sorry?'

'What's the relevance? It has to have some. So read it as if it has something to do with you.'

I reread. 'And?'

Charlie stands up and points to the screen. 'It says, '*Genetic pattern consistent*'. Is your ability genetic?'

'I've no idea. My mother died in a fire. Then my dad left. I was young.'

'You've said before.'

'Did I ever tell you I thought I was responsible?'

'What, for the fire? You were eight.'

'I watched as the house burned. But deep inside I saw it as my fault.'

'Of course you did. It's natural. We all need someone to blame. It's easy to blame yourself.'

'No. It wasn't that. Isn't that. I just feel that it was all down to me.'

'Or your dad?'

'Why would you say that?'

'Genetic. Maybe your dad had something of what you have.'

My father had been away that night. Out on business. At least that's what I was told. But years later I bumped into an old neighbor. She had a different recollection of events. One in which my mother and father had argued as I'd slept. I found out later that the police had questioned my father. He left me six months later. Bastard.

Charlie stretches his arms above his head. His muscles from his bodybuilding days may be less detailed but he still cuts an impressive shape. He snaps a few joints. 'Shit, Craig. You need this sorted. How long can you keep running? How many questions need answering?'

'Suggestions?'

'The locked file would be a good place to start. It might give us a bit more to go on. Anyway we need to get mving. If those idiots can find us, who else is on our tail?'

I nod. We return to the house. Packing is the order of the day. It takes less than an hour. We run light. Furbie and Chubby watch us, but say nothing. I keep my gun well out of reach. But it's the last thing I'll pack. I want them to see it. To keep still. Be compliant.

With the SUV full it's time to run. I throw my jacket on the back seat. 'I'm going to sort out Furbie and Chubby.'

'How?'

'I have an idea.'

# Chapter 7

'I need to pee.' Furbie's lips screw up as he speaks.

I'm standing over him. 'I'm sure you do but we have a little sorting out to do first. Then you can whizz to your heart's content.'

I bend down. I begin to remove their shoes. Chubby tries to pull away. I sigh. A slap on the head chills him. 'I'm taking these.'

'How do we walk?' Chubby looks like he's going to cry.

'The very fact that you *can* walk is a step up on from where things could be. Easier to shoot you. Leave you in the woods. The local wildlife are always hungry. Ain't no-one coming up here for months.'

Chubby doesn't reply.

I flip the shoes off. 'So I'm fairly sure that you'll figure a way to get free. You'll improvise on footwear. You'll need to – your car's out of gas. A long walk ahead. But there's some food in the cupboard. Needs must and all that. But a hundred grand is a big pull. You're going to squeal as soon as you can. So here's the deal. I'll take your wallets, cards and PIN numbers. We'll clean you out. How much do you have on your cards?'

Furbie shifts. The need to pee is strong. 'A few hundred dollars.'

'And you?'

Chubby mutters. 'Not worth it. A few dollars.'

'I don't believe you.'

'Go find out.'

'I will.'

Being on the run is harder than it sounds. Neither Charlie nor I are flush with cash. Our bank accounts have enough to sustain us for a few months more but accessing them now would be suicide. We have husbanded our resources as best we can, but things are tight. I'd hoped that Furbie and Chubby could be counted on for a few dollars. We could probably cruise on their plastic for a while. After all, who checks signatures? But cash is king when you're on the road. And in a land where dollars count, we're down to loose change. I take a moment to consider the situation and have a change of heart.

'New plan. We need cash and I don't trust you to give me the right PINs.'

I slit the tape on Chubby, before re-wrapping Furbie. I urge him up. 'Put your shoes back on. You're coming with us.'

Chubby looks confused. 'Where?'

'To get a loan.'

I push Chubby out the door.

Furbie moans. 'I still need to pee.'

I shrug, then relent. I grab a pot from the kitchen. 'Your friend will be back to join you once we have a little folding to be going on with.'

A few minutes later Charlie gives me some kind of look when I load Chubby into the SUV. I hold my fingers to my lips.

An hour and a half later we hit Havre. It's the nearest town of any size. I flick open Chubby's wallet. The cards are Bank of America and Wells Fargo. On the next corner the red Wells Fargo logo tells me I'm in the right place. I pull up at the sidewalk, encouraging Chubby to join me as I jump out.

The streets are quiet. The sidewalk is empty but at least the bank is open. A cold wind cuts in from the north, blowing dust into the air. At this time of year the atmosphere rips the fluid from your body like someone milking your skin.

I pull Chubby with me as I walk towards the bank. 'We're going to make a withdrawal. Any nonsense and three things happen. First, we all get out of here. Second, we drive back to take care of you and your friend. Third, we vanish. Alternatively, you do what I say. If I were you I'd do what I'm telling you. That way you can go claim part of your hundred grand.'

I leave him standing on the sidewalk as I tap on the SUV's passenger window. Charlie hits the down button.

I lean in. 'I'll get him to clean out his account before returning him to the house.'

'Craig, if he screams in there you could be in the crapper.'

'I've explained the consequences. He's not stupid.'

'Craig, he *is* stupid. And he's scared.'

'I've got it covered.'

As I encourage Chubby through the bank doors I look around the interior. I thought it would be quiet. There are few cars outside. But people clearly walk around here – there are a good fifteen inside.

Only one teller is working. The line is seven long. Around me others are talking to employees or filling out forms. I wanted to be in and out quickly but that isn't going to happen. Chubby and I join the line.

I whisper to him. 'I want you to clear out your account. Don't close it. Leave a few dollars. No checks. Cash.'

He doesn't look happy, which makes me think there's a damn sight more than a few bucks in his account.

A second teller opens to deal with the line. She's an elderly lady with hair so severe that it looks painted into place. The other teller is a young kid, acne front and center on his face. Around us the bank is library quiet. We move up one space. The six in front of us are in their own world. Fifteen minutes later and we're next.

'Now, no tricks,' I warn Chubby.

The customer in front finishes. Chubby moves in with the speed of a fatally-wounded tortoise. When he reaches the teller he looks at me. I do nothing.

He turns back to the teller. 'I want to withdraw most of the balance of my account.'

The words take an age to come out but the young kid has been trained to wait. 'How much will that be?'

'A thousand dollars.'

That will help. The kid is handsome. Blonde, thin-faced. Once the craters have gone he will knock – probably already has knocked – the other sex dead. His accent is local. He takes the bank card from Chubby and runs it through the machine. His face crinkles.

I step forward. 'Come on, don't be an idiot. Your dad needs the cash. Don't short change him.'

Chubby doesn't know what to do. I'm guessing there's more than a thousand dollars in the account. It's the discrepancy between 'withdraw most of the balance of my account' and what he has asked for that has caused the crinkling of the teller's face.

I smile at the teller. 'Can you let him have the balance? But leave it open with ten bucks.'

He looks at Chubby. Eventually Chubby nods. The teller scribbles a number on a withdrawal slip. He hands it to Chubby. I look over his shoulder. Eight thousand, four hundred and twelve dollars. Better.

The young kid nods towards the far end of the bank. 'I'll need the manager to sign this off. It's more than five thousand. Do you want cash or a check?'

I answer for Chubby. 'Cash will be fine.'

The teller checks Chubby's ID. Satisfied, he calls the manager over. A portly man – decades around his waist – wobbles towards us. He looks down on the slip and, with an 'I'm the boss' pause, he nods.

The young kid follows the manger across the floor. They vanish into an office. He returns a few minutes later with the money, counts it and places it all in a Wells Fargo-branded cash bag. Chubby takes it.

We turn to leave. A blind man behind steps forward quickly, almost pushing us out of the way. A bit too quickly for someone visually impaired.

He's wearing a wafer thin coat. His face continues the thin theme. Emaciated would probably be a better description. He's sporting a wispy beard. The diminishing black hair on his head is dropping dandruff on his shoulders. He kicks a large carryall until it hits the teller's point. Again an odd action for someone holding a white stick. He bends down. We have taken three steps when he pulls a sawed-off shotgun from the bag. The Thin Man points it at the teller. 'Ok, let's make this easy. Hands in the air.'

He spots the teller moving his hands beneath the counter. He rams the gun into his face. 'No alarms. Arms in the air or you die.'

Around us people are slow on the uptake. Fear is like that. When you're not ready for it fear can work against you – slowing you down, confusing you. I size up the Thin Man. This guy's on another planet if he thinks no one will trip the alarm. There's probably a button near every employee. Someone will have hit one by now.

Keeping the gun in the teller's face he pulls the carryall up and drops it on the counter. 'Fill it.'

The young kid doesn't move. The gun has him frozen.

I turn towards the Thin Man. He catches the movement. 'If you want to be a hero, feel free.' The gun swings in my direction.

'He's scared.' My voice is steadier than I feel.

'Fuck off.' He turns back to the young kid. 'Fill it.'

The teller stays stock still. The Thin Man spins the gun round, cracking the butt into the young kid's forehead. The teller catapults backward as the Thin Man leaps the counter.

I watch, with a deepening sense of dread. As if the bank haven't thought about this. The till will be an empty chest of gold. Enough to handle the day-to-day but too little to make robbery worthwhile. That's why the kid had to go get our cash. The Thin Man's going to be disappointed. Before he gets stuck into the cash he points the gun at Chubby. 'And you made a healthy withdrawal. Hand it over.'

Chubby looks at me. I don't care about the money. I need out of here. The police will be on their way.

I push Chubby's arm. 'Give him the cash.'

Chubby doesn't move.

I take the bag from him. 'Here.' I hand it over.

Chubby looks like he's just chewed a wasp.

'Smart man.' The Thin Man smiles.

I step away, moving towards the door.

The Thin Man watches me. 'Where are you going?'

'Fresh air.'

'Fuck you. Stand still.'

I obey.

Around me the world is a still life study. The line, now only two people long, is fixated on the bank robber. The three desks next to us are occupied. All are locked onto what's going down.

The nearest desk has an older lady dressed in a thick, dark coat. The next one has a young couple wrapped in Puffa jackets. The final desk has a well-dressed man. All the employees on the other side of the desks are male. All suited and booted. And every one of them is staring at the Thin Man.

To my right an elderly couple is standing at a stomach-high shelf. They had been completing a form but are now, with everyone else, concentrating on the gunman. The only other person I can see is the manager. He's sitting in a glass office at the far end of the tellers' counters. He has a clear view of what's going down. He loosens his company tie a touch, running his hands through black, swept-back hair. All in all that makes eighteen of us.

I glance at the window looking onto the sidewalk. The concrete is barren. So is the road beyond.

'Where the fuck's the rest of the money?' The Thin Man has tried all four teller points. No one answers him. By the look of things Chubby's money is the fat end of his haul. Without it he might have a few thousand. And a few thousand is nothing when you know that armed robbery is twenty-five to life. He looks nervous. His eyes are flicking. Too fast. He's on something or coming off it. Either way he's unpredictable.

The silence following his question is broken by the distant howl of a police siren. If this becomes a hostage situation I'm stuffed. I'd love to do the hero thing, to save the day, but a junkie with a gun is no easy target. Running is an option. But he might shoot. I'm thirty feet from the door. A couple of seconds to cover the distance. Then a few more to open the door. Maybe five seconds and I'm gone.

I don't move. I can't. I would need to pass the elderly couple. That would put them in the firing line. If the Thin Man shoots, the spread from his sawed-off would hit them.

'Who hit the fucking alarm?' The Thin Man jumps back over the counter. 'Who?'

I turn to him. 'I'd put the gun down.' He raises the weapon towards me as I talk. I hold up my hands. 'Trust me, when the police get here it'll be a lot easier if you don't have the gun.'

'Why? I'm not going to jail.'

'Yes you are. It's just a matter of for how long. At the moment you might get out while you can still raise a smile. Pull that trigger, point it at a policeman or take us hostage and you're never getting out.'

'Who the fuck are you? A lawyer?'

'No. I just don't want shot. No one does. In fact, if you hit the road now you might beat them to the door.'

He's shaking. I reckon he has ten seconds to make the call.

If his luck is in he might give the police a run for their money.

I'm wrong on the time front. A patrol car slides to a halt outside. I'm as good as caught. My heart is racing. And that's not good news. I open the bottom of my rib cage, taking the actor's deep breath. I hold. Count to ten. Then exhale.

'Who did it? Who hit the fucking alarm?' The Thin Man's voice is shrill. All the staff are avoiding eye contact.

The man in the glass box opens the door. 'I did.'

Brave man. The Thin Man walks towards him. Right up to him. He smashes the gun into the manager's groin. The manager drops like a pair of wet jeans.

'Calm down.' My voice is still steady.

The Thin Man looks at me. 'Do you want some?'

I shake my head. 'It's not going to get better. Hurting people isn't going to help.'

A second patrol car arrives. I hope Charlie has had the sense to get the hell away. The Thin Man raises his gun again. He sweeps the room. For him, escape has gone.

It's time for my Plan B.

Be a hero.

# Chapter 8

I take a single step. 'Look, this is going nowhere. Put the gun down and we can all get out of this.' I keep my eyes on his. Action is in the eyes. Eyes before hands. Every time.

'Fuck you. I'm not going back inside.'

'I can't do anything about that but you can make it easier on yourself. See sense. Put down the gun. Walk out. I'll go with you. That way they won't shoot.'

'Piss off.'

He crosses to the window. A third police car arrives. I see a gun appear over the hood of the first patrol car. Drawing a bead on the building. I step towards the Thin Man. He doesn't see the movement. He's too wrapped up in the scene outside. I take another two steps. He's still watching the movie unfold on the street. One more step and I'm now less than six feet from him.

The gun is by his side. His fingers wrapped round the butt. Resting the barrel on his thigh. He's looking away from me. Towards the police vehicles. A slight tremor rolls through his body. I lift for one more step. He spins round.

The barrel rises. Instinctively I throw myself to one side. I hit the ground but there's no explosion. I look up.

He's pointing the gun at my head. 'Want to be the hero do we?'

'No. I just want us all out of this alive.'

'So do I. So here's how this is going to work. You're going to step outside. You're going to tell them to drive one of those pig wagons up to the front door. They have two minutes. Tell them no more. If the car isn't here by then, well, we draw straws for who dies first. Now go.'

'They won't play ball.'

He jams the barrel under my chin. 'I don't care what you

fucking think. There are others in here that can pass on the message. They'd be happy to. So here's your chance – once you're out the door you can run for all I care. As long as you pass on the message.'

That would suit him. I'm the only one who has talked to him. I'm a threat. He wants me out.

He shifts the barrel to my thigh. 'Or I can put you out of action. Your choice. I'll count to five.'

My heart has picked up again. I need to keep the beast caged. Letting it loose in here will mean death. The Thin Man is trig-ger-happy. If the others kick off – and they will if I don't keep my head tight – he'll start blasting. I go for another actor's breath.

He twists his head slightly as I breathe deep. 'What the fuck are you doing?'

I let the breath out. 'I'm going. Just getting my shit together. I don't like guns.'

I stand up. Slowly. Around me the still life behind me has changed little. No one has moved.

I point to them all. 'Look, let the others sit down. We'll be here a while.'

The Thin Man pushes me with the barrle. 'No. I'll be here for a hundred and twenty seconds. Then I'm gone. We can all wait it out.'

He steps away from me, pointing to the door. 'Now.'

The door handle is cool. I push. A rush of cold air hits me as the click of a few guns being prepped bounces across the road. I step out.

To my left three patrol cars sit across the intersection. Each has an officer crouching behind it with a gun pointed at me. To my right a new patrol car is sliding to a halt. Sirens in the distance suggest even more are on the way. On the sidewalk opposite an officer is clearing onlookers. The space where Char-lie should be is vacant. Good man.

I let the door close behind me. I put my hands in the air. No point in risking being seen as the perp.

I turn to the intersection and shout, 'The man inside wants a car to the door in two minutes or he'll start killing people.'

An officer pops up with a bullhorn. *'Say that again.'*

The noise booms off the shop walls.

I cup my hands over my mouth. 'The man inside wants a car to the door in two minutes or he will start killing people.'

The bullhorn opens up again. *'Who are you?'*

'A customer.'

*'How many are inside?'*

'Including me? Eighteen.'

*'How many robbers?'*

'One.'

When the gun goes off I hit the floor. The door behind me shatters as glass sprays around me. The officer ducks. I roll under the bank window.

The Thin Man's yells, 'Ninety seconds. Cut the fucking chat. Bring me the fucking car.'

I lie still. The situation is fluid. If I were the police I'd want the Thin Man out of the bank. Deal with him where there are no hostages. So why not send in a car? How far can he get in? Then again, out here he could take to random shooting.

After a few seconds the bullhorn sounds again. *'Come out with your hands up.'*

The second shot takes out the plate glass window above my head. A wave of broken glass cascades over me. The Thin Man screams. 'Sixty seconds.'

I hear him reload the shotgun. I'm a mummy wrapped in shards and slivers. I shake my head to clear the debris. 'Get him a car.' My lips are peppered with glass as I shout.

The bullhorn is quiet. People are thinking. I hear no chat. The two gunshots have released a quilt of hush. I'm trapped in a sea of glitter.

'Thirty fucking seconds.' The Thin Man is still screaming.

Another gunshot. This one sounds like he's shot the ceiling. He screams. 'I want a fucking car or people start dying.'

I push up. My hand stippled by glass. I look into the bank. The Thin Man has grabbed the elderly woman, dragging her towards where I lie. He's shouting in her face. 'What's your name?'

She's too scared to reply. Her husband is stepping forward. Brave but foolhardy.

The Thin Man senses the movement and swings the gun, connecting with the husband's cheek. The old man falls. Skin splits. Blood sprays into the air. The lady is crying. I'm up to kneeling. The Thin Man has all of his attention on the old man he's just hit. I push up. Glass penetrates my knees. I ignore the pain. I focus on the Thin Man. My head is pounding. The beast within is not far away. Gasoline and a hangman's noose didn't set it free – but this will. I'm about to make a bad situation far worse.

The Thin Man is turning his back towards me. The elderly lady is in front of him. They are both a few feet from the window. Momentarily the lady is blocking my view of the Thin Man. She moves. He's raising the gun to her head. Behind him one of the tellers screams. It breaks the trance. Others join in. I aim for the old lady. I fire a starting gun in my head.

Launching forward, I catch the old lady in the midriff, pushing her to one side. My momentum hurls us both into the Thin Man's gun arm. I focus on the gun. Nothing but the gun. Remove it and I have a chance. My head is beginning to split. The beast is on its way. I throw my weight into the tackle. The Thin Man spins, his face registering what's going down. I focus on the gun.

I have the gun. Hold the gun. Tight. I pull. Pull hard. The

gun flies free. I take the fall on my shoulder then lash out with my foot. The Thin Man grunts as I catch him on the hip. I throw the old lady to my left. She lands with a thump.

I can feel the kernel in my head heating up. I keep on rolling. Holding the gun. Holding it tight. The Thin Man turns. The elderly lady lies on the floor behind him. I don't have time to level the gun. To use the gun before the Thin Man is on me. I hug the weapon to my stomach. My vision blurs. A blue blur as something flashes past me. My head is about to explode. I rise up on one knee.

A police officer has the Thin Man.

I drop the gun, slamming my head on the ground. White light. Pain. I suck it up. Embrace it. Move the focus from inside my head to outside. I raise my head to slam it once more. The world dulls. An officer stops me from making it a triple. I flop. Let my muscles go. Let everything go. Hold the kernel in my head. Blow on it. Cool it. Stop it cracking.

'Are you ok?' The officer's voice is distant but it helps. I concentrate on it. Southern states. Not a homegrown boy. High tone. Slight lisp. 'Sir, are you ok?'

I nod. I feel the kernel cooling. Chaos retreating.

For now.

# Chapter 9

The police station is not where I want to be and I definitely don't want to be a bloody hero. But it's where I am and it's what I'm being billed as. Everybody wants a piece of me. TV and press are outside. So far I've used my situation to act confused. Giving a first name, but no surname. I've told them I'm on vacation and was in the bank with a friend. I have no idea what Chubby will say. I've had no chance to talk to him.

The hero worship will give me some time. Time to figure a way out. But not much.

I'm in the chief of police's office. Lying on a leather sofa. The paramedic at the scene cleared me. I tred to tell him that I was woozy. He told me it would pass. I wanted to be taken to hospital but the elderly lady, her husband and one of the tellers held priority with the two ambulances. The chief offered me a ride.

I'll be on TV by now. The local CBS crew was on scene as I left. I was center stage. A star.

I know time is ticking. Furbie and Chubby are snail mail compared to a slot on prime-time TV. It's exit time for Craig McIntyre.

The corridor outside is a sardine factory of bodies. The room has one door and it's half glass. Beyond lies the throng. A slatted shade, hanging over the only window, keeps the early afternoon sun at bay. I pull the shade from the wall. The window behind can swing out but the gold-colored lock that keeps it in place needs a key. I try the handle anyway. Solid. The window looks onto a blacktop parking lot. A few police vehicles litter the space.

I scan the room for something to break the window. The sheriff's desk has a full-size curling stone on it. An engraved plaque signals he won the Havre 2008 Open. It lacks subtlety but would be effective.

The noise racks up outside the room just as I cross to pick up the stone. In walks the sheriff.

His name is Mike Colinski. Six feet five in his stockings. You would need two hundred and fifty pounds of beef to balance him on a teeter totter. Clean-shaven, his hair is the quaffed bouffant so many balding men seem to favour. He's a born and bred local.

He smiles when he sees me on my feet. 'Feeling better?'

His voice is soft. At odds with his bulk. I shake my head. 'Still feel sparked out. I thought standing up might help. It's making it worse.'

'Maybe you do need a trip to the hospital.'

I nod.

'Ok, give me ten, but you're going to run a gauntlet. The TV crew got in. I'm having a hell of a time throwing them out. They want to interview the hero.'

'Tell them I'll talk all they want once I get checked out.'

'Will do.'

As he leaves I can feel the digital timepiece of life throwing seconds away. My face will be across the airwaves by now and Tampoline has the longest of arms. The hospital will present a better escape opportunity but Mike is not going to hang out on the key questions for much longer. I sit to take a moment and know that, even at the hospital, things will be hard. *Name? ID? Where do you come from? Have you medical history? What do you do for a living? The scar on your skull – is that recent?* None of which I want to answer truthfully.

Mike returns to find me with my head in my hands.

'I'm feeling sick.' My voice sounds pathetic.

'I've cleared everyone but the station crew. We have a car out back. The hospital's down on 13th. It's a mile away. We'll be there in five minutes at this time of the day. Are you up to walking?'

I nod.

I'm given a round of applause as I walk through the station. We exit into the parking lot.

A fire station sits to the right, beyond it a church. Everything around me is low to the ground. I'm helped into the back of a patrol car. Charlie's car is across the road as we exit. It falls in behind.

I consider digging the beast out. The sheriff and the driver are chatting. Good friends is written into their chat. I do good friends so well. But I need something to set me off. A knife would be good but they're rare in the back seats of patrol cars.

'So, Mr Hero, where are you from?' The sheriff leans over the seat to ask.

'New Jersey.'

'And your name?'

'Craig.' No point in lying. My brief TV appearance negates that. 'Craig McIntyre.'

'And what brought you here?'

'I was taking a break.'

'And your friend?'

'Who?' Mistake.

'In the bank. The man who drew out the eight grand.'

'Oh, Chubby?'

'Who?'

'It's my nickname for him.'

'He says he's called Sandy Taylor.'

'I call him Chubby. You only have to look at him to see why.' I try a weak smile.

The look on the sheriff's face is not good. He can smell bullshit a mile away.

'Why was he drawing out so much cash?'

'He didn't say. I was along for the ride.'

'He says that you met in town.'

Shit.

The car swings to the right. Where in the hell is the hospital?

'So talk me through the bank?' The sheriff has all his focus on me. Something is winding up his radar.

I drop my head and make a noise. It's supposed to sound like someone on the edge of throwing up but comes over as a half-arsed burp. 'Sorry. Feeling sick.'

The car swings into a parking lot bordered by a two-floor cream-coloured building. I've never been so happy to see a hospital.

I keep my head down. 'Can we carry on this chat after I get checked up?'

'Sure.' The word comes out like *'hell no'.*

I lift my head as the sheriff gets out. Charlie is pulling in behind us. I see him and he raises a thumb. I'm helped out and we cross to the hospital entrance. A sign welcomes me to the Northern Montana Hospital. Charlie is ready but I'm not for running just yet. The patrol car would hunt us down in minutes. We need time.

As soon as I get in to the building I turn to the sheriff. 'Where's the bathroom?'

He points to a corner. I walk over, slowly. Once inside, I head for the only window. It's locked. I put my elbow to it and the window shatters. If anyone comes in I'll pretend I stumbled, but there's no rush to the door. I clear the glass and climb out. I drop to the ground. Crawling a few yards, I stop at the corner of the building.

The patrol car has moved off to park. Charlie is fifty yards away. He spots me as I walk out from my cover.

As he pulls up I get in. 'Drive, Charlie.'

He powers us out of the car park. 'Where to?'

'Anywhere. CCTV will give them your tag. We need new wheels.'

A black SUV slides in behind us.

# Chapter 10

'I see them.' Charlie is focused on the road. 'I thought I saw one at the station.'

'Fuck but they're quick. We need to lose them.'

'I know.'

'Charlie, this is going south with speed. Agency, police, the media... We'll make OJ Simpson look like a sideshow. They all want us.'

'They all want *you*. I'm just the help here.'

'How do we dump them?'

'I'm with you on the need for new wheels. I'd suggest that some retail therapy would be in order.'

'Shopping?'

'I saw a Wal-Mart on the way in. Change of clothes. Change of car. Best I can do.'

Charlie keeps inside the speed limit as we slide past an airport. The sign tells me it's Sands Ranch Airport. A mile later he hangs a left. The SUV stays tucked in behind us.

The Wal-Mart is fronted by a huge parking lot. Charlie parks as close as he can to the front door. We both take a few breaths before we exit the car. Charlie grabs a bag from the back seat. We enter the shop. Behind us two suits have left the SUV. They are heading our way.

I pull Charlie towards the clothing section. I intend to get lost in the maze of cloth before they can enter the building.

'Quick, a jacket.' I grab a blue parka as I speak.

Charlie gets the gig. He lifts a black half-coat.

'Excuse me, is there a changing room?' The assistant turns at the sound of my voice.

'Eh, sure, sir, follow me.'

He escorts us to the back of the shop and points to a door.

'In there, sir.'

We both duck into the changing rooms. Seconds later we're out again. New jackets buttoned up to the top. Our old jackets left behind.

We skirt the shop. Charlie diverts down an aisle. I have to stop and double back to follow him. He's searching the shelves for something. We're in hardware world.

'Got it.' He grabs a box cutter. 'Craig, here quick.'

He lifts my jacket and cuts off the security tab. He does likewise to his own coat. He spins the knife in his hand, thinking about keeping it.

I shake my head. 'Put it back, Charlie. Bringing a knife to a gun fight is never a good idea.'

He drops the knife back on the shelf, pushing the security devices in with it. We get moving again.

At the end of the aisle I look out. The two suits are standing near the main exit.

I pull back. 'We need another way out.'

We cut back into the store. At the rear wall the entrance to the back shop looms. A giant sliding door rolls up as a young man emerges, pushing a cage full of electrical equipment. Before it can shut I jog in, Charlie in tow.

We're in a massive store room. There's no one in sight to challenge us. The golden rule, now, is to look as if we're supposed to be here. We slide past racks of goods. More giant, sliding doors are open at the far end of the space. Beyond them a semi is being unloaded. It's nearly empty.

'Our carriage awaits.' My whisper is low.

A last pallet is dropped from the back of the truck as we watch. The driver closes the rear doors. We step forward. A forklift swings by. There's no one else around. I grab the truck's rear door and pull it up. Charlie crawls in. I follow, pulling the door down behind me.

I wait for a shout but we're on board for free. With minimal delay the truck growls into action. I pray we're in for a long haul – that the driver isn't local.

Twenty minutes later we're rumbling along at a fair speed. Probably on the main highway. Charlie and I sit opposite each other. To keep us steady both of us wrap around our waists some of the strapping that litters the truck wall. Charlie reaches into his bag and takes out the laptop, fires it up.

We say nothing. There is nothing to say.

An age slides by. Then the truck swings hard. Pulling itself from the highway. A few seconds later the engine dies. I count to one hundred before opening the door. We find we're in a truck stop. The late-afternoon sun signals that food time is on the cards. We slip from the back.

I look for CCTV but see none. A coffee will do no harm. I have eight dollars in my pocket. A few hours ago I almost had eight thousand. Once inside the restaurant I find my dollars buy a plate of fries and two unlimited cups of black.

We grab chairs against a wall that allows us a view onto the parking lot. Our driver is next to the window. A young waitress is delivering him fat on a plate.

Charlie hauls his bag onto the table. He removes the laptop again. 'I've been thinking.' Charlie's strong point – not mine. 'We can't keep this up. We're too high profile. Even here. Lying low doesn't work. When would it end?'

'And where does that take us?'

'We need to take control of this.'

'Agree. How?'

'Ok. So here's how it is. Whatever way this goes down a lot of people want a piece of you. Tampoline. Probably other people in Tampoline's set up. They know what you can do. The police and the media are looking for you for a different reason. You're a bank hero who has gone on the run. Intriguing. I wouldn't want

57

to bet against Chubby dropping us in it.'

'I would put odds on it.'

'So any way you look at it, we're wanted and high-profile wanted.' He spins the laptop screen towards me. 'I've read and reread the note that they found with your file and I have some ideas. So live with me on this.'

He slugs some caffeine before continuing. 'It's only a guess, but I think the note is referring to some programme. Military or otherwise. The only reason it would be on your file is that you would be part of it. Or it has something to do with what you can do. If true, we need to find out more. So we need to crack this laptop – to get to the other file.'

'And you know someone who can help?'

'As it is, I do.'

'And this person lives just round the corner.'

'No, he lives in Italy.'

'Figures.'

'But we don't need to go to Italy. We just need to email the file.'

'That easy?'

'Yip. Get me some Wi-Fi and I'll fire it over. It may be encrypted but my friend is good.'

'Cool.'

'So I suggest we drink our coffee and leave. This is the middle of nowhere. We need a lift to somewhere more lively.'

'There's no Wi-Fi around here?'

'None that the laptop sees. I checked.'

The truck stop is small. The eatery is the only building. If there's no Wi-Fi here then I can't think where else it would be.

I turn back to Charlie. 'If we go somewhere more lively we might be spotted.'

'What do you suggest? Sit here and wait?'

Good point. We zap the coffee before heading for the parking lot. Our driver is in no hurry so we're in need of a new ride.

I spot another rig firing into life. 'Time to thumb a lift.'

I knock on the truck door. The driver opens it. I look up at him. 'Excuse me but you wouldn't be headed west would you? We're hitching to California. Even a few miles along the track would be good.'

'Not keen on hitchhikers.' His checked shirt suggests he's an old hand at this. As do the thousand crags and million wrinkles that are all being washed down with dirt-blonde hair.

I nod. 'Fair enough. I just thought we'd ask. We just came in but we have to be in Sacramento in two days and lifts have been a bit thin.'

'There's a bus that pulls in here.'

'If they take fresh air for payment that will be fine. Both of us are flat broke.'

He hesitates. Always a good sign. He sighs. A better sign. He beckons me in.

I spark up again. 'There's only two of us.'

He still beckons. Job done.

The cabin is huge. TV, bed, the works. The driver is small. Five feet – maybe less. The steering wheel is like a trash can lid in his hands. Stubble is threatening a full beard. Pizza and beer are the air freshener of choice. The beer is winning. As we pull out he reaches over to shake our hands. The truck wanders onto the highway. More by luck than design.

'Kent. Rudy Kent. From Kansas City. On my way home now. Where are you from?'

He trips two lanes and back one as he talks. His eyes take in everything but the road.

I tap Charlie on the shoulder, nodding at our driver. Charlie nods back. Rudy finds second gear when fourth would have been one less than we need. He grinds it out. This is a bad idea. Sixteen wheels and a skinful of booze don't mix – and Rudy is full to the gills.

I volunteer some information. 'New Jersey. My friend here is from LA. We're doing some 'us' time. Hitting the road. Seeing where we end up.'

Rudy cuts up a station wagon, finding third while the engine pleads for mercy. He speaks, more of a slur. 'Been on the road three weeks now. Wife and kids back home. I need to see them.'

In heaven at this rate.

We are mainlining the outside lane, lurching along until, with the subtlety of a silk cloth falling on a light bulb, day becomes night. It welcomes us with air that flosses our teeth as we breathe in. Rudy has his window wide open. The clouds are on strike and the northerly wind will drop the temperature by a degree or two an hour. So says the dashboard thermometer. And my feet.

A horn flares as we get within an inch of taking out the car in front of us. Rudy hangs out a finger as we slide past. We are – no word of exaggeration – a forty-ton missile on self-destruct.

'Rudy, what way are you headed?' I don't want to distract him but it would be good to know where we're going. 'Back home you said?'

He turns to answer. The action sidewinds the truck. 'Not yet. Soon. It depends.'

I don't want to ask what it depends on but he obliges by mind reading.

'I'm behind schedule. Had a small pit stop in Havre. I'll keep going until my eyes shut. Then over for a rest. And back on the road as soon as I can.'

Still no indication of where he is going. I also think pit stop is a euphemism for drink. I don't follow up. I need all his attention on the road. Next to me Charlie has closed his eyes. The man can sleep in a hurricane.

I keep my eyes on the road. There's nothing I can do if Rudy decides to commit suicide but I'm determined to see my last seconds on this planet.

We slam through the night. Rudy flips on the radio and we enter old-school country and western through the front door. Johnny Cash bemoaning being named after a girl.

For a while I keep an eye on the wing mirrors. It's frustrating, the angle is wrong. I can see little more than the side of the trailer. If the police, media and/or agency (take your pick) are after us, the first we'll know is when they get up close and personal.

Rudy has settled into a fifty-mph trance. We might get pulled for a little weaving but it won't be for speeding.

At some point my need for sleep overtakes my need to be awake when I die.

# Chapter 11

I awaken screaming. Rudy is wrestling the wheel. And losing. The world feels unstable. My nightmare is topped by a more worrying reality. The lights dead ahead are white. They should be red. We're on the wrong side of the road.

Rudy is hauling the wheel to the left. A pair of headlights flash by. A horn goes into overdrive. We leave the highway. The truck bounces hard on the dirt. I'm flung against my seat belt. Charlie shouts. Rudy joins in. We are rushing across the landscape like a crab on speed. The highway is receding. We pile-drive scrub before grinding to a halt.

Rudy is leaning on the wheel. Charlie leans on me. I lean on the dashboard.

Our exit from the highway will not have gone unnoticed. I grab at Charlie's arm. 'Time to go.'

I tap Rudy on the shoulder. 'Are you ok?'

He looks at me, his eyes wide. 'Fuck, I fell asleep.'

'When the police get here your breath is going to offer them a nice DUI.'

'Fuck.'

Charlie opens the door. The night air is a chisel of ice. I follow him out. When I hit the ground I turn round. 'Rudy, some advice. I'd make myself scarce. Kill all the lights. Pray no one reports it. And head for town. Claim your phone was screwed. Tell them you were heading for help. Maybe it will give you time to sober up. If not, hit a bar. It's an old trick.'

There's no reply. Charlie pulls at my arm. There's a flashing blue light on the horizon. Rudy's screwed.

We head away.

It takes a few minutes for our eyes to adjust to the dark. The lack of cloud coupled with the near-full moon helps a little.

Charlie eases up next to me. 'Where to?'

'Anywhere.'

'Again?'

'Again.'

'But away from the road. How far do you think we got from town?'

I look back. 'Hard to tell. I was out for the count.'

'So the best guess is this is the middle of nowhere.'

'True, although we have company.'

Off to our left there's the soft glow of light. About a quarter of mile into the scrubland we are walking on.

I stop. 'Looks like cars. Circled.'

'Hell of a place for a meeting.'

'Could be our way out of here.'

'Could be trouble.'

'Middle name.'

'Craig, it's your whole friggin' life. If I look up the dictionary under the word *disaster* I'll find nothing but your photo as an explanation.'

'And I love you too.'

'I know. It's why you can't walk an inch without me to hold your hand.'

I place my hand on Charlie's chest. Stopping him. 'Let's give this twenty minutes.'

'Why?'

'Look back.'

Whirling blue lights are bordering the highway where the truck exited. I steer us away. 'Let's circle to the far side of the cars and see what goes down.'

We start out to the right. Keeping the car lights at the same distance. It's cold. I pick up the pace to generate heat. 'Charlie, why do you hang in with me?'

'Deep-rooted love and affection.'

'Apart from that.'

'You're good looking in a quirky kind of way.'

'I'm not sure how to take that.'

'A compliment.'

'Seriously. This is shit. All of this. Being on the run. Why hang on?'

'Seriously?'

'Seriously.'

Charlie looks behind him. The red and blue is still beating out a pattern in the night sky. A flashlight has detached itself from the scene. It bobbles in the night. It's not heading for the truck; it's heading for the circle of car lights. I swing a little more to the right. In the dark. We are all but invisible, but no point in cutting it too fine. 'Go on.'

Charlie returns his attention to me. 'You walked into my bar on a Monday night. The 1st of February; I remember the date. First time I ever saw Lorraine. You don't forget the first time you see a lady like that. She looked stunning. You looked like shit. More hair but shit. I couldn't figure the gig between the two of you.'

I couldn't either. Lorraine was so far up the NFL draft that she had the pick of the country. I was already on the disabled list.

Charlie keeps going. 'You looked uncomfortable. But she had eyes for you that told everyone else to take a hike. That lady owned you. Lock, stock and miserable bastard that you were.'

'I'm glad we started this conversation.'

'You won't be. For months I poured JD and Coke down your throat. I knew you were ex-military. Ex Hatch Role. I was there as well, remember.'

My tenure at the nut house for military psychiatric cases was not good.

'You became a fixture in the bar. Too much of a fixture, with too much JD, but I ran a bar not a medical advice forum. You ran up a hell of a bill.'

'And you never called it in. Why?'

'I'll get to that. Anyway, what you didn't know was that I was in financial trouble. Buying and doing up the pub ripped me of more than twice my budget.'

Charlie's pub had sat on Melrose Avenue in LA. Not really central Hollywood but close to some of the supporting businesses.

Charlie mows on. 'I wasn't worried at first. I thought the site was good. Edge of movie land. Plenty of cash. But the recession rolled in and booze may be a temporary cure for some of life's ills, but drinkers were still thin on the ground.'

'Fridays were jumping.'

'True, but that was on the back of cut-price booze and a band. I barely broke even on those nights. I slid into a money hole that was too deep. At one point I thought I was winning. I marketed the hell out of the place. Ran Karaoke, open-mike nights, comedy...anything that worked. But it was for nothing. I owed the best part of a hundred grand to the bank. With all my efforts I was breaking even on my running costs but not making a dent in the loan. The bank knew it. They started to put pressure on me. Pay-up-or-else type pressure. And I couldn't pay. Even selling the place was a no-no. I would still have been in the hole.'

'Lorraine said you had other property.'

'Lorraine was wrong. I might have bummed myself up a bit when I was chatting to her.'

'And Tina couldn't help?'

'Her house was mortgaged to the hilt. She wanted to help but she didn't have the dollars to give me. She would have but she couldn't.'

I want to ask what happened to Tina but this isn't the time.

Charlie keeps his foot down on the talk pedal. 'I hung on in there. Paying the bank enough to keep them at bay. But it was for nothing. There was no way out.'

'You never said.'

'Oh I said ok. You just never listened. Back then the only subject that had merit in your world was Craig McIntyre. Anything else was for the birds.'

Ouch.

Charlie looks at the car lights, before truning his attention back to me. 'I had a few ex-army friends. One night I collapsed into a bottle or two and fessed up to one of them. He listened but didn't produce a check book. What he did do was talk to some other people. People I didn't know he knew. People of the 'not nice' variety. Two nights later a pair of goons showed up. All suit and muscle. They bought a few beers, standing out like a virgin in a brothel. But in LA if you throw out the oddballs you'll have no business in a week. So I served and smiled. At closing time one of them approached me and asked for a word. He said that he knew I had some financial worries – that he was a representative of someone who could help. He explained that he could make my cash problems vanish. I didn't ask how; I just politely refused. He shook my hand and left.'

The flashlight is closing in on the circle of lights. We are five hundred yards away. Almost level with the circle. No sound comes from the scene. Strange.

I return my attention to Charlie and keep my voice down. 'I take it they came back.'

'Three times. On the last visit they got a bit pissed at me blanking them.'

'Weren't you worried?'

'A little. But they never outlined in any detail what they were offering. Just that they could help. I thought they would get the message and call it quits.'

'But they didn't.'

'A month after the third approach they came back, but with a new friend. An evil-looking dude. Thin as a drink of water. Dressed in dark from top to tip. Eyes sunk so deep they looked like black holes. He didn't waste time. He told me he knew I was in the crapper, that he knew the details. Said he had the bank money in his pocket. I coud have it and pay off the bank. In return he would take fifty-one percent of the pub. I would work for him and my business would improve tenfold.'

'Laundering cash.'

'Exactly. No more punters but a shed load of dollars flowing through the till.'

'And you said no.'

'I tried. But the guy didn't have *no* in his vocabulary. He told me he'd be back. A fucking mini terminator as it turned out. The next night a Molotov cocktail took out my front window.'

'I remember that. I thought you said it was gangs.'

'If I remember correctly I told you I had some local trouble. I think I even asked your advice.'

That, I don't remember.

He frowns. 'I was lucky. Molotovs are simple but don't always work. The gasoline didn't spread far enough to do much damage.'

'Why would he risk destroying the pub?'

'He didn't give a flying fuck.'

'Who was he?'

'A full-on prick called Jimmy Salino. A New Yorker who thought we still lived in '30s Chicago. I told the police what I knew. No reason not to. They knew who he was and pulled him in but he had a thousand alibis courtesy of a My Chemical Romance gig. Anyway, it would have been one of his muscle-bound lap dogs who did the deed. I told the police that, but I may as well as have been pissing on a volcano.'

'I take it Jimmy didn't take well to being questioned.'

'And some. He was smart enough to stay away from the pub for a while. But when I got home the following week I found him in my apartment. Muscled-up. I took a beating.'

'The hit and run incident.'

'That was my story.'

'They did that to you? Shit, you were in hospital for a week.'

'Yip. But I still didn't sign.'

'Brave.'

'I was lucky. One of the neighbors saw him break in. Half-way through, Jimmy and the beat squad did a runner when they heard the police coming. Otherwise I think I would have been dead meat. I told the cops who it was and Jimmy went to ground. For a few months it was quiet. I was still earning enough to keep the bank one step from calling in their note. If I'd been clear of the debt I would have been making a good living.'

'What has this to do with me?'

'Nearly there. I need to tell you a few more things.' Then he stops.

Voices. From the direction of the lights. I can't make out what's being said. We've nearly completed our half circle of the spot. We stop and listen but the sound is too indistinct. The police officer has arrived on the scene.

I nudge Charlie. 'Lie low. When we see the flashlight move we'll let the cop get back to the road, then go in and scout.'

Charlie nods. 'Want to hear the rest of the story?'

'You've got me hooked.'

A gunshot.

It's time to stop storytelling.

# Chapter 12

I drop flat to the ground. Charlie with me. Nothing to do with our army training. Just a normal reaction to being shot at. More gunfire and then engines start. I look up to see the huddle of lights dispersing. There's no order to their direction. All are tearing up ground to be gone.

A last shot rings out. A single dot of light is left. It wobbles. Then it's extinguished. The other lights keep spreading out. Putting distance to best use. As they fade, the distant sound of engines and rubber from the highway tarmac becomes our backing track.

I rise. Keeping my eyes on where the lights had been.

Charlie rises too. 'What went down?'

'Hell knows. But if that last light was the police officer then I think he's in trouble.'

'Time to walk away.'

'We can't.'

'Why?'

'We can't leave him.'

'How do you know it's the officer who's down?'

'One light went in at walking pace. All the rest left at speed. It has to be him.'

'He will have called for back-up.'

I can still see the spinning blue light back near the truck. No other light is making its way towards us. 'I don't see help rushing in.'

Charlie shrugs.

I stand. 'I'm going to see.'

Charlie falls in behind me.

As we reach the spot, I see a figure lying on the gorund. Spread around is the debris from what looks like a party. I approach the prone figure. 'Are you ok?' Better to announce my arrival. I don't want shot.

Nothing. I bend down. 'Hello.'

Still nothing. 'Are you ok?'

Zero. It's a police officer. He's young. Fresh out of the refrigerator. I reach for his neck. Taking a pulse isn't as easy as it looks. You have to know where to feel. The slick of blood around his collar doesn't aid me.

'Help.' The whisper from the soil negates the need for a clinical diagnosis. He's alive.

Charlie drops next to me. 'Let me.'

He checks the officer before rolling him on his side. 'Head wound but not from a bullet.' He points to a rock with blood on it. 'He hit his head when he went down.'

The officer lifts his arm. 'I need to call it in.'

I don't want him to call it in. If there's no gunshot wound then he might make it without us. 'Charlie, are you sure there's no gunshot wound?'

The officer answers. 'I've not been hit. I tripped once they bugged out.' His voice is a low rasp. 'I thought they were packing. As soon as I appeared they started to run. One of them reached into his jacket. I shouted but he kept reaching. I fired but missed.'

Charlie chips in. 'We heard multiple gunshots.'

'All me. When they saw me, suddenly they were running all over the place. I thought I was being attacked.'

'Who were they?'

'Not locals. I know the locals. Just out of town girls, boys and beer. Old story.'

'Heck of a place for a party.' Charlie is mopping the officer's head wound with the arm of his shirt.

The officer is older than I first thought; late twenties. He has a Village People moustache going on and it's not Movember.

His hair is non-regulation.

'You need this stitched.' Charlie presses the officer's hand to the wound. 'Keep it there.'

The officer reaches for his radio. 'I'll call it in. I'm feeling ok. Who are you guys anyway?'

'You need a bandage to stem the flow.' Charlie keeps the officer on the ground with a friendly hand on the shoulder.

The officer pulls out a handkerchief.

'That'll do.' Charlie gets him to hold it on the wound.

The officer sits up. 'So who are you?'

'Out for a walk.'

The officer looks at Charlie as if he's just spoken Swahili. 'Out here?'

'It's good to get away.'

'At this time of night?'

'Cool and quiet.'

'And where did you say you were from?'

'We didn't.'

The officer slowly gets to his feet. 'So talk to me.'

We blank him. Now he's getting nervous. His gun is ten feet to his left. Charlie is between him and it.

He looks at me. 'What's with the silence?'

We keep blanking him. Then I see a bag. A black sports bag. Just beyond the gun. In the half-light, provided by the Moon, it seems to be leaking something through a hole in the side. The officer follows my gaze, sees it and picks up his flashlight. He keeps an eye on us both as he flicks the flashlight into life. He plays it onto Charlie's face. Charlie throws up his hands. He does the same to me. I follow Charlie's lead. Then he shines it on the bag. White powder is flowing from the hole.

I don't think it's Tide.

A car engine breaks from the background noise. We all spin and see lights coming towards us. This takes no figuring. This has been no 'lads and lassies' night going down. It's all about drugs. And they're coming back for the good stuff.

The bag is bulging. I don't know street values but even the make of bag isn't cheap, regardless of the substance oozing from it. It's been left by mistake. It's way too expensive to dump. Whoever has the brave pills to come and get it also knows the officer is carrying. And that means they are probably – definitely – armed.

The officer is ahead of me. His eyes flick from the approaching vehicle to the bag and back to us.

I step back. 'I'd let this one go if I were you. I doubt that they are light on weapons. This isn't worth dying for.'

He looks confused.

I rock on the balls of my feet. 'We don't want any trouble. We'll just head off. And if I were you I'd do the same.'

'You'll stay right there.' He stares at his gun on the ground. He'd have to rush Charlie to get it.

'Leave it.' I hold my hand up. 'Please walk away with us. Let them pick up the gear. Go back and get your gun later. You've no idea what you're dealing with.'

He shakes his head. 'Stay there. I'm going to get my gun. Then we'll see what's what.'

He moves towards Charlie.

Charlie's bodybuilding physique is an imposing barrier. He matches the officer's movement. 'My friend is right. Just walk.'

The car is a few hundred yards out. It's showing no sign of slowing. They're coming in hot. A single shot rises above the engine noise.

Charlie looks round. 'Craig, let's get the hell out of here.'

'Stay where you are.' The officer is trying to round Charlie.

'Look, Officer, it's time to cut your losses and run.' With this Charlie breaks off the head-to-head. It's too dark to see his eyes. Yet I know they'll be alive with fear. Mine are wide open, seeking an exit. Charlie runs towards me. I take off with him. We are trying for sub eight seconds in the hundred-yard dash.

The car roars in behind us. I keep my head down. I hope the police officer is copying us.

I trip. My arms flail out to try to keep me upright. They fail. I crash to the desert floor. My face grabs dirt as I try to roll with the fall. Then the night spins. Car headlights flash into my life. My life is all engine noise. More gunshots. A cry. A tire sliding in a cloud of dust, halting inches from my head.

A voice. 'Is he a cop?'

Voice 2. 'Doesn't look it.'

Wheels spin. The car leaps away.

Voice 2 stays with me. 'Take it easy.' The voice is edgy. Nervous on steroids. 'You a cop?' I shake my head. 'Your friend?' I shake again. 'Fuck up.' The words aren't meant for me.

Voice 2 presses me down. I hear car doors slam. The engine picks up again. It throws the headlights back over me as it returns.

'Get him in.' A new voice. Less jumpy.

Hands grab me. I'm lifted clean from the ground.

'You okay?' Charlie's voice.

A slap. Not for me.

'Yes.' I'm on the receiving end of a slap this time.

Voice 1 sparks up. 'Both of you shut it. Where's the cop?'

Voice 2 shouts, 'He's back there.'

'Is he dead?'

'No.'

'Leave the cop.'

I try to resist. A second slap. My head hits the side of the car. I lash out but catch fresh air. Another slap. A quarter of a second ticks over. Just a quarter. Enough to warn me...

My head detonates. Buried deep inside, the kernel shatters. No warning. It wants out. It wanted out back at the bank and won't be denied this time. My world enters *FF* and *Pause*. I'm dropped to the ground. Face back in the earth. I roll away. No one tries to stop me. My head pounds. My hearing dulls. I start crawling.

Away.

The pain ratchets up a notch, forcing me to stop moving. I wrap into a ball. I know a blue world will soon roll in. It always does. A world where the pain vanishes but my beast still roams free.

My head is being chiseled out from the inside. My eyes flash brilliant white dots across the landscape. Each point is accompanied by a needle to the soft tissue in my head.

Then the blue washes in. Glorious pain-free blue. Night vision is switched on. I know this game well. I have until the blue world goes to sort out my shit. Once it leaves I'll be next to useless.

This shit drains me.

I take in the scene. The car is a Range Rover. Top of the range. Inside, two men are ripping lumps out of each other. It's what I cause people to do. Afterwards they won't remember. Charlie is lying next to the rear passenger door. Face down. Another man is kneeling near the front wheel. Head in his hands. I look back to where the officer was. Two bodies are on the ground. No movement.

I jog up to Charlie. 'Get up.' He rolls over. 'Get up now.'

The two men in the car have stopped attacking each other. I yank open the nearest door and pull one of them clear. He flows out on a sea of blood.

'Charlie, get in.' I run round to the other side.

As I grab the driver's door the other man moves for the lock. I haul the door open before he can reach it. He follows his friend into the night. I get in.

Charlie jumps into the back. I shout at him. 'Get in the front.'

I select drive and press hard on the accelerator. Charlie crawls in beside me. I aim for the two prone bodies.

I switch off the headlights. With my night vision I don't need them. I stop next to the bodies.

'Charlie, get the officer.'

He jumps out. With some ease he uses his muscles to throw the officer into the back seat. As soon as Charlie's in, I point us to where the truck is sitting.

'Charlie, get ready to take over driving.' The blue world is fading and my energy with it. 'Take the wheel. If the officer is ok drop him at his car, then head west.'

I crawl into the back. The blue vanishes. I slump into the seat well.

I feel the car stop. Charlie gets out. Returns a few minutes later. 'He's fine.'

I'm not.

We cross onto the highway.

# Chapter 13

Charlie keeps us moving for two hours. By which time I no longer want to die. But only just. I climb into the front seat. The blood around me is drying. I buckle up. Irony would be getting stopped for no seatbelt.

We're cruising the inside lane. The landscape outside is a mystery. Apart from our fellow vehicles the only clue is glimpses of scrubland picked out in the headlights.

We're not in the cheap seats when it comes to a ride. The Range Rover has all the toys. Leather beats wood. Wood beats plastic. Leather fights blood on the smell front and it's a tribute to the coachbuilders that leather is winning out.

'How are you doing?' Charlie sighs after the words.

I look at him. His face is blue in the dashboard light. I could do with the blue world back. It's pain free. The more I do the trip to Chaosland the more it robs me at the end. 'I'm still here. Wherever *here* is?'

'Far enough along that we can call it quits for the night soon.'

'How was the cop?'

'Puzzled.'

'Figures. Did he get our number?'

'Doubtful. I dropped him in the back of his car.'

'I had an event.'

'You don't say.'

'I'm not sure I can live with this.'

'Like you have a choice?'

'Charlie, it's no way to break bread.'

'I agree.'

'I need answers.'

'And?'

'The file on the computer.'

'The laptop's back there. We can go back if you want?'

'Right. Well at least we have the note.'

'The one about Alfred.'

'It has to be to do with me.'

'Gone. All in the bag. Guns and all.'

'Seriously.'

'Yip.'

'Well at least the note might point to the fact that I'm not a natural born killer.'

'You could have fooled me.'

'I'm man-made.'

'You're made of something.'

'Funny.'

'Get to the point.'

'It's to do with Tampoline.'

'In what way?'

I take an extra breath. I haven't been straight with Charlie. Not as straight as I should have been. 'Tampoline had something to do with what I can do.'

'Do elucidate.'

'When we kidnapped him and his brother, he more or less told me so. I'm an experiment. And not the only one.'

'There are others? Oh joy.'

'A guy I tied up with. Placed with me by Tampoline. Guy called Martyn. He has a neat trick. He can knock you out by looking at you.'

'Cool. So you're part of some sort of superheroes gig. Is that it?'

'Closer than you know. Army-induced. The search for the superior soldier. Maybe?'

'The next generation of humans.'

'This isn't a surprise to you?'

He flicks his eyes from the road. 'Tina had an inkling.'

Tina used to work at Hatch Role.

'When did she tell you?'

'A few days after you rolled into my bar.'

'Back then?'

'Yip.'

'And you said nothing?'

'Would you? What was I supposed to say? Hi Craig, I hear you're Superman's first cousin twice removed?'

This needs more chat but first things first. 'So the note.'

'Well I was hoping my friend in Italy could have helped but that's dead now. But it seems to me that you might have someone better placed now.'

'Who?'

'Martyn. Isn't he one of you?'

'Shit, you make it sound like I'm a member of the KKK.'

'Well you're a member of something. And I'm not sure it's the human race.'

'Why Martyn?'

'You say he's from the same mould. Tell me.'

'He was the subject of some experiments. At least that's what he told me. On the back of what I can do Tampoline had someone play with his head. He told me they placed an implant in it.'

'When?'

'Not long after the TT.'

'So you're the original Ground Zero.'

'Could be, but I was out of it in Iraq when they played doctors on me. I can't remember. I know they didn't ship me straight home after the deaths.'

'Deaths.'

In my short army career I was responsible for a few dead people. To top it off, I'm sure I spent a lot of time in a hospital, but my memory is vague. A few people did the AWOL thing around me back then.

As my ability manifested itself over the years I was at the front and center of a string of nonsense. Some small and some, like the TT, big. A diplomat I was bodyguarding in Iraq was killed by his escort. That was when Tampoline got interested in me again. It was years since Iraq but he had keept an eye on me. He even tried to turn me into an assassin. All that went tits up when the fans at the Tropicana Stadium shredded each other. The TT. That's where Tampoline lost his eyesight and most of his manhood. The discovery of Martyn confirmed I was a black ops programme participant. One who initially looked like a failed experiment. Only I patently wasn't such a failure.

I tap on the mahogany dash. 'I'm not clear on what they did to me.'

'But did to you they did.'

'My best guess is yes. Again, maybe.'

Silence.

'Charlie, I need to figure out what I am.'

'Will that help?'

'I can't keep running.'

'And how will finding out help?'

'I've no idea.'

'Maybe I do.'

'Go on.'

'Take this back to square one. You're a living, breathing example of a new breed of person. Crude. Unpredictable. Uncontrollable. But you have something that's new in the shop. Whatever it is, it's major. We've had nuts running off at the mouth about psychic ability for eons. But in the cold light of day you never see one on the six o'clock news. It's the same with ghosts, telekinesis, mind reading, levitation, aliens, fairies and the assassination of JFK. Loads of theories. Lots of evidence that vanishes when you shine a spotlight on it. All gone. Nothing there. Except you're here and you're not a theory. You're the real deal. Professor Xavier would love you. A real X-Man. A genuine Human 2.0.'

'Maybe 1.1.'

'You underestimate yourself. It doesn't matter how bad you think your powers are. They're there all the same. You're the living proof that all things are now possible. If you, then what else could be true? That's how this will be looked upon. On a good day you could be a billionaire inside a year on the media rights alone. And since you now know there's not just you, no one can say you're a fluke. It means that we might all have it. Whatever the hell *it* is. All of us. Me included. Think of the implication. Think if we can tap it. How much would that change the world?'

'A lot?'

'Completely. We're no longer in a world where physical inter-action, as we know it, is required to influence each other. We just think it. You might be a babe in arms compared to what others can do.'

'Or I might just be the best there is.'

'True. Even then, it won't stop people looking to build on it. Forget nano technology or quantum physics or the echo of the Big Bang – you provide science with the biggest challenge yet. What are we really capable of? Or where are we going? You could be the wet dream for Darwinists and a nightmare for creationists.'

'A bit OTT.'

'Really?'

The first spatter of rain smacks the windshield and Char-lie stops talking as he figures out how to switch on the wipers. 'Screw this. There are more switches in this bloody car than in a nuclear plant.'

Then the wipers kick in. 'That wasn't me.'

'Automatic wipers.' I smile as I say it.

'Go figure. How does it know?'

'No idea. Magic.'

'Just like you.'

'You think I could make it big in Vegas?'

'Sure. You'd be up there with the best. A residency with Craig McIntyre. Not sure you'd get more than one show though. Kind of hard to attract the punters when the tutor kills and maims the students.'

'The S & M brigade might like it.'

'Cool. Niche markets are always a bit of a gold mine.'

'What would you call the act?'

'The Craig McIntyre Experience?'

'Dull.'

'Will You Get Out Alive?'

'Better, but sounds like the strapline.'

'The Catalyst – Will You Get Out Alive?'

'Works for me.'

'Sold.'

The rain puts on its running shoes to flood the windshield. Charlie drops the speed. His caution means the entire high-way is overtaking us. I chew over some useless options and get nowhere.

*

The rain is easing an hour later. Charlie kills Radio Fleetwood Mac. He signals to cross the highway and parks in front of a low-slung building called the Trailhead Saloon Casino.

The front door has a sign, scrawled on a scrap of paper, saying *No Casino*. Good start. There's light coming from two small rectangular widows either side of a door. The building looks like it has drawn its inspiration from a Swiss Alpine chalet – at least the woodwork covering the front does.

'I need a beer.' Charlie opens his door.

'Where are we?'

'East Glacier Village according to the sign we passed.'

I've seen worse bars from the outside. A beer sounds good.

The bar's a local's paradise. It's late, the music old-school. The residents don't even look up when we enter. Charlie orders two beers. We slide into a booth. I kill all but a finger of my beer in one. Charlie goes one better and is ordering refills before I'm finished. We haven't said a word since we crossed the threshold.

The bar door swings open. An elderly lady trails in; a waterfall of rainwater empties onto the floor from her coat. She adds to it by removing her trapper hat, ringing it out on the bar floor. No one objects to the new swimming pool. She shuffles to the bar, eyes on the barman. She orders up a large Scotch without anything to dilute it. She downs it without interrupting her drinking for breath.

Her face in profile pings a memory cell in my head. 'Got an idea. Can you make change? I need to dial 411.'

Charlie roots. I take the offered cash. 'Good old Mrs Rubenstein.'

Charlie looks at me. 'Who's she? An old flame?'

'Hardly. I visited Martyn's home once. I met a neighbor. I'm going to phone her.'

'Why not his mother?'

'She runs under her maiden name and I don't know it.'

I dial 411, get Mrs Rubenstein's number, then make the phone call. She is reluctant to get involved but eventually gives in and agrees to get Martyn's mum. I've to phone back. As I replace the receiver I watch the barman lift the empties. As barmen go he's from the age of drink, no food and more drink. His gut holds the history of a thousand nights on the wrong side of the bar. His face is puffed and red. His nose an explosion of small, burst veins. Each one a river of purple. A network that's threatening the rest of his face. He throws me a work smile and turns away, wobbling to the next booth.

I spent enough time in Charlie's bar to know there are two types of bar people on this planet. Those who still have a choice and those who don't.

The former are in it for the dollars. Paying their way to the next job. How long they've been at it makes no odds. They do it to watch cable, screw on a Saturday night and eat takeaway. They come in as late as they can get away with and leave as soon as they can. Their demeanor is one of servitude. Be nice and receive the punter tips. Tips are the oil that allows the system to work. Keep the pay low, keep the tips high. That way the bar men and women of the world smile, ask how your day has been and keep the drink coming.

The barman is the latter. This is it. There's a wanted ad where his life once stood. Our barman is as much part of this establishment as the stains on the floor. He doesn't come in late or leave early. He just is. There when he needs to be. Hours are not a measure of his working week. They simply count down to the day when he no longer pours cold ones but becomes one. Lying two steps down or flash-fried to ash.

I look at Charlie as he spins out the beer. He was the former. Then I ripped him from the womb, depositing him away from his beloved home.

It wasn't a conscious plan. But it's meant Charlie has had my back when I've most needed it. And when my life went south he came along for the trip. Along the way he killed Lorraine. And for that I can't forgive him. But neither can I blame him. He knows it was me, not him.

But the way it works in my world is there has to be a little history for two to tango. I once asked Charlie about him and Lorraine and I got the answer I deserved. Charlie had tried it on with her. He's never quite said what happened but I know it was bad enough for Lorraine to stay away from him from then on.

Lorraine was my sunbeam. Gorgeous in a way that made her

being mine impossible. I was a reject from the army, with more psychological problems than ten *Jerry Springer* shows. Lorraine turned heads as men threw me a sideways glance. Brother? Work colleague? Surely not her lover? She was reluctant but supportive when I surgically removed myself from Charlie's bar to start the job in Iraq. When I returned less than six months later – my short-lived bodyguarding career lying with my dead boss in a dusty alley in Basra – she was still there for me.

And now it hurts. It hurts that there is no more Lorraine. It hurts that my best friend killed her. It hurts that she would be alive but for me. It hurts that had she never met me she would be turning heads in another part of the world as I sit sipping beer. It hurts that she was doomed from the beginning of our relationship. I am a badly-scripted movie in which no matter how good things look they always end in the toilet. Even now there's no ending that makes me think I'm off this rollercoaster of pain. It's only a matter of time before Charlie joins Lorraine.

I kind of think that he knows this. That somehow this is him paying back for the loss of my wife. He could – should – be far from here. After the TT he did vanish, but then he came back. Somewhere in Charlie is an animal trying to tear itself in two.

I return to the booth. 'Charlie. Why do you stay with me?'

# Chapter 14

'Do you want me to finish the story from our walk on the wild side?'

'Will it answer my last question?'

'Maybe.'

'Shoot.'

'You remember the night the pub got broken into?'

'And some. The place got trashed.'

'After that I was screwed. It was the way my Italian friend signed off and left me to sink.'

'But you got back up and running.'

Charlie drains some more beer. 'All because of your wife.'

'Lorraine?'

'You had another wife?'

'Funny.'

'So, two days after the carnage she walks in and drops ten k on the bar. As cool as you like.'

'What?'

'Straight up.'

'Cash?'

'Yip.'

'Ten k. Are you serious? She gave you ten thousand dollars?

'In new notes.'

'Are you kidding?'

'No.'

'Fuck. Ten k. We didn't have ten k. I thought she hated you.'

'So did I.'

'Ten k? Really.'

'You never knew.'

'We didn't have ten bucks. Ten K – I mean...'

'She swore me to secrecy. I used it to put things right. She trusted me to pay it back.'

'And that's why you stay? For ten k.'

'Do you want the politically correct answer or the bare-naked truth?'

'Strip for me.'

'She would have wanted me to.'

'Wanted you to do what?'

'Look after you.'

'I'm not sure on that.'

'I am. She said as much.'

'What, when she gave you the ten k?'

'Well before that.'

'When?'

'About a week after you first appeared at the pub. She came down and introduced herself. Told me you were recovering from some sort of breakdown in the army.'

'She did?'

'Craig, skip the "she dids". I'm not making this up.'

'Did you tell her about you and Hatch Role?'

'No. I figured she was on point for you. She was a good lady. All she wanted to do was to put me on notice.'

'And?'

'And nothing. The conversation must have lasted about five minutes and she was gone.'

'So you were to be my guardian angel for ever and a day?'

'No. Just to keep a weather eye on you. The ten k sealed it. I'd have done it for nothing though.'

'And?'

'You know the rest.'

'I do?'

'I'm not going there. But you know why I'm here. Events overtook a casual promise.' Charlie pauses. 'Why the sudden interest? Do you want to get rid of me? Do you want the cash back? I'm good for it.'

I hear a splash as the barman drops a whisky into a glass full of beer. It's for himself. He turns from us as he downs it in one slug. He puts the glass down, turning to see if anyone saw. I did. Charlie didn't and everyone else knows he does it all the time. It's that sort of bar.

'Do I want rid of you, Charlie? That's a hard question.'

'I'd have thought it easy.'

'Put yourself in my size twelves. Being with me won't end up well. It hasn't been a day out in the country so far. So if you leave I might feel better. Distance between me and you reduces the risk for you. On the other hand, I'd probably be dead by now if you hadn't been there for me. And I don't see attempts on my life vanishing anytime soon. So you being around has to be good for me.'

'And that's got your boxers in a twist. I stay and it's a plus for you. I go and it's a negative for you. I stay and it's the wrong end of a crap-covered stick for me. I go and I might get to live out my dotage in some bar down by the Gulf.'

'Good summation.'

'And how is that your problem?'

The barman has doubled down on the beer with a larger Scotch. I sense a pattern here. 'Charlie, how's it not my problem?'

'Because it's my choice. I'm not staying because you want me to. I'm not even staying because you need me. I'm staying because the alternative is worse. I'm staying because I'm a selfish bastard.'

'In what way?'

'You die. I spend the rest of my life in the guilty box. You live. I might see that bar down Florida way and not have to take to religion to gain forgiveness.'

'So you don't give a shit about my feelings?'

'Not strictly true, but close.'

'And here I am worrying that you're doing this from some mile-wide altruistic streak.'

'Maybe a few inches door to door. So put your concern in your back pocket. Leave it there.'

I watch the barman load up again. 'And that's it?'

'Unless you've got something to add?'

I do. And I need another beer before the bartender reaches the point at which he can't dispense to his needy clients.

I check the pub clock. According to Schlitz it's close to midnight. I lift myself from the booth. I order up a beer and a Coke for my designated driver. I have twenty minutes before I need to phone Mrs Rubenstein back. I place the drinks on the table.

Charlie lifts the Coke. 'Are you interested in an observation?'

I nod as I sit down.

'Do you know what I can't get my head round?'

'String theory?'

'Apart from that.'

'No.'

'You say that you and Martyn are the next generation of humans.'

'You said that.'

'Ok. But, given the unlimited resources at Tampoline's disposal, why waste it on you?'

'I'm not following.'

'Well think on it. You and Martyn can't be the only two on the planet. I can't believe that all work on whatever project you are part of has come to a halt. Far from it. If I were Tampoline I'd have opened up the purse strings and gone balls out. I mean Martyn proves you're no fluke. Insert a chip and press go.'

'And that makes you wonder why he doesn't let me blow in the wind and get on with the big show.'

'Exactly. You were the warm up act. The main act is waiting in the wings. Hell, they may even be here.'

'So for some reason I'm still important. Is that it?'

'No. That's not it. I can see why you're important. You know stuff that can sink his presidential ambitions. I get that. But in that case the best option would be to kill you. No screwing around. Whatever it takes, just nuke you. But they haven't. They've tried to capture you.'

'I've been lucky.'

'No. I don't buy that. There were opportunities at the police station if he really wanted to.'

'A bit OTT.'

'Is it?'

Charlie has a point. A year back I was being hustled down by Tampoline's brother, a fat clone of Tampoline who ran a nasty organisation called Factor. He had pointed out that, if need be, Tampoline was capable of using Predators on US soil to kill us both. I had laughed. He hadn't. Tampoline really was that powerful.

I push my glass around. 'So where does that take us?'

'He wants you alive.'

'Figures. But the killer question is why?'

'You still hold some value that outweighs your danger to him. Any idea what?'

'Tampoline is a devious bastard. He blows with the wind. His is the politician's way. And he's good at what he does. Very good. But he knows I'm not as dangerous as you say.'

'You could blow out his presidential career.'

'I could try. But my story is so extreme that it takes some swallowing. Add to that my own demise if I try, and it's not such a big threat.'

'True you'd need to give them something solid. A small demonstration.'

'And then think where I'd be. My Vegas stint would be small fry compared to the media circus that would follow.'

Charlie rubs his already red eyes. 'And if you really did fess up, Tampoline would step in and alleviate you of the trouble of breathing.'

'I'm still a risk though. And I can't see the downside in making me vanish. Who would notice?'

'Me.'

'Except you'd probably join me in a body bag.'

'You say all the nicest things.'

'Thanks. But it's true. If I've an ace up my sleeve I don't know which sweater it's in. Whatever he wants from me it could give us some leverage. Or at least it would if I knew what the heck it was.'

'It has to be to do with your party trick.'

'And I thought it was to do with my charm and electric personality.'

Charlie smiles. 'That too.'

I rise. 'Time to phone my girlfriend.'

I need to make change with the barman. He's a few more into his drink routine. If he wonders why I'm not using a cell he isn't saying.

# Chapter 15

*'Hello.'*

'Mrs Rubenstein it's me. Craig.'

*'Coleen's here. She's not happy.'*

Welcome to my world. Coleen is Martyn's mum.

I take a deep one. 'My name's Craig McIntyre. I know your son Martyn.'

*'I know. You're the one who talked him into kidnapping the senator.'*

Not quite true. It was Martyn's idea. An insane punt about a year ago that set me on the road once more. 'I'm sorry. I'm sure Martyn explained the background.'

*'Not really but for whatever reason no one seems to have done anything about it. For the life of me I can't figure it out.'*

I can. We lifted Tampoline just after he announced he was running for president. It should have been impossible but Tampoline made it easy. He came out of the whole thing a hero. A blind man surviving a kidnap attempt. The story read that he talked us into not killing him. Martyn is safe as long as he keeps his mouth shut.

'I need to get in touch with Martyn.'

*'He has a cell. Try that. He's never home.'*

'I can't. He's still being watched.'

*'By who?'*

'Some not very nice people.'

*'Is this to do with the kidnapping?'*

'Yes.'

*'Then why would I help you?'*

'Because, if I can meet with Martyn, I can get the people off his back.'

*'Look, Mr McIntyre…'*

'Craig.'

*'Mr McIntyre. My boy's no angel. He's brought down the devil on our house. He probably deserves what's coming to him. Lord alone knows I've wished it on him often enough. But he's still my son. And I'm not handing him on a plate to no troublemaker.'*

'You don't need to hand him to me. Just give him a message. That's all. He can decide what to do.'

*'Do I sound like a prima face idiot?'*

The phrase throws me a little. 'Eh. No.'

*'So give me a good reason why I shouldn't just phone the police and tell them about this call.'*

'That wouldn't help Martyn.'

*'Why not?'*

'Martyn is walking free because the nasty people don't see him as a threat. If he keeps his head down then they might let things lie.'

*'Good, so we let things lie.'*

I can hear the tiredness in her voice. A lifetime of weariness in each breath. Martyn told me he had brought a lot of grief into his mother's life. He had worked for Gaylord in Factor and being a member of Factor was not a job that you walked away from. It was also not the sort of job that involved rearranging roses in an old folks' home one day.

'I said *might*. They *might* let it lie.'

*'And, you sticking your nose in, that won't stir it up?'*

She has a point. The last thing Martyn needs is to be seen with me. Or even be in the same state. Tampoline wouldn't waste a second before using Martyn to get to me. 'Maybe. But if they don't know I'm in touch then maybe not.'

*'You're not selling this very well and I got out my bed to take this call.'*

I'm selling it like a devout Muslim selling the benefits of alcohol. 'Can you give me two minutes to explain? If you still don't agree to help then put down the phone and I'll never bother you again.'

Silence. More silence. Then, *'Ok, two minutes.'*

'OK, Martyn got in with a bad crowd. You know it and he knows it. But since the kidnapping they don't want to know him. And that's a good thing. You don't want them back in his life. For reasons too long to go into, Martyn's old boss has lost interest in him. And we don't want that to change.'

I hope the 'we' in the sentence helps me bridge a few gaps.

'But here's the rub. Martyn's old boss is friends with the senator we kidnapped.'

*'He's his brother.'*

'Yes, he's his brother and you know that blood runs thick. Well I've good reason to believe that the senator wants me. For obvious reasons I don't want to be on his dance card.'

*'And what has this to do with Martyn?'*

I can hear the negativity. She is close to hanging up. 'Nothing or everything. I think Martyn can help me figure out what the senator wants me for.'

*'Kidnapping?'*

'No. He wants that door firmly closed. The truth about the kidnapping is a lot less helpful to his campaign than the version he has spun.'

*'I'm going to hang up.'*

'Please, just a little longer.'

*'Thirty seconds.'*

I draw a breath and let rip. 'If I can find out why the senator wants me I'm fairly certain I can help Martyn.'

*'Help him to do what?'*

'I'd love to say he'd be on the straight and narrow for the rest of his life but you wouldn't believe me.' Nothing. I go on. 'But I'm willing to bet there has been little or no trouble from him since the kidnapping.'

'He has a job.'

'That's good.'

*'It's not much.'*

'But it's legit and pays.'

*'That it does.'*

'And that could end tomorrow.'

*'How would that happen?'*

'If the senator gets desperate to find me. He'll use everything at his disposal and more. And that will include Martyn.'

*'Only if you get back in touch with him.'*

'Even if I don't get back in touch.'

*'Ten seconds.'*

'Tampoline will pull every trick in the book to get to me. Martyn and – sorry to say – you, are on the home page of his list of contacts.'

*'So me having this call with you has put us in danger.'*

'No.'

*'Yes.'*

'How?'

*'Up to this call I could safely say I never talked to you. If they're that smart they might work out you've been in touch.'*

'There's no way.'

*'Mr McIntyre, there's every way. If these people are watching Martyn they could well be watching me.'*

'Have you seen anyone?' I pray the answer is no.

*'Do I have to? How hard would it be to put in a bug or two to an old lady's house?'*

She is right.

*'And'* – her voice has picked up a notch -*'they might wonder what I'm doing at Mrs Rubenstein's house after midnight. And they might just check phone records. And I'm betting you're not phoning now because you're bored. I'm betting something has happened. Otherwise why not phone at a more sensible time? And if something has*

*happened and this phone call originates from somewhere in the vicinity then it won't take Hercule Poirot to put two and two together.'*

'That could be true.' She is as smart as Martyn said.

*'And?'*

'Ok, so I hang up and leave you alone.'

*'Mr McIntyre, what good would that do?'*

'I'd be on my way and you can still tell them I called if they appear. They can check it out.'

*'And do I tell them you were looking for Martyn?'*

'Do you have a choice?'

*'You know I don't. What other reason could I give for you phoning me?'*

This call is racking up as a seriously bad idea. I considere ending it. Hitting the road and running.

*'Mr McIntyre, are you still there?'*

'Yes.'

*'So now I need to put you in touch with Martyn. Don't I?'*

'No.'

*'Yes is the right answer. If these guys are as bad as you say I'm already in the cow dung. And so is Mrs Rubenstein. I'm not sure what they'll do to two old ladies. But I'm sure it won't be on my bucket list. So now I need to put you in touch with my son.'*

'You don't.'

*'But I do. You've said as much. If you really can get them off his back then they'll be out of our lives. What's the other option?'*

'They could leave you alone.'

*'They'll use me to get to Martyn if he goes on the run. This call, Mr McIntyre, has been a Pandora's Box. Only it's not about the ills of the world. Just me, Mrs Rubenstein and Martyn.'*

Coleen is as sharp as a butcher's knife on this. And I'm not sure that, had I spent a little more time working it all out, I might not have reached the same conclusion. And then the question is: would I still have made the phone call? I consider where this could go. 'Give me some time to think on this?'

*'Time, Mr McIntyre. To think on what? The alternatives. You call the senator and explain? You call Martyn's old boss man and explain? You call the police? What are you going to think on? Unless you're full of shit and can't fix Martyn's problem, then we're all in the tumble dryer. You take all the time you want, but unless the story you have just run off at the mouth with is all bullshit, I don't see much of an alternative.'*

I have zero to say.

*'So now we have a clock that's running. I get a message to Martyn. He meets you. Assuming he can lose his friends. And then you figure out what you need to figure out and do something. To be honest, Mr McIntyre, it all sounds weak.'*

As weak as my throwing arm. I look round. Charlie is nursing an empty glass. The barman is now sitting on the wrong side of the bar. He's no longer hiding his drinking. He has a double with a chaser on show. The other locals are gone.

*'Mr McIntyre.'*

'I'm here. Look, put me in touch with Martyn and I'll sort this out.'

*'A promise you can't keep.'*

'I can and I will.'

*'Good words but talk is cut-price. Deeds are what count.'*

'I will sort this out.'

*'You had better. I'm still away to give this a night's thought. If I don't see any other way, I'll put you in touch with Martyn. Phone here at nine tomorrow morning.'*

With this she hangs up. I stare at the phone feeling like there were a million different ways to have handled this better. I return to the booth.

'And?' Charlie is rubbing his eyes. We both need sleep.

'I've to phone back in the morning.'

'Why?'

'Because Martyn's mother is a damn sight smarter than me and I've been told that's when she might agree to put me in touch with him.'

'We'll need somewhere to sleep.'

'The Range Rover will do. You could sleep a baseball team in there.'

'And then there's the issue of money.'

'That I don't have an answer for.'

'We will need some soon. The gas tank is flirting with empty.'

'First things first. Sleep. Then onto the problems with a fresh eye.'

'And we just kip by the road side.'

'Sort of. As long as we're near a phone in the morning.'

We don't wave at the barman as we exit. He's past caring anyway. As we step out into the night I see a road that T-bones the main highway. It vanishes under a small bridge in the distance.

I point. 'Down there. I know you're tired but we're still on a main route out. I doubt the barman will remember us but if they're looking for a Range Rover, someone will have seen it outside the pub. Sorry, Charlie, but we need a few miles.'

He just nods. Once we are in the car I take the opportunity to search it. I flip open the glove box and do a double take. 'Charlie. Money for nothing.'

'Dire Straits.'

'No, look in the glove box.'

He looks over. In the light of the dash the glove box reveals a surfeit of small green-and-white bundles of money.'

I put my hands together in a prayer. 'Tell me that's not fake.'

I pull one of the rolls of notes. A rubber band is tripled on it to keep it tight. I slide it off and flip through. All twenties. Maybe five hundred dollars in total. And there are at least fifteen rolls stuffed into the cubby hole. I hold a note up to the light. I'm no expert, far from it, but they look real enough. I sniff it. Not that that will tell me anything; I just don't know how to check for forgeries.

'They could be real.' I start to count the roll.

Charlie starts up the SUV. 'How much?'

'Give me a minute.'

As we cruise under the bridge I pull out the others, checking each one. All twenties, all in five-hundred bundles. 'Seven and half grand. Give or take.'

'And is there more anywhere else?'

'Isn't that enough?'

'Craig, there's no such thing as enough.'

I flip off my belt and clamber into the back, my hands sticking on the blood. The rear seats are empty. I open the shelf to the trunk. In the quarter light I see a small bag. I unzip it.

'Charlie, what's the term time for being a drug mule?'

'Ten to life.'

'I think we're in for life.'

I check the rest of the trunk but it's bare. I climb back to the passenger seat and place the bag on my lap. 'It's full of white powder in bags.'

'And so we have, in no particular order: grand theft auto, drug smuggling, leaving the scene of an accident, a couple of hundred misdemeanors and the attention of the US government. Did I leave anything out?'

'Manslaughter?'

'May as well throw it in.'

'We should throw this bag out.'

'Why?'

'Come on, Charlie. It's drugs.'

'And that makes things worse how?'

'I hate them.'

'So do I. That's why we're not throwing it. Who knows who

might find it?'

Fair call. I don't argue further. 'Does the GPS work on this thing?'

'Try it.'

I fiddle with an array of buttons that would do NASA credit. I find us on the map. I fly around, but the GPS is second rate to a good old Rand McNally for an overview. After a fashion I find something of interest. Too far away for tonight but it gives me an idea. 'Another few miles, then we dive into some backwoods to find a place to stop.'

'We'll need gas soon.'

'Tomorrow.'

Thirty minutes later we are both bedding down for the night.

# Chapter 16

I'm awake before the sun. I need to pee with speed. I open the rear door. The cold hits me like a blow to the eyeball with a spike. I take a leak on the rear tire and jump back in – quickly. This is bear country. It's not much warmer in the car. I shake Charlie awake and ask him to fire up the engine.

He obliges and we look at the surroundings as the warm air builds. The car is nestled in a small clearing. It's still too dark to make out much. Charlie gets out to relieve himself. It's not far short of six o'clock. We have a few hours but first we need to get rid of the drugs. I'm sure if I scatter them to the wind it will work but what if I coat a Grizzly's next meal? I'm sure the locals would love a junkie bear for company. I heard a stream nearby but same again. For all I know there's a camp full of scouts out on a winter's trek. I don't want to spike their water. Bury it? Then some deer or wolf digs it up. Spreads it around. It gets back in the water. Burn it? With what? And the smoke will be seen for miles when the sun comes up. How hard can this be?

When Charlie gets back in he has no better ideas. So I place the bag back in the trunk. Charlie retraces our steps, with the fuel light going all disco on us. Soon we hit the road once more.

I flick at the GPS. According to the satellite there is a Cenex not far from here.

We hit the gas station but it's shut tight. The sign on the door gives us forty minutes until it opens.

I scratch an itch on my leg. 'We should wait. We need gas. And this place has a payphone.'

Charlie shrugs. 'Better park up and away from here. It'll look strange if we're waiting for the place to open.'

He drives us back up the road we came down. Parking beyond the bridge we passed under last night, ensuring we're out of sight. The fuel light is having a cardiac. Charlie shuts down the engine to let us freeze for half an hour.

As the light comes up we head back. East Glacier Park is small-town America personified. The gas jockey pays us little heed. The Range Rover gulps twenty gallons before it's happy. I add a few bags of chips and Coke to the order. The breakfast of kings. I use the drug cash to pay.

The station payphone is free but we're two hours too early.

'Back up the road again,' I say as I jump in.

The Range Rover obeys and we settle in for another wait. At least we are warm. As Charlie demolishes a bag of sour cream and onion, I brush my teeth with Coke.

'So where are we going after the call?' Charlie has finished the bag of chips.

'I have an idea. Let me talk to Martyn's mom first.'

Around us are low-rise trees and scrub. Cars slide by on the occasional basis, but we're are out of sight of them. Only their engine noise betrays their presence. The morning is spring-water clear. The temperature won't rise much but, in the sun, it'll be a nice day for walking the dog. I've never had a dog and I don't want a walk. But the image is nice.

A rustle in the bushes near us sends a bird flying. Nothing appears to suggest what spooked it. I keep an eye out for bears. Do they attack cars? The only bear I've ever had a close encounter with was the teddy bear that sat on my bed when I was a boy.

G Ted he was called. My father had got him on a trip some-where. He was welded to my side for years. Then he vanished. I cried for days. My mother told me someone had stolen G Ted. I was too young to believe otherwise. Later I found out it was true. My father had stolen him. He viewed it as a child's thing. In my dad's world, a four-year-old boy was supposed to let go of such things.

The time crawls. I feel my nerves stretch. Partly due to the desire to get moving. The rest is down to the caffeine in the Coke disagreeing with me. Caffeine does that to me. It sours quickly. Vibrates my nerves, plays with my head.

★

At ten to nine Charlie takes us back to the station. If the gas jockey thinks it's weird that we have come back to use the phone he doesn't show it. The iPhone in his hand holds too much interest to let me impinge on his life.

I dial. Mrs Rubenstein answers. *'Hello.'*

'Hi, Mrs Rubenstein, it's Craig.'

*'Coleen is here..'*

There's a pause. *'Hello.'* Coleen sounds tired.

'Did you decide what you want to do?'

*'Not want. Need. You've given me no choice. I'll pass on your message to Martyn. What is it?'*

'We stayed in a hotel last time we were in New York. Tell him I'll meet him there two days from now. Midday on the 20th. He'll know where I mean.'

*'Anything else?'*

'Yes. I'm sorry this has to involve you.'

# Chapter 17

We plough up the highway with me playing tunes on the GPS and telling Charlie about the call.

Charlie waits a few minutes before becoming my interrogator.

'So where are we going?'

'A place called Chief Mountain.'

'Where?'

'It's a town on the map. On the border. North of here. A couple of hours.'

'Never heard of it.'

'To be fair I'm not sure it's even a town. It's marked as the crossing point on the 17.'

'Hang on, I think I've seen the mountain. Looks a bit like the one from *Close Encounters of the Third Kind*. But we can't use an official crossing. Tampoline will have that covered for sure.'

'In this animal we don't need to. We go off road and circumvent the Canadian customs officers.'

'That easy.' Charlie grimaces.

'Probably not, but staying this side of the border is living on borrowed time.'

We slide north through serious lake and mountain country. Passing the oddly named Lower Two Medicine Lake, an artificial pond heading towards St Mary Lake and Lower St Mary Lake.

The scenery around us splits the eyeballs. Demanding attention in too many places at once. White caps top out craggy explosions. The air is so clear that the locals must be able to recognise each other at two miles. An eagle catches my eye. Riding a current to the north. On the hunt. Its wings are fixed. Minimum effort to keep aloft. Then trees block it from view for a while. By the time we are back in line of sight it's gone.

I drift into the landscape. Using the time to leave my problems behind. I open the window, wanting to in suck cold air, to breathe the clouds. My heart slows to tick-over. I pick up a tune from yesteryear. *Float On* by the Floaters. An almost one hit wonder.

*Float on, float on, float on, float on, float on, float on, float on, float on.*

Not the most challenging lyrics in the world. Nice melody. I float on as Charlie drives on.

After an hour I zone back in. 'Charlie, what happened with you and Tina?'

'Same old same old.'

'Tell me more.'

He looks over at me. 'Things got messy. The whole TT thing. Me on the run with you. It was never going to last.'

'So it's down to me?'

'Yes.'

'Thanks for the honesty.'

'You asked.'

'What did she think of it all?'

'Not a lot. She said I spent too much time with you. She knew you were trouble. It wasn't destined to end well.'

'Have you talked lately?'

'No. I don't want her involved. You know what Tampoline's men are like. She's probably got a shadow anyhow.'

'This is a real mess.'

'That it is.'

The car unwinds the road. Small pine trees whip by. I check on the GPS. We will need to pull in soon to try and figure our border crossing point.

There are no obvious routes marked on the map that show a way into Canada. No surprise there. We need to stop well south of the crossing point. We can't be the only ones who fancy an unobtrusive entry into Canada. But, with the longest land border on the planet, there has to be the odd hole.

I stop fiddling with the GPS. 'How good do you think this thing is off road?'

Charlie points to the array of instruments. 'I think it's happier in mud than on concrete. This is as good as it gets without hijacking an army vehicle. Why? What are you thinking?'

'The main road is out. We've no passport. Our names will be on a watch list. Anyway, a random search and we are doing twenty-five for drug smuggling. There have to be backwood tracks. I suggest we work our way north through the boondocks. This road still runs east before it bends north for Chief Mountain – so north will cut the corner. If we're lucky we can make it over the border in a few hours. There.' I spot a small dirt track. 'On the right. Let's take that.'

Charlie dumps us off the highway. The Range Rover drops onto a rutted track with overgrowth that looks mildly under control. Maybe used once in a while. Even so, Charlie has to ask the box of tricks under the hood for help. We slow down as the bumps kick in.

We're not in thick forest yet, but flitting between patchy runs of trees. According to the GPS we could have taken the 89 and tried our luck further east but this looks less used. And, hopefully, less watched. I keep my eye on the GPS as Charlie threads the needle.

We pass a wooden hut. It looks well maintained. Next to it sits a Skidoo. Waiting for the winter snows.

A few miles further on the track is so thin that it's more a wish than reality. Charlie keeps us moving. We hit a stream. He pulls left to find a crossing point. The Range Rover handles it like a pro.

We start to climb and around us the trees begin to thin.

'Charlie, stay off the summit. We could be seen.'

He obeys. At times we're down to a crawl. At others we're able to lift the needle above the ten mph mark. The early afternoon sun makes things a little easier. In the dark this would be more of a problem.

I sense more than hear the noise. 'Charlie, stop.' I listen. 'Kill the engine.'

As the power plant dies the sound of the wilderness, muted by the car's glazing, takes over. On top of it there is a distant beat.

'Get us out of sight.' I point to a clump of trees.

Charlie squeezes the car into a copse.

'Deeper.'

He shakes his head and pushes the nose in further. The paintwork takes a beating. I slide the window down. The sky is visible – but only just.

'What is it?' Charlie kills the engine.

'Chopper.' I think.

He listens. The beat picks up a more insistent rhythm.

Charlie leans forward. 'Police?'

I shrug. 'Could be mountain rescue, loggers, private – who knows. Give me a hand.'

I jump out and start to pick up fallen branches that are scattered around. I throw them on the roof of the car. Trying to break up the white expanse. Charlie does likewise.

The helicopter is closing in.

'How far to the border?'

I lean in and tap the GPS. 'We're as close as makes no odds to being on it.'

'I don't see any "Welcome to Canada" signs.'

'Funny that.'

I keep throwing sticks on the car. I can't see how we've been spotted. But I've never tried to slip over a border. Up here it seems easy. Mile after mile of nothing. But satellites, remote sensors, patrols – they all have to be in use. Or maybe not. Maybe the chopper is looking for Bigfoot.

A few minutes later the helicopter begins to hover over one spot. I can't see it but the sound is steady. I walk to the edge of the trees, dropping to my knees. A mile away the helicopter is the size of a dragonfly – still in the air. Montana police markings are clear. It starts to crab towards us. They're definitely looking for something. I crawl back to Charlie to tell him the news.

Charlie listens. 'They could be up here for anything.'

I want to agree but something is niggling. If we've graduated to mainstream media then the gas station might have clocked us. There are only two roads north from there. It wouldn't take a member of MENSA to figure out where to look. I stare at the gaps in the trees as the noise rises. Then it fades as it slides to our left. A few moments later the noise is on the rise again.

I realize that the rain from the night before threatens to betray us. The Range Rover is no lightweight. Our tracks are clear to see. I can only hope that they're less visible from the air. We should brush them out back to the last set of trees. But there's no time. Anyway, if they've spotted movement in this direction our tracks are a small worry. Infrared will find us.

Infrared. Crap.

I pick up dirt and throw it on the hood. 'Charlie. Pile it high.'

We work up a sweat as the helicopter zigzags the area. It rolls in over the clearing. I push Charlie down and under the car. The car has a good clearance from the ground but, even so, Charlie struggles. 'What are we doing?'

I urge him further under. 'Heat signature. If they have infrared on that thing we'll be two blobs of molten lava. The car engine will make it three. The earth should block the car a little. And I'm praying the car blocks us.'

We squeeze in tight. The downdraft from the chopper is stirring up the debris on the ground. It's a few hundred yards away from our location – in a dead hover. Something is causing them to stay. From under the car I can see a little of the clearing. The blades are driving a mini hurricane. The noise is a club thumping into my ears. Then the storm starts to drift to the right. The pilot pulling the craft ninety degrees to where we lie. The note of the engine rises as power is fed in. She lifts, starting to roll west of our position. A few seconds later she takes up a hover again. I look at Charlie. There is nothing to be done but lie and wait.

The chopper engine whines. Off again. Only a few hundred yards. But it's moving away, and that's a good sign. I scrabble to the edge of the car. I signal Charlie to stay. The chopper moves on again. Methodical. Suggesting real focus. Our tracks can't be clear. If they were, the chopper would be on our head by now. I look up through the foliage. The sky is a patchwork quilt of blue and the helicopter is too far away to see.

I slide back a little. Still afraid of the infrared. I slip back to Iraq. IR showed the hidden. We used night goggles back then. You still needed positive ID though. It was easy to let off at a local by mistake and, even though we were armed with all of the toys that the military boys liked, we were often left shooting at zip. A pair of sandals, a dish dash and an AK47 and the enemy could move like a skater on a pond. We carried a hundred and fifty pounds at times.

They were also cunning. Hiding under a car was one of their tricks. Burnt-out car shells littered Iraq. They would dig out a hole under the car and slip in. Sometimes two to a car. IED's on the trigger. We would hammer by. A flick of a switch and the IED would rip into the protective metal around us. Over the stretch of the first months we learned to beef up the protection. In turn they ramped up the explosive punch.

In the beginning we would empty out of the vehicles after an explosion. They would mow us down. We stopped that.

Others would come to our help. We stopped traveling solo. But at some point you had to get out of the vehicle. That's when they would take their best shot. We would rake the burnt-out cars in advance. They stopped using them.

IEDs got harder to spot but we got smart at spotting them. Then they got smarter again. They changed tactics and moved to suicide bombers. We were taught to spot them. And, if we got the chance, run or hug. Hug to stop them releasing the trigger. Then they stopped holding the trigger to their chest and put it in their pocket. If you hugged them they could still let it go.

Each day we inched forward on the protection front. Each day they inched a little more ahead of us. I hadn't been there long but it was all engraved on the inside of my skull.

The helicopter swinging away brings me back.. This time it doesn't stop and sweeps out west. I slide from the car and stand up. The air around me is a cloud of debris. Settling. I walk back to the clearing. Keeping low. I look out but there's nothing to see. A ridge to my right hides the horizon. I take a breath. Holding the cold air. Warming it. I drop it through my stomach, down to my toes, imagining the hot air bathing my feet. I pull it up my legs. Back through my stomach. Into my lungs. And out.

Charlie appears next to me. 'Do you think they were looking for us?'

'I'd like to say no.'

'But?'

'I'm not sure. Seems too much of a coincidence that they would be up here. Yet if they had us on satellite we would be dead. Maybe they saw us go off piste and wondered what we were up to. Maybe it's nothing to do with the suits?'

'It's still trouble. If they did see us they'll report it.'

I agree. 'We need to get moving again.'

'I'll check the ridge. See if they're still around.'

Charlie half jogs up to the ridge. He keeps low but with his bulk it just makes him look bigger.

A few seconds later he's back. 'It's heading back down the valley.'

'Given up?'

'Could be. Any way up, we should get a shift on. Distance is our friend.'

I nod and we head back to clear the car. One ear open for the sound of a returning helicopter.

# Chapter 18

It's a long way to New York and we haven't got much time. We need to be there in two days. The driving will be a killer. We can make it but it'll be nonstop. And we have to re-cross the border. A flight would be better but we can't use our ID.

I have a thought. 'Charlie, why not forgo the Range Rover and let the train take the strain?'

'Is there a station nearby?'

'There has to be one somewhere. I once took the train from Newfoundland to Vancouver. Wonderful trip.'

'Could work.'

We stop at a mom and pop. It's solid local. Right down to gingham-cloth-and-white-pinnie-fronted waitress. We coffee-up. I order the steak sub and Charlie doubles up on that. We sit in silence as we chew, watching the cars and trucks roar by.

'What do you think *Alfred* referred to?' The question catches Charlie cold.

'Alfred?'

'On the note. Whoever signed it had their name blanked out above the word *Alfred*.'

'Not unusual. Most signatures have their name in print below. Standard practice.'

'But this was just one word. Just *Alfred*.'

'Do you remember the rest of the note?'

'More or less.' I wasn't blessed with a photographic memory but whatever they have done with me has changed how I think at times. I close my eyes to dig around my head, looking for the note. Sometimes this works. Other times it fails. Then it appears – a few inches above the cloth. I ask the waitress for a pen and piece of paper. I conjure up the note.

Subject: Dynamite.
Date: ███████

MI: Coded DNA. Full issue on all counts. Positive
on ██████████ samples. Genetic pattern consistent.
Connection with subject aura highly likely. Highest
correlation with ██████████ and ██████████
Replication possible but technology not available.
Maybe ██████████ years. Recommend annual revisit as
tech unfolds.

Highest priority.
Signed: ██████████

Alfred


'Does that look right?'

Charlie pulls it toward him. 'As good as gold.'

I look at Charlie. 'Weird how that works.'

When I was at school I flunked so often that they called me Retake. It was all I ever seemed to do. Retake exams. I even retook an entire year when I was eight. Not that I was dumb. My last IQ was 124. I just had no real interest and my memory was shocking at times. My mother would send me to the shops for milk and bread. If I didn't have a note, I'd come home with no milk and no bread. I could forget my own name in a crisis.

It nearly floored my army ambitions. I was never going to progress up the ranks. I couldn't remember the date of the exams, never mind pass the things. Yet I could strip a gun. I could run a unit on patrol. I could read the lie of the land better than anyone in the unit. But I couldn't remember the telephone number to dial home. Now, since the monster has risen from the deep, I'm better than a Xerox on a good day. On a bad day I may as well have cardboard for brains.

Charlie nods at the paper. 'What do you think this all means?' He's munching on the last of his sandwich.

I read it again. Slowly. Pulling out detail. Trying to fill in the blanks. 'Let's do this from the top. Dynamite. Why Dynamite?'

Charlie pulls the paper towards him. 'Project name?'

'A bit old-school.'

'But plausible.'

'It may mean nothing. We had a mission in Iraq called Flat Iron. Turned out the ops team leader had a thing for the Flat Iron building in New York.'

I point to MI: Coded DNA. Full issue on all counts.

'MI?'

Charlie is still chewing. Hes stops. 'Most Important.'

'You think?'

'We used to use it at briefings. MI was the stuff worth listening to. All MI was life critical.'

'*Coded DNA?*'

'Deoxyribonucleic Acid.' The voice comes from over my shoulder. I turn to find the waitress standing with the coffee pot. 'More coffee?'

'From a chemistry expert I would love more coffee.' I smile. My best smile. She's pretty. A bit too many of the 'homemade donuts – the best for miles' but I am judging from a point where my weight is way, way south of my prime.

'How did you know. Chemistry Major. MIT.' She smiles back.

'No kidding.'

My look of surprise is a bit of giveaway. She tilts her head to one side. 'Why can't a waitress have brains?'

'Sure, but MIT. It begs questions?'

'Why I'm here?'

'Kind of.'

'Family restaurant. I start a job with a company called Cal-Chem in a month. Mom's short on staff and things are busy.'

She really is pretty. Hazel eyes. Rounded cheekbones. Full lips. Blonde. And that matters to me. I'm a blonde man. Lorraine was blonde. 'Do you know much about DNA?'

'A little. I took a sideline in genetics. CalChem are hot on genes.'

'Would this phrase make sense?' I point to the first line.

She checks around. No one else is looking eager for her attention. She pulls out a chair and sits. Charlie says hi as we exchange names. She's called Terry.

She reads the whole note. I'm not sure us allowing it is the best idea on the planet but I'm weary of the deal at the moment. I want answers.

She flicks her hair back, reading and rereading. I spend the next few seconds watching her eyes roam over the words.

She sits back. 'What *is* this?'

'That's the money question.' I keep my smile on.

'If you ask me it's tied up with passing on something between people.'

'Why do you say that?'

'Ok, remember I'm no genetic expert, but take *coded DNA*. It doesn't make sense. All DNA is a code but if they mean the DNA sequence has been decoded then that would tally. It might just be shorthand.'

'You said 'passing on'?'

'Yeah.' She does the nice hair flick thing again. Charlie notices me noticing. He lifts his eyes to the ceiling. I shrug.

*'Genetic pattern consistent. Connection with subject aura*

*highly likely,*' she reads. 'It sounds like there's some connection between the subject's aura and genetic pattern consistency. In other words, whatever pattern consistency they have found has a direct correlation to the subject's aura – whatever that is?'

'And the bit on replication. Is that why it sounds like something is being passed on?' Smart point on my behalf.

'No. That looks like they mean they could replicate the natural process but they're short on the tech to do so. Note *recommend annual revisit as tech unfolds.*'

Smart point squashed.

She reads it again. 'I'd say the writer has found something unique in a subject. They may have discovered that others with the same genetic pattern have the same *aura.*'

Charlie points at the paper. 'And what is aura?'

'I don't know what they mean here but an aura is aura.'

She smiles and my heart takes a little kick up.

I push her on. 'And does any of this make sense?'

'Well if the author is talking about passing something on through genes it's a well-worn path. It's why we are what we are. Our genetic code is passed from parent to child. That's in simple terms. It's actually far more complicated than that. But I think this is something else.'

'Go on.' Smile still on.

'See *Full issue on all counts?*'

I nod.

'That suggests a hundred percent success rate. Whatever they are looking at is guaranteed. *Positive on blank samples* suggests they know where the positivity comes from.'

'Positivity?' Charlie slurps at his coffee.

'The blanked out bit will probably refer to the subject under test. Could say "dog", "mice" or even "human" – could be anything. It's why it's blanked. It would tell the reader how far along they are with the test.'

'What makes you think it's a test?'

'*Full issue on all counts*. It's a phrase used in testing to indicate a solid link.'

'You must have been top of the class at MIT.'

'Patronizing me is one way to get me to leave.'

'Sorry.' My smile has gone.

'Apology accepted.' She does the hair flick thing again.

'Anything else?' Charlie's tone is a reprimand to me.

'The middle sentence – *Highest correlation with* – would be a big reveal but for the blanks. Fill those in and it would be a lot clearer. Where is it all from?'

'A friend gave it to us. A puzzle. He loves this nonsense. We're on a hundred bucks if we can figure it out. We've never beaten him yet.'

She frowns.

I probe. 'If this is about passing on stuff, would they be able to fiddle with DNA to copy what they've found?'

'You don't know much about DNA, do you?'

'Obviously not.'

'You can't copy DNA as such. But you can insert strands of it into animals, plants and people, like they do in gene therapy. Take plants. Genetically modified crops are big news at the moment. We play with strains of plants. We cross-pollinate them. We insert genetic material from other plants and try and make the recipient plant better – less prone to disease, better able to cope with drought, quicker growing. But the real money is in animals and humans. Animals to make them more productive, humans to help us live longer, fight disease, get better quicker and so on. In essence, all genetic information is stored as a four-letter code in nucleic acids. All living organisms use DNA to sore their information and DNA is made up of two strands of nucleoids that are twisted together to make the famous double helix.'

'Nucleoids?' I reintroduce the smile.

'Think of them as the codes. There are four letters: A, C, T and G. They can only combine in certain ways. Do you want to know what the letters stand for?'

'Go on.'

'Adenine, cytosine, thymine and guanine. The sequence of these determine your DNA.'

'Didn't we decode the human genome?' I'm not sure where this comes from in Charlie's head.

She nods. 'We did. We worked out all the code.'

'And that helps us how?' I tap my finger on the paper.

'It doesn't. But I wanted in on the conversation.' Charlie shrugs.

Terry smiles. I want that smile. She doesn't oblige. 'Anyway, whatever they're playing with here sounds like they're looking for a way to replicate the effect they achieved. By the way, did you know that Alfred Noble invented dynamite?'

'No.'

'It's just the note refers to dynamite and Alfred.'

'Was that on the MIT course?'

'No. *Who Wants to be a Millionaire* last night.'

'Terry. The garbage cans need emptied.' The voice rings out from the kitchen.

She stands up. 'MIT or no MIT the garbage still needs dumped. I hope I helped. Whatever the puzzle is I think your friend has you beat again.'

I want to ask what she's doing after work but that's a bad idea. She doesn't look devastated that I don't. So much for my manly charms.

'Catch you later.' She smiles and I let me heart trip up a few more beats.

When she's out of hearing range Charlie pulls my face from looking at her. 'She could be your daughter.'

'But what a daughter.'

'And all the trouble you would bring down on her.'

'I know. But she's gorgeous.'

'You are a walking disaster.'

'Fair call.'

Charlie studies my scribblings. He scratches at his left bicep. Muscle. No wobble. He still puts in an hour a day. Come rain or shine. Tearing fiber. Letting it rebuild. As a champion body-builder he was determined not to run to fat. He has succeeded in part. His gut is not great but the rest is cool. He's too old for the circuit. Or at least too old for the main circuit. The seniors. Or do they call it masters? That's where his head is. The older circus is now a big-time draw. Guest appearances by the likes of Lou Ferirngo. Arnie back on screen. Hulk Hogan still ripping off his vest. It all points to life after fifty. Charlie was a quality act. He was no steroid junky. Or so he claims. He was never world-class. But he was the next step down. On the office wall of his old bar sat a picture of him at his finest. Ripped. Tanned. Happy. He pulled a state win on that day.

I watch him as he rubs the sheet of paper. I was the one who poured some fat on his stomach and put the brakes on his ambition.

He keeps going. 'So let's assume your new love is right. What does that tell us?'

'I'm part of an experiment. One looking to create clones of me. Martyn exists and he was 'created' after me.'

'And where does it all come from?'

'Where does this stuff usually originate? The government? Or governments? State anyway. Look at the history. Area 51. Project Blue. Remote viewing. Psych troops. Type *enhanced soldier* into Google and see where it gets you. A few years back a senator managed to extract a high-end dollar figure for research into telekinesis for the armed forces. The number would make a developing country cry.'

'And "aura"?'

'Not sure. But you would have to say that I have a certain aura.'

'Sure, when you forget to shower.'

'Funny. But when I let rip you could call that an aura.'

'And Alfred and Dynamite?'

'You called it on Dynamite – a project name. And Alfred could be a location.'

'Where?'

'Sweden? It's where Alfred Nobel is from.'

'A US project on Swedish soil. Possible but they're not our greatest friends. They've always had to walk a line between East and West.'

'Still possible though.'

'And a long way away if that's where the answers lie.'

'Every journey starts with one step.'

'Confucius?'

*'Sesame Street.'*

# Chapter 19

The next morning I have our transport sussed. We are about eighty miles from Lethbridge. The Canadian Pacific railroad runs all the way to Toronto from there.

We cross to the mom and pop for breakfast. My new love is missing. I'm not amazed to find I'm disappointed. We pancake and syrup our coffee into submission before heading for our wheels.

Charlie seems to like driving the Range Rover. We crack the windows as we drive. The dried blood is not the best air freshener.

'As a matter of pure curiosity, where in the hell are we?' Charlie doesn't lift his eyes from the road.

'Southern Alberta. Heading for Lethbridge. Home of the largest railway structure in Canada.'

'And that would be?'

'The Lethbridge Viaduct. Also known as the High Level Bridge. Made of metal and built in the early twentieth century. It's a mile long and rides over the Old Man River. Supposed to be quite a sight.'

'Wiki is good.'

'Can't fault it for the sheer volume of nonsense.' It cost me a couple of dollars at reception. I was sure to wipe the history when I finished.

'And does the rail line that crosses this magnificent viaduct take us nearer New York?'

'All the way to Toronto.'

'Cool.'

The highway is quiet. Charlie keeps the speed down and I keep my eyes open. 'We'll be at the town in less than an hour. We need to drop the car before then. An over-chromed, white

Range Rover is a bit of a fashion statement for me.'

We're cutting through a green-grass valley and the GPS tells me we need to find a cutoff soon or we are going to be downtown. The High Level Bridge looms up. Ok, it's impressive. Wiki was right.

'Charlie, get off now.'

We spin off and start flying along some back roads; me playing the GPS as if I know what I'm doing. We run out of road. I instruct Charlie to play hide and seek until we pop out at the river. I'm out of the car and into the trunk before the engine is dead. I pick up the drug bag, heading for the river bank.

'Morning, sir.'

I freeze. Bag in hand. I turn my head. Slow. Real slow. Blue. The man who is speaking to me is wearing blue. Dark blue. Red stripe running down the pants. Leather belt. Gun. Baton.

Police.

Shit.

I don't respond. This doesn't help.

'Can I help you, sir?'

I scan the area. We're in grassland. Running to mud. No picnic area. No roads down to the river side. His patrol car is parked fifty yards away. There's no reason for it to be there. But it is.

'Good morning, officer.' It seems like a good start.

'And you would be?'

Not a good question.

'Mike.' It's close enough for coffee.

'And can I ask what you're doing here?'

Another good question. Not one you want when you have a life sentence of drugs in your hands. 'Taking a break.'

'Really?' His face has the look of a well-worn question mark. He's in his early fifties. Tanned. No gut. Clean shaven. Eyes as dark as the water sliding behind me. He's waiting on a response.

It needs to be a good one…but I don't have one.

When I left college I was short on cash. Always short on cash. For six months I worked as a gopher for a private investigation firm based in New Jersey. Camden Bellow was a small but effective set-up owned by two school friends. Chris Camden and Mel Bellow. Chris was the brains and Mel the brawn. I spent most of the time with Mel. Backup in case of trouble. Although what use I would have been was dubious. I was never needed. Mel was an XXL version of Charlie. He carried a gun at all times. He spent his downtime learning martial arts in alphabetical order.

On the days Mel didn't need me I was assigned to Chris. Mostly to pick up admin and be a runner for coffee from the shop on the corner. Double espresso – heavy on the cream. He was born to the job. His manner was easy. He breathed trust. He could have been a billionaire if he had sold cars. I loved watching him interview people. He would elicit information in a fw minutes that others would have taken a month to find out. People liked Chris. Women loved him. He appeared as honest and as vulnerable as a newly-blessed priest. His face placed him ten years south of his real age. He chose clothes that said taste, but not money.

The fact that he was a pig of the first order was only known to those who spent more than a few hours in his company. A compulsive liar. A charlatan. He was that and more. But he could do his job. The two houses in Florida, the '72 Cobra and a powerboat in Miami were just a few of the toys he had earned the bad way.

As the officer stares me down I take the one bit of advice that Chris swore by. If you don't know what to say – say fuck all. So we play silent bunnies for a few seconds. Charlie doesn't move. I can see him playing the audience to my one-on-one.

The officer shuffles his feet. 'So what's in the bag?'

Something is a little off here. Not the question. That's legit. I'd ask the same if I were in his shoes. The shuffle. It signals nerves. Why? I can't figure what he's doing here in the first place. We are a good half-mile off the road. This is no tourist spot. There's no sign of life. The ground is loose dirt. My footprints are clear. They have no brothers or sisters. The patrol car is parked in front of a small track leading into the bushes behind it. Maybe he's on a few minutes R & R.

I drop the bag to the ground. 'A towel and some food. Care to join us?'

'A picnic?'

'Kind of. As I said, we're on a break.'

He looks around. I know what he's thinking. This is the worst picnic spot in Canada. I'm ten feet from the river. It's a slow-moving beast at this point. A few more steps and the dry earth turns to mud. I take Chris's advice again.

A train whistle cuts the morning air in half. High, shrill, determined. The High Level Bridge is just round the next bend. Diesel engines build up the noise as the train approaches. I'm hoping there are frequent freight trains through Lethbridge. I'm counting on Charlie and I hitching a lift on one, heading east and picking up the passenger train at some point.

The officer waits. In *High Noon* they stand like this for an age. Waiting for the moment to act. In reality no one waits that long.

The officer shuffles again. 'Sir. Where are you from?'

I decide to go on the offensive. 'Can I ask you a question?'

'You didn't answer my question.'

'New Jersey. Now my turn. Why are you here?'

'Sir, could you open the bag?'

I keep up the offence. It's either that or comply with the request. 'You didn't answer *my* question this time.'

'I saw you come down this way.'

Bullshit. His voice is assertive. He knows this game well. But he's pinch hitting. He's hiding something.

I push. 'Tell you what. I'll show you mine if you show me yours.'

'Sir, can you please open the bag.'

'Tell you what. I'll be happy to do that. But let's do it down at the station. I could go a cup of decent coffee. And, if there is one thing I know, it's that police know coffee.'

'There is no need for that. Open your bag and we can both be on our way.'

The police car rocks a little. I smile. I relax a little. I've got this game.

I put the bag down. 'I once knew a police officer. Same age as you. He loved his job. Turned ten hour shifts into twenties. Lost his wife. Lost his house. Lost his bank account. But loved his job. Reckoned the police owed him some. The pay packet wasn't as a good as it needed to be. So he ran his own rules. Long hours meant he took breaks when he fancied it.'

The police car rocks some more. His eyes want to look back but that would be a giveaway.

I continue. 'Anyway, with his wife humping a decorator and relationships a little hard to come by when you're never around, he still had his needs.'

The officer steps forward. Just one step. Trying to take control. 'The bag, sir.'

Charlie opens the door. The officer catches the movement. He turns.

I cough to gain the offcers attention again. He turns back. 'So my police officer friend works out some local action. No cash involved. Just a little reciprocation with the local ladies of the night. He turns a blind eye and they provide a few freebies. All in all a good deal. No messy emotional stuff. Just straight sex.'

'The bag?'

'But where to do the deed? Eh. Hard when you're a cop. People know you. There isn't a hotel for miles around that you can use and you sure as hell can't let the neighbors see what's going down.'

The officer scowls but doesn't close in. Charlie steps out of the car. We're definitely two on one here. The police car has stopped rocking but the scrunch of blonde hair between the front seats is still bobbing up and down a little. Trying to get a view.

I keep mouthing. 'So my officer friend figures it has to be the car. Park up in some out of the way spot. Let rip. Get it all done in the back seat. If someone sees him he simply tells them he has lifted the lady. Perfect.'

'The bag.' His voice is now weak.

'So I say we head down to your station. There I'll show you the towel and cheese and ham subs. Then we can ask the young lady in the back of your car for an explanation as to why you're down here.'

His face is set. Trying to figure the next move.

I push on. 'Or I can sit down, enjoy my lunch with my friend and you can wave us goodbye. But if you really want we can play twenty questions back at the ranch. I'm sure you have the story worked out. By the way, what way was it that we came?'

Nothing.

'Come on, if you followed us you must have seen which direction we came from.'

'I want you gone in twenty minutes.' He turns on his heels and marches back to the car.

Charlie walks towards me. The police vehicle revs into life, spraying dirt as the officer hammers it. The blonde in the back looks at us. Nice looking guy.

I turn to Charlie. 'Let's dump this stuff.'

We spend ten minutes slitting the bags and pouring the white powder into the river. I wrap all the used bags – wiping them for fingerprints – into one before placing them back in the sports bag. I fill the bag with dirt and stones, zip it, clean the handle and fling it as far out into the flow as I can.

I let out a big sigh of relief.

# Chapter 20

We dump the Range Rover in a multi-story a mile from the rail station. There's a long-stay section. We spring for that. If we're lucky it will be weeks before it's noticed. We leave quickly. I want on board the train. I want moving and I want moving now.

A police car streams by. I keep my eyes fixed forward. If it's our river friend he might have taken brave pills and be intent on pulling us in. The car vanishes. We keep walking. Before we got out of the car I split the money between Charlie and myself. If things get hot I want us both able to keep moving. Cash helps.

We're in backwater Canada, industrial land. Around us is a sprawl of dirt-cream buildings. Each with the architectural merit of a lump of manure. The sky is cloudless; the sun is warm on my back. With the drugs now giving the fish a high I feel better. No doubt the bag will wash up at some point. And I'm sure CSI will be able to extract my DNA, pant size and mother's first boyfriend's middle name if they find it. More likely it will end up as twenty-first century jetsam. Or maybe a handy addition to a down-and-out's wardrobe. It wasn't a cheap bag.

I turn my head to Toronto. I lived there for a while but it isn't somewhere I've been for twenty years.

In an attempt to find work after college I took up my aunt's invitation to stay with her. She lived in North York, in the north of Toronto. Her neighbor, Kartan, was from the Balkans. He had contracted polio as a kid. Both of his legs were in calipers. He was permanently short on dollars. As was I. He spotted an opportunity within a day of my bag landing on my aunt's bed.

He pointed out that Pizza Pizza were looking for delivery boys. '967 *Eleven Eleven, Call Pizza Pizza.*' I can still hum the tune from the ad.

He realised he couldn't deliver the pizzas, whereas I could.

But with his driving skills – he fancied himself as cross between Steve McQueen and Mario Andretti – he reckoned we could earn more than twice what a single driver could earn.

Every night for months we would rocket across northern Toronto, ignoring most of the road signs. I would be ejected from the car before we had stopped. I would sprint to the door, deliver the pizzas and be on my way back to the car while the customer's front door was still closing.

We were on thirty minutes or free for pizza back then. In those days the order was phoned to a central point – then sent to us by fax. We got the order with twenty-five minutes left on the promise. Take off ten minutes to cook. Add on three delivery points and we needed to average five minutes per delivery. Over an urban sprawl of two miles by two miles that was near impossible. Yet night after night we did it. We brought in more cash than any delivery team and we always got the late, late jobs. The ones that were too tight.

Me and Kartan spent four months pulling in as much cash as we could. We picked up parking and speeding tickets. Kartan would play the disability card and get off more than he got fined.

I'm not planning a sightseeing tour of old haunts in Toronto but I'm growing in certainty that New York is not going to happen. Way too tight on time already. I need a plan B and, as I walk, I begin to think Toronto is it. If for no other reason that it's a lot closer and *not* in America.

Charlie spots him first. Our police officer from the river. Charlie grabs me by the arm to haul me out of sight.

I screw my eyes up. 'What's going on?'

'Your police friend is in front of the rail station.'

'Seriously.'

'Large as life.'

'Crap. How would he know we are coming here? It's a freight yard.'

'Maybe we've been spotted. Maybe he put an APB on the car. Maybe they've found the car. Where else would we go? This is the nearest jump off spot.'

I disagree. 'There's Red Arrow, Greyhound, flights, hire cars. All a lot more obvious than jumping a freight train.'

'So you tell me why he's standing there.'

I look round the corner. The police officer is next to a colleague. Two more guard the other side of the main entrance. They're eyeballing everyone.

I pull back. 'We'll never get on the train with him there. We should move on. Let's hope we can jump on the train out of town.'

Charlie shakes his head. 'Not likely. The days of bumming a ride on a passing train are all but dead. The whole train will be locked tight. We need to find an open wagon. That's only going to happen at a station.'

Charlie's right. I take another look. The old station in front of me looks mid-ninetieth-century – white clapperboard up top and red brick below. I kepp my head out a fraction too long. The police officer spots me

I duck back. 'Run.'

We run back the way we came, as a patrol car zips into view. Charlie sprints right. The officer shouts from behind. I look back. Turn to follow Charlie but the patrol car is cutting me off from him.

I run down the opposite road. The patrol car goes for Charlie as it spots the police officer cutting right to catch me.

I need off the road. I choose the first store and dive in. It's a launderette. A few customers are sitting, bored and tuned into channel washing on the machines. They look up as I enter. I fly across to the rear. I crack open the door. Inside is dark. A splinter of light indicates another door. I kick it open. A back alley lies beyond. Instead of running out I go into reverse , throwing myself to the right. I clip a small desk. I tumble to the floor, as the door from the launderette bursts open. The officer rushes through and out the rear door.

I'm up, doubling back, through the laundrettet, onto the street. I run back towards the station.

There are only two police offciers left at the station. Both are on the far side of the small square. I slow. Breathe. Walk out. Desperate to look back. But don't. I want to check if the river officer is there. I don't. I just try and look as if I'm meant to be there. Part of the world. I reach the steps to he entrance and, as I pass through the double door, I expect a shout to go up. Nothing.

I pass into the body of the kirk. The tracks spread out before me. A triple-engined Canadian Pacific locomotive with a thousand wagons stretches for a country mile in front of me. Most of the wagons are oil or grain. I can't hide in any of them. At the rear one of the caboose's doors is open. Two men are loading boxes. I look back for Charlie or police. I see neither.

The train driver pulls on the whistle. The loaders are lifting the last box. It's the size of a coffin. They're at their limit trying to get it in. The taller of the two – a man with tattoos instead of shirtsleeves – has his back to me. The other, a smaller man, is head-down. I keep walking. No time for subtlety. The door is twenty feet away. They place the box on the ground to try and find a better grip. The smaller man bends to grab the box. The taller man is already bent double. I nip in behind them, climb the ramp and enter the darkness.

The car is stuffed with crates. I clamber over them, find a spot and drop out of sight.

I hear the men struggle to get the box on board. Use of the F-word is compulsory. The last F is thrown as the door is ground shut. I have no idea where I'm going. No idea what has happened to Charlie. But with luck I'm off the grid.

# Chapter 21

The train seems to accelerate with the same fervor as a sloth on dope. I'm so underprepared that I wonder what the hell I was thinking. No food. No drink. No change of clothes. Nothing to keep warm. I had planned to do a little shopping on the way but we passed nothing. I'm freewheeling.

I settle in for the ride. I wonder if Charlie'll talk if he's caught? Unlikely. We're not in Cold War Russia here. They have nothing on us. Charlie will say nada.

I decide to go exploring. Fingertip-searching in the dark and rolling landscape. I clamber around, trying the tops of random crates, hoping to find something to ease the pain of the trip. I strike lucky half an hour in. One of the crates is less than solid. There's a gap between box and lid. I work at it with my fingers. It gives a little. I scramble around the floor, looking for something to give me a little leverage. I come up with a small metal strip. Some long-lost fixing. I force it into the gap. The lid cracks. A sharp sound over the rolling thunder of the train. The lid releases. I dip my hands into the open container.

I pull out packing. Soft balls of cloth. A lot of them. I pile them to one side. It will make good bedding. Then I hit something rigged with wires. I try to manhandle it out but it's packed tight. I play around with my fingers.

A new quiz show for prime time television. *In The Dark.* Contestants are given mystery boxes to examine in the dark. They get ten seconds to guess what's inside. If they get it right they win a thousand bucks. If they get it wrong they get another ten seconds and the prize fund drops. After a minute they're done. But at any point they can stop the clock and forgo the cash for the object. Of course not all the objects would be worth winning.

I play *In The Dark*. Material gives way to more wires and bolts. Hard plastic next. Then a cold metal housing and a prop. I'm guessing a powered hang-glider. Might come in handy if I need to do a James Bond out of the car door.

I keep up my game. Six boxes on, as the train feels like it has hit the dizzy heights of ten miles an hour, I find one stuffed with plastic bundles. I burst one with my finger. I rip it open, pulling out a thick woolen sweater. It's too dark to see any pattern but at least I won't freeze.

★

As the day crawls by I doze. My head is circling on the same old same old. No fresh news. Just flashbacks of the last few years. Lorraine's death. Being on the run. Hatred for Tampoline. Martyn. Back to Lorraine. Always back to Lorraine. My lifeblood. I feel wet on my cheek. I let the tears flow. My guts tighten as the sobs drag out. They deepen. Take on an edge. The dam bursts and I cry harder than at any time I can remember. I so want to change the past. Go back. Undo. Redo. Live in a better world. My sobs ease and I rock myself to sleep.

When I waken I need to pee. I clamber around to find a spot at the back. I aim at the wall, hoping the stream will run out of the car. I'm hungry but that's not going to get better soon. I finish my pee, bed down again, settle in for the wait.

I fall asleep again. Dreamless. A rare occurrence.

★

Deceleration knocks me from my slumber. The train slows to a crawl before shunting to a halt. Voices carry from outside. Then the lock of my car is thrown. I leap back into the interior as light floods in.

'Fuck. It smells like someone has pissed in here.' The voice has a heavy Canadian twang. 'If I find a bum in here I'm going to cream his backside.' The voice is loud. I lie still. 'Geoff, have you got the list?'

132

'The big box at the front. Paulo at Lethbridge says it was the last one they loaded. They screwed up. It's supposed to be on the westbound train.'

'Assholes.'

'At least they realized before the thing got to Toronto.'

I hear them shift the box. It takes a while.

I make a call. I can't ride this any longer. With no food or water this is nuts. I slip from my hiding place and crawl to the front.

I squat by the door. Beyond is nothing but trees and space. The two workers have removed the box. I slide forward. The workers are wheeling the box back to a small platform. I was expecting a goods yard but the stopping place is no more than a halt. A highway cuts across the tracks about a hundred yards back. A small truck is idling at the crossing point.

I drop from the train and clamber under. Halfway through I slip, landing on my back between the tracks. What if the behemoth moves? I crawl at speed – throwing myself out on the other side. I look back at the steel wheels. The train stretches as far as I can see to my left. To my right there's only the caboose. The two workers are heaving the box onto their truck. Behind me some small pine trees clump together. I dive into them.

A mile up the track a whistle goes. A few seconds later the wagons shudder. Then, almost beyond detection, the train begins to move. As it leaves I'm tempted to hitch a ride from the two box men. But it wouldn't take a smart person three seconds to figure where I'd just come from.

I watch as the truck drives off. Time for Shanks's Pony. My rendezvous with Martyn is fading into the distance.

The highway gives no clue as to the best direction to take. It stretches at right angles to the railtrack. Either way could be good. I consider walking the track. I might be lucky – might be close to a station. But I doubt it. The box men would have let the train stop on a full platform if they could. My instinct is to head in the opposite direction to the way the pickup went.

As I set off I'm glad of the sweater, although the giant red rose motif on the front is a bit disconcerting. Who the hell would see this as a good fashion choice?

A couple of miles on and I'm none the wiser on where I'm at. Two rides have flown by. Both ignored my raised thumb. I turned towards them to show face and thumb. I kept my chest away from the vehicles. The rose isn't an aid for hitchhikers. Nada.

I hear another vehicle approaching and a white compact rounds the corner. I try and hide the rose, flip my thumb and smile. I wait for the brush off but the car slows. It draws level with me.

A small man with round wire-framed glasses stares at me. 'Where are you going, son?'

He has one of the worst comb-overs I've ever seen.

*Son* is a bit of a surprise. I would say we are in the same age neighborhood.

'Anywhere east.'

'How far east?'

'As far as you can get.'

'You're not one of those killer hitchhikers are you?'

'How did you know?'

There's no smile. I may have blown it.

He leans out a little to give me the once over. 'I used to hitch-hike. Never in such a wild sweater though.'

I risk the humour line a bit more. 'Us roadside nutters all dress this way. Makes us easy to spot.'

This time his lips flick a small smile. 'Jump in.'

I climb in, welcoming the interior heat. The smell in the car is pure sandalwood. Strong.

He notices me sniffing. 'What you're smelling, son, is the

angel's own wood polish. *Honey 2 Honey*. My own invention. You might have heard the radio ads. Been pushing it local. *Honey 2 Honey. And your wood is free.* He sings it. Dire Straits might be due some royalties for the use of the *Money for Nothing* melody.

I shake my head. 'Sorry, I'm not local.'

'Never no mind. The name's Johnston Honey.'

My eyes say *seriously?*

'I know. My mother married a guy called Henry Honey. Her maiden name was Johnston. I'm the original spoilt, single child.'

This guy likes the sound of his own voice. He also has a thing for speed. The compact is a Chrysler-something and has had its engine swapped out for a jet. Johnston takes the first two corners without lifting from the gas. We pass seventy miles per hour with little more than a nod to the fact that he seems to be just winding up for the pitch. His eyes only occasionaly look at the road in front. 'And you would be?'

'Craig.' No point in inventing a name. At six feet five and bald as a coot I'm not going to slip from people's memory with ease. If he asks for a second name I'll pick something easy to remember. Maybe Smith.

'Nice to meet you, Craig. Now you said east. I'm heading for Toronto but it's a long trip.'

'As far as you feel good to take me will do, Johnston.'

'Let's see how we get on.'

Outside is a blur. I pull on my seatbelt. I'm not sure talking is a good idea but I'm curious. 'Why Toronto?'

Johnston looks over. 'Got a shipment of *Honey 2 Honey* for export. Never had any go abroad before. I want to wave it off.'

'Really?'

'Sounds dumb?'

Our speed seems to have found a new level. We are already slamming by one of the cars that blanked me. I nod. 'A bit.'

Johnston seems at ease with the velocity. 'I know it does, but it turns out my distributor in Ontario has a brother in Glasgow who has ordered up ten pallets. Half a container. Shit, that's more than I sell in a month on the road. I need to see the distributor in Toronto anyway, so I thought I would try and get there before the order ships out.'

At this speed he'll get there before the ship's built. 'Is it shipping out from Toronto?'

'The Port of Toronto. Never been there but it can't be hard to find. Not really a main port. It seems that all the major stuff is offloaded at Montreal. Big ships can't make it into the lakes but mine can. The Canuck B. Can you get with the irony? *Honey 2 Honey* and Canuck *B*?' He laughs.

'Can you make it in time?'

'Easy. She doesn't ship out until 8.00am.'

'And you had time to stop to pick me up?'

'I need someone to keep me awake. I need to pull an all-nighter if I'm to get there with time to spare.'

We take the next corner on little more than two wheels. Then he rips us up an on-ramp and onto a freeway. He settles into the groove. 'Now we can get some miles under our belt.'

He pushes the needle up and flicks on some heavy duty dance music.

Highway patrols don't seem to figure in his world.

# Chapter 22

We hurtle through the Canadian landscape, trailing high energy music in our wake. Johnston has no need of a gas pedal. All he requires is an on and off switch under his right foot.

We stop for gas. I fill up on fizzy drink and snacks. Johnston stacks up the Red Bull. Then we're back on the trance highway with a vengeance. Johnston trying to make up for the time lost on the pit stop. As night closes in he swigs from can after can of caffeine, all the time dragging more dance music from the stereo.

We streak on. Eating miles. I fade in and out of the world. My ears are numb but I don't complain. A flight would have been slower. I worry that Johnston will get zapped for speeding but he seems to have an in-built radar for the police. The process is always the same. I'll feel the pressure on my chest build as we leave warp speed. We see a police patrol. We are legal. We lose them. Then back to the lightning.

Outside is dark, then I see a sign for a rest stop. Tapping Johnston on the shoulder I point to my groin. His face drops but he signals right to land the plane on the gas forecourt. I use the washroom before making for the shop.

I enter and scan for a payphone. Cell phones have done for most of them. The man behind the counter is dressed in a company T-shirt. His name is Dave. Not David but Dave. Next to him is a phone.

I rub my pounding ears as I approach him. 'Could I use your phone?'

'Not for the use of the public.' The words are monosyllabic.

'It's a bit of an emergency.'

'Police, fire, ambulance?'

'Not that bad.'

'Phone's not for the use of the public.'

His head is a swathe of blonde. Bottle born. His nose is a sharp hook that's turned down on me.

I put on my best puppy eyes. 'It'll only take me two minutes.'

'Phone's not for the use of the public.'

'I got that, but I need to make a call.'

'Cell?'

'I'm the last holdout on the planet.'

'Pity. Payphone is ten miles back. Last-but-one turn off. Graham's Bar. You can't miss it.'

Johnston won't be up for that. 'Come on. One call.'

He points at the camera. 'My boss watches the tapes for fun. He sees me giving you use of the phone – I get fired. Phone's not for the use of the public.'

I'm not going to win this one. The door opens, Johnston appears. 'We need to go.'

I nod. I'll just have to risk using Johnston's cell.

Johnston points to the car. As if I need to be reminded. Behind him a young man rolls in. Hoody up. I smell trouble enter with him. He shuffles past me.

'Jez, get out.' Dave is speaking to the hoody.

Either Jez doesn't hear or doesn't want to hear. He walks up to the counter and turns to look at me. He's waiting for me to leave. Johnston clears out. I should follow but I don't. I play with some chips, looking as if I'm sizing up flavors.

I keep my eyes on Jez. He keeps his eyes on me. I back up a little. I clip a shelf. A jar of peanut butter swan-dives, smashing on the floor. It splashes on my feet. I jump to one side, landing in a puddle of peanut mud. My left foot takes off. My right follows. I'm airborne then, with a crack, my head meets the shop window.

The world lurches. I slide to the floor. I lose contact with reality for a few seconds. The blue world settles around me then it's gone. Dazed, I settle in the peanut butter and glass. I hear a shout as I rub the back of my head. I'll have a hefty lump. I lie for a second. Another shout. A crash, then a yell. Then a sound I can't place. I keep still. Letting the planet find me again.

The door opens. I hear Johnston say, 'What the fuck?'

I stand up.

Johnston's looking in the direction of the counter. He is stepping back, grabbing the door.

I realize that he's going to leave. I call to him. 'Johnston.' He doesn't look at me. He keeps his eyes fixed on the counter. Whatever is there, is keeping his attention big time. The shelving blocks my view. Johnston plays with the door handle. Rubbing his hand up and down the metal.

'Johnston, what is it?'

The sweet smell of peanut butter is filling my nostrils. Johnston has the door wide open now.

I move forward. Jez's feet appear. Puma sneakers. One gleaming white. One with a wash of pink through it. A puddle of red is flowing around the pink one. As I emerge from the shelving I see a stream of blood running away from Jez. Thick. Rich. It starts at his neck. His head is bent at an impossible angle. Lying by his neck is a Bowie knife. A blade of nine inches. Solid wooden handle. Serrated edge.

The knife is floating in the sea of blood. Jez's head is attached to his body by his spinal column. And little else.

It took some force to do that. No casual stroke. No accidental swipe. Severing a head is a major job. And Dave has come as close as makes no difference to achieving it. I flick my eyes to the CCTV. Jez would have been in the prime spot for the recording with Dave the guilty party. I'm probably on the tape now. Johnston will be there. We wouldn't be in the frame for the murder. But that's not the major worry in my life.

I look at Johnston. He's still backing away. I swing back to

Dave. He turns his attention to me. His eyes are wide. His mouth clamped close. He has no words. He just looks confused. Burned deep. No understanding. Reality has been replaced by madness. I've seen it all before. Some remember. Some don't. Some see their actions as justified. Others are left tortured. Some vomit. Some collapse. Many cry. Whatever it is that I do, there is no defined way for it all to finish. But their world will never be the same.

He opens his mouth. A single word. 'Me?'

A question. One to which he wants a negative answer. For me to point to someone else. And then all will be right in his garden.

I neither shake nor nod. I have no answer. For no answer will ever suffice. He will never know why. All he will know is what he sees. He will watch the playback on the grainy CCTV. Watch himself slice Jez. He will probably watch it again and again. And yet he will never believe it. As if some cruel Candid Camera show is playing with his head.

I don't usually have much to do with the aftermaths of what I do. I'm rarely around for long after an incident goes down.

Dave reaches out, his hands rising slowly. Beseeching me. This time I shake my head. I lift my hand and place a thumb on my ear. A pinky on my mouth. I mouth 'police' then spin away.

I exit and, with gathering speed, follow Johnston.

He's heading for the car. He quickens and I have to break into a jog. He leaps into the driver's seat. I'm twenty yards away when he fires up the engine. I'm ten yards away when he puts the car into gear. I'm five yards away when the car moves. I change direction. Angling towards his planned route. The car jumps forward.

I leap across the hood. Grabbing at the car. My head hits the windshield. I scrabble for a hold. Johnston's eyes lock onto me. He keeps his foot down. We accelerate across the forecourt. I have little to hold onto. As soon as he swings left or right I'll be thrown free.

I thump my fist on the hood. 'Stop.'

My yell is lost in the engine noise. He has his foot hard to the floor.

We swerve left. I start to slide. I throw my hands at the windshield and grab at the wipers. The car straightens. My biceps groan as my fingers, circling the wipers, try hold me in place. I shout again. Telling Johnston to stop. And, to my surprise, he does just that.

I slide forward, hands ripped from the wipers, rolling on to the ground. I expect him to accelerate again. I scrabble out of the way. The car sits. Engine ticking over. Exhaust fumes clouding the rear in the cold air.

Johnston is looking towards me. He opens the passenger door. I slide in. He pushes the car out onto the highway. Then we're part of the conveyor belt of vehicles.

Johnston has lost his appetite for speed. We cruise. No mad rush. I sit. Staring straight ahead, trying to figure what Johnston is planning. He slips his hand to his head. Unconsciously rearranging his comb-over. An act he must perform hourly. He stacks and packs. His hair settles. It looks contrived. He ages with the style. He would be better cropping it all off.

He fingers the blinker stalk, as if contemplating pulling off the road. We slow. A rig gives its horn a haul as it's forced to avoid us. Our speed falls some more. Johnston flicks the blinker and we bump onto the dirt. He finds neutral but leaves the engine running.

I wait.

'We need to go back.' His words are quiet.

'We don't.'

He turns to me. 'Of course we do. I just witnessed a murder.'

'And can you bring him back to life?'

'I shouldn't have left.'

'What could you have done?'

'Tell the police what I saw.'

I don't want to go back. I change tack. 'You nearly killed me.'

'I didn't know what I was doing. I just wanted away. But it's not right. The police will know we were there.'

I'm not sure where to take this. Everything about the situation demands we return. And everything about my situation demands we don't. 'Look, drop me off and you go back.'

'But you should go back as well.'

'They don't need me. I didn't see anything. I was behind the shelving when it all happened. They need *you*.'

'You can't just leave a murder scene.'

'You just did. It happens all the time.'

'They'll want to know where you've gone? Who you are?'

'And what can you tell them?'

'Not much.'

'And, trust me, that's a good thing.'

'Why?'

'You don't want to know. Just take me along to the next sensible place you can stop, and drop me.'

'And what do I tell the police?'

'The truth. You witnessed the murder then panicked. You saw sense but I wouldn't come back with you. No drama.'

He thinks this over. Chewing at a nail on his right thumb. 'I want to go back right now. The police could be there now.'

'I'm not going. Drop me here if you want but all I'm asking is that you find the next exit and let me out. You can't cross the meridian here anyway.'

He nods. Without hesitation he nudges us back into the traffic.

Two miles later there's an exit. He swings up and stops at the top. I open the door and get out. There are no goodbyes. I watch as he speeds back the way we have just come.

# Chapter 23

I walk down, back to the highway, heading away from the scene of the murder. Around me is darkness. I can't see a single light indicating a house or any sign of life in the vicinity.

Car lights throw shadows in front of me. I'm far enough over not to be in danger of being hit. Unless someone loses it. Someone always loses it. It's just a matter of time. A heart attack, spilt coffee, kid screaming, sneezing fit – any major distraction. Eye off the wheel, vehicle off the road. I wouldn't see it coming. Hit by a car. Slammed by a truck. Rammed by a rig. Better to go out quickly. No warning. Roadkill. Someone else's cleanup job. Not a nice one. But someone has to do it.

I read, or heard, that there are companies that specialize in such cleanups. Cleanup after suicides. Cleanup after murder. Cleanup after accidents. They know stuff. What works to remove brain matter from a woolen carpet? Do shredded guts need an acid or alkali removal agent? How do you get the last of those stubborn spinal fluid marks from the back of the fridge? Who knows what else?

I rub at my eye. Crack a knuckle. Flick at an invisible hair on my jacket. I don't revisit the madness. I spend too long in that world. The whys and whats that have no answer. The insanity of it all. I want my head elsewhere. A new focus.

I start with my foot. My left foot. I concentrate on it. Focus on my toes. Work out what they're feeling. I can feel the pressure from my shoes as I walk. I raise my thoughts to my ankle. Notice it's hot. My lower leg. An itch. Thigh. Nothing. Stomach. Food needed. Chest. No heart attack. Head. Headache – but a gentle one. In the background. An Advil moment soon. Then back to my other foot and repeat the journey. Add in my arms then onto my breath. Cold blue in. Hot red out. Concentrate on the breathing. Nothing but the breathing. Envisage my lungs expanding and contracting. My mind wanders to the gas station. I drag it back to breathing. Where's Charlie? I return to my breathing. Think about breathing. Always breathing.

It's part of mindfulness. A nonsense that I now observe. For the moment I gorget what has gone. |I don't look to what will be. It's time to just be. To live in the now. A footstep is a precious commodity. Within it a second of living is counted. A heartbeat you cannot get back. So enjoy it. Work to immerse yourself in it.

My mind cuts free. Floating. Always take it back to the breathing when your mind wants to crawl over stuff. No past. No future. Only now.

Soon, thoughts vanish. Replaced with an unruffled peace. A dead calm in the center of a storm. A spinning light joins my breathing. Pulsing to the movement of my lungs. My eyes watch the pulse. It spreads across the land. Lighting the flora and fauna. I keep pace with it. Marching to its silent rhythm.

A mile becomes two. Two doubles. Four. The light keeps me moving forward. My head tries to squeeze thoughts in. I fight them. Gently. Pushing them down. Down and out. Away.

And now we have music to accompany the light. Trance dance. Music from Johnston's car. A pounding rhythm. Repetitive. Hypnotic. Drum and bass in unison. High end keyboards striking out on a mission to encourage movement. To urge me to move from walk to bop. Armin Van Buuren. Paul Van Dyk, Underworld, Jam and Spoon, Above and Beyond. Euphoric breakdown. Chill. AM. PM. Dawn. All in my head. A personal rave.

The miles creep past. I'm no nearer my destination in any useful sense. But I'm now in the hands of fate. My head allows a few random thoughts back in as the light vanishes. A new beat kicks in. Not trance. More Mamas and Papas. Not in my head. A cold white glow rises up. The home to the music is a hundred yards away. I take in the new. I let go of the old. A third voice joins in. Not a mama or a papa. Not in tune.

Ahead is an RV. Side door open. Light spilling out. A shape is bent over near the front. Singing. I walk up as the music flips to Jimi Hendrix. The sound is coming from inside the RV. The bent form is a man. He's heaving on the nuts of the front wheel. A flat lying next to him.

I keep back. Near the door. 'Hi.'

He jumps a little. Spinning round. 'Jesus, man. You gave me a fright.'

'Sorry. Flat tire?'

He's in his thirties. Goatee. Thin face. Dandruff. His Afghan coat looks like an original '60s. He looks up at me. 'It could have been worse. It didn't blow out. I felt it start to vibrate and pulled over.'

'Can I help?'

He looks past me. 'Where did you come from?'

My lack of transport has changed his tone. Curiosity with an edge of caution.

'Hiking.'

'At this time.'

'Couldn't find a bed. Short on cash. So I just kept walking.'

'This is a hell of a place to be. I mean, it's the middle of nowhere, man.'

He sounds like he's slipped from a comic book. A version of a Santa Monica surfer just after the Beach Boys stopped being cool.

I look at the open door. 'Are you alone?'

'Always, man.'

'You wouldn't be up for giving an old man a ride.'

'Where are you for?'

'East. You?'

'Same.'

We're in a negotiation.

He stands. 'A couple of questions, man?'

'Sure.'

'You wanted by the law?'

'Yes.'

He doesn't bat an eyelid. 'You been shat on by the law?'

'A bit.'

'Man, are you gonna bring me trouble?'

'Maybe.'

'Bad trouble?'

'Maybe.'

'Honest dude, aren't you, man.'

'Best policy. I take it I'm walking.'

'No, man. Get in.'

'Risk taker?'

'Friend. Too many run-ins with the law back home, man. Happy to help.'

It seems that telling some people you might be the next Son of Sam doesn't put them off you. Go figure. I help him store the busted wheel before I get in the RV.

The inside is a shrine to psychedelia. Love's eponymous album cover is pride of place on the space above a tiny wash-bowl. The RV's color scheme is early Scooby Doo. The carpet is shag pile pink. The ceiling is night sky blue, studded with tiny lights – an indoor star field. The driver's wheel is fur-lined. The seats are coated in more of the same material. A bed has a cover with Jimi Hendrix picked out in stitching. The music is coming from a cassette player. It's now playing Garth Brooks. Out of step with everything else. Even the joss sticks suggest we have time-warped.

The man turns. 'Welcome to my pad, man. I'm Artie.'

'I'm Craig.'

I climb up front with him. I'm not surprised to see a wobbling figure of Marylyn Monroe siting on the dash.

'You really dig the '60s?' Rhetorical question really.

'I was born in the wrong era, man. My mom and dad were flower children. My dad was at Woodstock. Saw Jimi. Artie was the name of one of the originators of Woodstock.'

'Was more of a Janis fan myself.'

'Cool, man.'

I'm wondering if this guy is taking the piss. Even in the '60s no one was this '60s. 'Where are you from?'

'My heart lies in Haight-Ashbury.'

Question avoided. I'd take a guess at somewhere more Mid-West. His faux West Coast accent slips now and again.

'You?'

'New Jersey.'

'Cool, man.'

He trundles onto the highway. Artie is the polar opposite of Johnston. Speed is an optional extra. I yawn. 'Mind if I close my eyes?'

'Be my guest, man. I'm awake now. Bust tire and fresh air will do that.'

I let the roll of the badly sprung RV act as a lullaby.

*

A flash of white. A man in a coat. Hanging over me. Syringe in hand. His face featureless. White skin pulled over a smooth skull. Strip lighting above him. Cold. Soulless. The smell is anti-septic. Hospital, hot and heavy. Sounds leak from other rooms. Crying. Moaning. Yelling. Screaming.

I'm restrained. Hands and feet bound to the bed. My head is locked solid. A second shape appears. A twin of the first. Tips the syringe skywards. Presses on the plunger. Liquid sprays into the air. Silver. A tiny rainbow forms.

This is Before. Before the first incident. Before I hatched a monster. Before my life changed. This is army time. I have grit in my teeth. I crunch on it. Tasting the saltiness. The dryness. Sand. Desert?

I don't struggle. I'm here but I'm not. A calm runs through me. A serene moment in a bad place. My breathing is shallow. My muscles pliable. Soft. chewed paper. No energy.

White Coat 1 rubs my arm with a wet swab. It cools my skin. I like that. He passes the syringe to his twin. The twin leans in, piercing me just below the elbow joint. The junkies' hot spot. There's no discernable impact. No rush. No fade. No lucid revelation. Nothing.

The twin steps back. I stare up. Above the crude strip lighting rows of corrugated metal sheets are bolted together. Temporary.

A voice in the distance shouts, 'Mother'. One word. A lifetime of meaning. Pain. A squeal. Then 'Mother' again. Loud.

A printer rattles. Paper being gobbed out. I count. After fifty I stop. But the machine doesn't. A dry clatter for each page.

My chest is wired up. My fingers are wired up. I'm leaking information. Feeding the printer.

I count the bolts in the ceiling. They are fresh and dull grey. If I could touch them they would have storage dust still on them. This place is a recent construct, built in a rush. One of the metal sheets is twisted at the corner. A bad fixing. A lazy join. The gap lets in a slit of light. Whiter than the strip lighting. But warmer. Deeper. Outside light.

A flake of aluminum drops from the broken corner as a vehicle roars by. A heavy roar. Tank? It rumbles. Taking its time. Then a second and a third. A convoy. The printer spits on. The shouts and screams keep up. Noise closes in on me. Yet I'm still at peace. No panic.

The tank is not just a roar. It's a recipe of sound. Gears crunching. Engine grinding. Tracks ripping the soil. Exhaust whistling. I dissect the sounds, lay them out, filling a mental table with images. Each related to its sound.

I search deeper. Digging within the gear changes for the catch of the clutch, for the clash of the linkages, for the drip of the gear oil. I expand the table. It's longer and wider than the room I occupy. It fills with objects. I shape each one individually. Taking care to dwell over the detail. The printer inks are flowing into the engine oil. The cries of 'Mother' are in perfect time with the breathing of the tank commander.

My eyes do not blink. My head becomes the table. Objects tumble in. Order becomes disorder. I dissect further. Shavings from the tank tracks. Slivers from the paper. Letters from the words. My table wraps my world.

Deeper still. To sub-atomic level. And beyond. Each step multiplying the contents on the table by wild factors. It groans. It dips. The legs buckle. And yet more stuff floods onto it. The photons from the light. The quarks. Charms. Higgs bosons. A Niagara of energy. Keep breaking it down. All is energy. Like the scientists, I'm no longer seeking matter. For matter down here is pure energy.

My head is open to everything. Receiving all. Sound. Light. Smell. All. I'm lifting from the bed. Passing through the restraints. Rising to the ceiling.

I speed up. Through the roof. Into the heat of the desert. Into the sky. Soaring. Straight up. Looking to the cloudless sky. It darkens as I rise through the atmosphere. Into ink. Out of air. Into real cold.

I feel a tug. Something slowing my ascent. It starts to hurt. Pulling at my skin. I reach round. Explore. A wire. Fused to my back. Yanking at my skin. Separating it from my skeleton. I twist, tracing the wire as it curves back to earth. A tether. My speed slows to a crawl. The wire at its limit. My skin close to splitting. Then, like a reverse bungee, I start back down.

I know the landing will hurt. All my dreams hurt in the end. I become a blur. Passing terminal velocity. Being reeled back in.

The desert reappears. The base. The building.

I wake screaming.

I know now when my world changed. When they found what they were looking for. When it was set free. I am in the moment, but of the moment. That moment.

★

Artie swerves onto the meridian. We're out of the night, well into the next day. He fights the RV to get it back on the road. He catches the slide and forces us back onto the highway. Thankfully the traffic is light. We slip onto the nearside lane as he eases off the gas.

He turns to me. 'Shit, man. What's wrong with you? You scared the hell out of me. What kind of nightmare were you having?'

'Sorry. It's not like me.'

'Well if that happens again I'd go and seek some help. I thought you were on a bad acid trip.'

'Where are we?'

'Getting there. But still a good few miles to Toronto.'

'We're near Toronto?'

'Getting closer.'

'Really?'

'Man, but I can get it on with this old driving wheel when I need. Don't feel tired. So I just kept us going. You've been out for the long haul man.'

'I need to go to the bathroom.'

'I could do with some caffeine.'

He signals at the next turn off. I expect him to find a diner. He doesn't. He pulls in at the side of the road. 'I've a chemical toilet at the back. Feel free. I'll brew some wake-up juice.'

# Chapter 24

It isn't the rest stop I envisaged. But needs must when the devil's pressing your bladder. I'm conscious of the noises I might make and stuff toilet paper into the pan to try to deaden the sound of descending pee. A handle sits to the left. Pulling it back and forth flushes some green liquid. The smell takes me back to the dream. I shiver.

I turn my mind to next steps. With Toronto now a real option I need to get in touch with Martyn and hope he can reroute.

I exit into the RV. Artie is worrying a pot of water on a stove. Coffee is still some way off.

'Do you have a cell?' I say this with the same expectation of a yes as for a date with Katy Perry on Match.com.

He turns round. 'In the front man. Next to the sound machine.'

Surprise, surprise. 'I need to make a long distance call. I'll pay.'

'Sure, leave what you think in the pouch. If you need to make change there's plenty. I pay for every call. Makes it easy to buy the credit.'

I wonder how a cell and hippie culture mix. Truth is that if mobile technology had been available in the Sixties they would have used it.

The phone is old school. No internet. Voice and text. I drop out of the door. We are a few hundred yards from well-kept homes. Brown wood and mown lawns. Paint up to date. No car over four years old.

Next to the RV is a culvert. I skip over it, trying to recall Mrs Rubenstein's number. On my fifth attempt I get it right.

I expect her to hang up but she doesn't. She agrees to get Martyn's mother. I ask if I can hold. I'll owe Artie a few dollars but I want Coleen on the phone as soon as possible. If they're tracing this call, holding on will make no difference. Traces are instant. No need to keep the perp on for a trace nowadays. Just press a button and ask the computer.

'*Hello.*' Colleen.

'It's Craig.'

'*Yes.*'

'I'll keep it short. I need to get another message to Martyn.'

'*Go on.*'

'I need to change the meet point.'

'*To where?*'

I take a breath. 'Toronto.'

'*And?*'

'Can you tell him to go to the Drake Hotel on Queen Street West.' It's the only hotel I can remember. I hope it is still there. 'As soon as he can.'

'*Ok.*'

'And ...' She hangs up on me.

Well I've telegraphed where I'm heading to anyone tuning in. I re-cross the culvert.

The smell of fresh coffee emanates from the not-so-fresh Mystery Machine. I wait outside. Artie emerges with two mugs. 'No cream or sugar. Black or black, man.'

He offers out both mugs.

I take one. 'Black is good.'

And it is. The caffeine gets to work and I feel a little more positive. 'So, Artie, which part of Toronto are you headed for?'

'Downtown. Got a guy I need to meet. A deal I need to do. You know, man.'

'And then?'

'Ah. No idea. Not 'til I meet the man. All depends on the man.'

'Life-changing deal?'

'Maybe. Maybe not. He has some promises in the wind. I'm hoping they don't blow away. Where's Nirvana for you?'

'East.'

'And when you hit water?'

'I'll do a Forrest Gump and head back.'

'Good film. Always wondered why they never made a sequel.'

'Don't mess with a classic.'

'Ain't the Hollywood way. Always want the successful sequel before they release the first film. Risky business the movies. Risky, man.'

I draw in some more coffee. 'You like the movies?'

'Love 'em.'

'What type?'

'Anything, man. Just about anything. From Bond to porn. Sci-Fi to highbrow. But I don't get to see much on the road. Back home I'm more VHS than HBO. You?'

'Never was big on movies. Books.'

'Ah, the written word. Cool, man.'

A Dodge slows as it approaches us on the far side of the road. An older man with a full gray beard eyeballs us as he slides along. In the passenger seat a pale-skinned woman stares out. She's shaking her head. As if Artie's van and a couple of coffee mugs suggest the neighborhood is in danger of invasion. I wave. She snaps her eyes to the front. Gray Beard flicks me the bird.

Artie catches this. 'Really? For what?'

He returns the gesture with a flourish. Gray Beard scowls and mouths off. I'm guessing that his vocabulary is not fit for the *hanging over the picket fence* brigade that live around here.

The car drifts towards the houses. The brake lights flare. Then the car three-points a turn.

Artie watches. 'He's coming back.'

The car crawls up.

The window drops. 'My wife is phoning the police.'

Artie sips at his coffee. 'Really, man. For what reason?'

'Vagrancy. We don't need your sort around here.'

'And what would our "sort" be?'

'Wasters.' The word has a ring of the well-used about it.

'Ain't no waster, man. Got my own home. Own wheels. Run my own business. What's your contribution to society?'

'Fuck off.'

I step forward. 'What's your problem? We stopped for a coffee and a breath of air. Why the attitude?'

'Joan, you got the police yet?' He's talking into the car. There's a mumbled reply. 'Law's on its way.' He smiles.

Artie tips the dregs of the coffee on the ground. 'Bring 'em on, man.' He walks onto the road.

Gray Beard hits the up button on the window.

'Leave it, Artie. It's not worth it.'

'Ain't no call for this.'

'I know – but we don't need this.' I don't need this.

Artie reaches the car. He raps on the window. The car moves off. Artie aims a kick at the door. He scores a hit and it dents. The car stops. The door opens. Gray Beard gets out. He's enormous. Three hundred pounds. At least. My height with it. Old. But not too old. His shoulders are massive. His hands are a full side of beef each. He slams the door shut. The car shudders. I watch Artie. He seems unfazed by the monster in his midst.

Gray Beard storms up to Artie, but Artie doesn't flinch an inch. He doesn't even lean away when Gray Beard invades his space in a big way. Gray Beard towers over him. Artie looks like a doll next to the bulk of the man.

Gray Beard looks down on him. 'Look what you did to my fucking door.'

Artie shrugs. A small movement. He says nothing.

Gray Beard growls. 'I'm going to rip you a new one.'

Artie looks up. He tilts his head to one side. And smiles. Gray

Beard lifts a hand. A prelude to a strike. But undecided. Artie's lack of concern has caught part of his mind. He's accustomed to people backing down. He exudes the confidence of someone used to winning. Artie is neither backing down nor looking like he's bothered about the man mountain's threat.

Gray Beard grabs Artie by the arm.

Artie looks down at the massive digits. 'Me. I'd remove the hand if I were you.'

It's said with a voice so low that Gray Beard leans in to catch the words. 'What?'

'My body. My choices.'

'Fuck you.' Gray Beard has such a spacious range of expressions. He lifts Artie's arm. Pulls Artie to one side. Artie's free arm moves. A jerk and he has his hand sitting just below Gray Beard's groin. Gray Beard looks down. Artie is clasping a knife. A blade, maybe six inches long, is just piercing Gray Beard's trousers. The tip nicking the thick blue denim.

Artie has never taken his eyes off Gray Beard's face. 'Man, you ever heard of your femoral artery?'

Gray Beard is sizing up the threat. Artie pushes the blade a little. 'Don't be thinking of moving, man. Trust me, you don't want to do that.'

Something in Artie's small voice freezes Gray Beard. An edge to his words. A self-assurance.

'You see' – Artie keeps the blade tight in – 'the femoral artery is a useful little thing. It's used by surgeons for inserting stuff. Catheters, wires, fiber optics. It's a main highway into the body.'

To catch the chat I put in a few steps. Artie is holding the big man's attention with barely a whisper. Gray Beard's face is set hard.

Artie moves in another few inches. 'It can take you to the kidneys, the heart – even the brain. And, when your blood pressure drops low, you can still draw from it. It's less of a highway.

More of a river. And, man, it's a brute if you cut it.'

Artie eases his arm from Gray Beard's fingers. He meets no resistance.

Artie's knife hand stays rock still. 'Now, if I apply a little more pressure at the point and split the artery – well that would be a bad thing. You're a big man. A man like you has a lot of blood. Look at me. Eight pints maybe. You? Maybe ten – more. Lots of blood.'

A car appears. Heading for the houses. The horn goes. The driver gives Gray Beard a hands up. Gray Beard ignores it. Artie has settled his hand on the inside of Gray Beard's thigh. The car moves on.

Artie keeps up the chat. 'You see I'm also betting that your doctor has warned you about your blood pressure. 140 over 90 and then some. Man, you must be on a thiazide-based diuretic. Aquatensen, Hydromox – maybe Zaroxolyn.' The last one gets a flicker from Gray Beard's eyes.

Artie sees it. 'Knew it. Makes you piss more often. Doesn't it? Anyway, high blood pressure ain't great if you get cut. Blood is bursting to get out, man. Just bursting.'

The passenger door opens. 'Richard.'

Gray Beard doesn't turn. 'Joan, get back in the car. It's all right.'

Joan leans on the door. Compared to Gray Beard she's a pebble to a boulder. Her hair is dyed and severe. Her face hardcore with lines.

I'm taking a fervent pleasure in the scene. I still have one eye on the road in case Joan has made good on Gray Beard's words about the police. But, for once, I'm no more than an interested bystander.

Artie is winning major plaudits from me. I wouldn't have booked him for standing up to a gust of wind. But he's taking on Gray Beard with an ease that suggests regular practice. His voice has a quiet menace. And it's the tone that's holding the man. Artie could be bluffing. He could be slow. He could be out of his depth. He could be on drugs. But he's none of these. He just knows how to hold someone's attention.

His face is alive. His eyes are fixed on Gray Beard but his teeth are grinding in his mouth. His jaw slides back and forth. It marches to the same pulse as his knife-free hand – which is tapping on Gray Beard's leg. Artie's left leg catches the counterpoint to mouth and hand. He is a rhythm machine. One with threat embedded in the pulse.

'Ok, Richard. Here's the thing.' Still almost a whisper from Artie. 'We've got what I call an LA standoff going down, man. You know that I'll open up your artery. You're not sure how you know this. But you know. I'm small. You're big. I'm a stranger. You don't know jack shit about me. You're thinking hard. Trying to suss out how this is going to end. You know it could be messy.'

Artie's three-point beat combo picks up a sparkier cadence. His leg taking the lead. 'But in that gargantuan brain you're thinking *when this man moves away I'll get my chance.* Let me tell you, it's not going to happen, man.'

Artie steps back. Three steps. Gray Beard watches. Artie lowers the knife. Gray Beard's face is taking on a red tinge. Anger? Embarrassment? Artie swings the knife in a loose arc, clipping his jean pocket with the handle each time he passes it by his leg.

Artie looks down. Takes his eyes from the beast. Gray Beard moves. His arm lifting as he steps in for the strike. I take an involuntary pace forward, thinking I can put myself between the two. But I'm too far away to be able to reach in time.

Gray Beard's arm pulls back. He's winding up for a punch. Artie shakes his head. Gray Beard throws the shot. Artie shifts his weight to the left. Ducks under the incoming blow and has the blade back at Gray Beard's groin. This time he presses it home. A few inches vanish into the big man's thigh. He pulls it back out and raises it up a little. 'That will hurt in a few seconds but it's not fatal. If I press now...' He tenses his wrist. '...then you bleed out.'

As he talks he matches the big man's movement as the momentum of the punch takes him off balance. With the choreography of a ballet dancer, Artie stays with Gray Beard until he regains his composure.

A red stain is spreading below the big man's crotch.

Artie snaps his fingers. 'I told you it wasn't going to happen, man. You big bullies are all the same. Rely on blunt force trauma. But your woman there. Now she's the real deal. Small but effective. I'm always scared of the small ones. You big guys live in a different time zone to us vertically-challenged individuals. Always running a bit slower. Slow enough for me to keep ahead of you.'

I'm liking Artie a lot. He looks like your worst dopehead but acts with the assurance of a Navy SEAL. His triple beat is back. Gray Beard has a stain flooding down his leg. But he doesn't move.

Artie sighs. 'So we need to end this. And I know that you're still chewing over ways to get me. Waste of time, man. I told you it isn't going to happen. Not today. So I'll give you an out. You turn round. Walk to the car. Get in. Drive. Don't look back. Looking back is fatal. No third time lucky for you. Next time your blood loss will make that stain on your pants look like a paper cut. How you explain the stain to your good woman is your concern. She's smart. She'll know you've had your fanny handed to you. Suck it up man. Put this one down to experience.'

I'm liking Artie an awful lot.

Gray Beard pauses. His head trying to put two and two together – looking for five and getting three. He turns. Slowly.

Artie follows him for the first quarter turn. Then steps back. Gray Beard limps to the car. Artie is on the move towards me. Crossing the road.

He grabs me by the arm. 'Time to go. The big man's not going to go quietly.'

'He looks tame to me.'

'Trust me. I know the signs.'

I drop in behind Artie. He jogs to the RV. We both pile in. He leaps into the driver's seat. He was right. Out of the passenger window I see Gray Beard starting to charge. I shout. 'Ok, Artie, time to go.'

'Cool, man.'

Artie fires us up and, as the man mountain slams into the side of the RV, we bump onto the road. Gray Beard lets rip with a series of well-punctuated threats. His face, inches from the window, is crimson.

'Artie. Some speed would help.' My words are superfluous.

'This is her on nitrous oxide.' Artie isn't smiling now. 'She wasn't designed to take on the quarter mile.'

Gray Beard grabs the door handle. I slam down the lock. Too late. The door swings open. The man mountain is running to keep up but we haven't the speed to lose him yet. He reaches in.

I slide away from him. 'Artie, any extra velocity would be welcome.'

Artie does better. He throws the wheel to the right, putting us off the road. Gray Beard is towed with us. Artie reverses the maneuver. Gray Beard has to let go or he'll be dragged under. He releases the handle and is spat out behind us. I watch in the wing mirror as he tumbles to the ground. He goes down hard. Somewhere a seismic institute will register a minor tremor.

I pull the door shut and lock it. 'Shit, Artie, you're a bundle of the unusual.'

'Had to learn to handle myself. Being a hippy has its downsides. Some people don't take to peace and love the way I do.'

'Did you take lessons?'

'What in? Fronting up to assholes?'

'Don't play dumb. That wasn't natural talent back there. The talkdown. The moves. The speed. You read the signs the right way up. Even at the end.'

'Yeah, well the end wasn't my best. I needed a few more minutes with him to make sure he didn't do an encore.'

'So why break off?'

'Cops.'

'Cops?'

'Saw them hammering up the main highway.'

I didn't see anything. 'Are they behind us?'

'Not yet. But they can't be far from the on-ramp.'

We have entered suburbia. Artie plays lefts and rights. Digging us good and deep into it.

# Chapter 25

Ten minutes into the drive, Artie pulls over. He ignores me and grabs a plastic bag from a cupboard. He retrieves a screwdriver before leaping out of the side door.

Five minutes later he's back.

He nudges us back onto the road. 'Dodgy plates?'

He nods. 'I've got three sets. All belong to RV's. All are registered in California. All with matching registration documents.'

I'm not that confident this will work, but as the miles start to unfold beneath us, I'm more than a little surprised at the lack of obvious pursuit.

Night slides in. The sun dips behind us. Artie switches on the headlights. We are now less visible. Finding us at night will be that much harder.

'Artie, you can handle yourself. Where did you learn?'

'On the street, man. Where else?'

'Haight Ashbury were big on gangs?'

'No, but LA was.'

'You're an LA kid?'

'Born and buggered in the city of angels. Hardest of hard places. Gang was family and family was the enemy. You either ran with them or died by them. I was small. An easy target. So I hardened up. A dude called Sick Ron, ex-Vietnam, taught me the main moves in return for a little man-love.'

He pauses, waiting for the obvious question. I don't oblige.

'Fought from Santa Monica to the Beverly Hills Hilton. Fought with everyone and anyone. Did some time in the cages. Beating up on guys for cash. Then one day, after handing an evil shit called Cass Moon a beating, his three brothers caught up with me in a back alley. I put two in hospital but they nearly put me in my grave. I was in ICU for three months. Tubes to feed me. Tubes to pour drugs through. A tube to breathe for a while. The hospital gave me a one in a hundred chance of pulling through. A one in thousand chance of not having brain damage. And they lost their bets on both counts.'

His eyes widen. 'Have you ever been real sick?'

'And some.'

'And how were you when you got out of the back end?'

I think back to the time when Tampoline filled me with so many drugs, in an attempt to control my little gift, that I nearly died. It took months to get back on my feet. Longer to feel right and, even then, I wasn't firing on all cylinders. 'Weak.' It's the best answer I have.

'True, man. Weak. Weak and then some. That was me in hospital. As a kitten on Valium. But my head worked. The doctors said it shouldn't have – that I'd have some damage. They tested me and declared me a miracle. I was a bit of a celeb. Interns. Junior doctors. Specialists. Of course I was hardly in the real world. Drugs ruled my life. When they weaned me off them I started the long journey home.'

'And that's when you found peace?'

'I wish. All I found was a burning desire to kill the bastards who had put me there. I lay in bed – hour after hour, day after day – planning my revenge. Breaking down the steps. Building them back up. Working out the angles. Always with one eye on the door. I knew that Cass Moon would be back. He would figure on revenge too. For his brothers. Remember, I'd put two in hospital. So I just got focused on how I'd put Cass's head in a vice and spill his brains.'

'And did you?'

'Oh I caught up with him all right. It was the anticlimax of the decade. Someone had got there before me. His family were dropping him in a six-feet-by-three-feet hole. Twelve stab wounds, so I was told.'

'And the brothers?'

'Only one at the funeral. It told me I had done a proper job on the other two. You don't miss your brother's funeral unless you've no choice. Afterwards I followed the family to Cass's house. Then I went back to a gas station and bought a gallon of the good stuff. I had plans to cremate his home.'

A blue flashing light flies through the night on the opposite lane. Artie watches it. So do I.

Artie waits until it's a speck before continuing. 'So I wait until it's dark. I grab the can and make my way to the back door. Nice house. Beating up on guys clearly pays well. There's a new extension. Glass all the way. It's lit up and a party is in full swing. Or rather the wake is in full swing. It's kids and adults. Maybe twenty brats – all running around like the house was already on fire. Well I can't torch kids, man. So I think I'll just bide my time. And that gets me to thinking about my own family.'

He pauses. 'I'd love to say I had the sort of dad who inspired me to be who I am. Maybe he did. If you call being a dick a way to inspire your son. He was an asshole of an order yet to be invented.'

'I thought he was a flower-power child?'

'He was.'

'And was that not all love and peace?'

'He believed in fifty percent of that. He was the world's biggest advocate of free love. Shagged for the state. Told my mum it was his duty.'

'And she wasn't happy.'

'If she was she said nothing. She couldn't. He would hit her.'

'Really?'

'Not all the time. Only when he was high. Like that was some kind of excuse. So I stood there, at the back window of the house, and looked at a family coping with grief and thought how much I'd have given for just an hour of that. Weird. A man cooling in his grave and I'm wishing I was one of the family. And then I realise I'm standing with a gallon of gas about to end it all. I couldn't. I walked.

'After that I hit the road. Never looked back. Morphed into an alternate version of my dad. Got hooked on the lifestyle.'

'Are your mom and dad still around?'

'Mom's alive and in better shape than history has any right to have placed on her. Dad's dead.'

'How did he die?'

'Mom killed him.'

'Sorry?'

The outside world vanishes completely. All is Artie's voice.

'Mom killed him. Twenty years back. He came home one night. Drunk was the new high. He raised his hand to complain about dinner. She raised the bread knife. The court found her not guilty. Self-defense. She had character witnesses, defense witnesses – more witnesses than to the miracle of the loaves and the fishes. All of them testified the same thing. All told of the abuse. The jury were out of the room for less than ten minutes. She didn't even go to the funeral. I did. I wish I hadn't. Sordid affair. A few of his drinking buddies and some woman that I didn't know. She lay on the side of the grave, crying. I didn't tell mom about that bit. Although I'm sure she knew.'

'And the road has been your home since when?'

'As close as damn it since then. I spent a few years in a retreat. Polishing up my reading and combat skills. Strange mix. Read Joyce in the morning and fight each other in the afternoon. Then one day I got bored. The road called and I hit it.'

'And what's in Toronto?'

'Like I said, I've to see a man. So enough about me. What about your life story?'

'Dull.'

He waits for more. I give him none.

'So what's next, Craig?'

It's a good question. I've been on the run so long it's become the norm. Martyn is my current goal but I've no idea if he'll make it to Toronto. No idea if he can help. No idea if he'll *want* to.

'I'll bail in Toronto and you can meet your man.'

'Cool with me. Where do you want to say our goodbyes?'

'I know a hotel. I'm going to spend a night in a hot tub with a beer or two.'

Arties nods. 'What hotel?'

'The Drake.'

'Classy.'

'You know it?'

'Not from the inside. A little out of my price bracket.'

The traffic around is gearing up. The edge of Toronto is still a distance off but we are slipping from agricultural to industrial. Artie is chatting. He has a way of talking that's compelling. I noticed it when he was fronting up Gray Beard. His voice is low but penetrates the sound of the laboring engine. Almost finding the gaps in the ceaseless firing of the cylinders. Using the tiny pauses to cut through.

'Maybe a couple of hours to the hotel.' says Artie.

We cruise the rest of the way in silence until Artie snaps upright. 'Next junction.'

'Well it's been short but eventful. Thanks, Artie.'

We slip from the highway and work the Mystery Machine through downtown Toronto. Artie has to be psychic. No map. No GPS. But forty minutes later he's found the hotel. A bemused commissionaire wonders if he should open the side door of the RV. I let him sweat while I turn to shake hands with Artie.

I reach to open the door just as a man wrenches it from my grasp.

As he gets in he pushes me, talking at the same time. 'Move over. We've got company.'

# Chapter 26

I slide over. Take in the new passenger.

'Hi, Martyn. Nice to see you again.'

Artie looks at Martyn. I look at Artie.

I decide on introductions. 'Artie, meet Martyn. Martyn, meet Artie.'

Martyn keeps his eyes on the street. 'Please, get going.'

Artie shrugs and signals. You can't faze the man.

Martyn is a cleaned-up version of the one who helped me kidnap the 'wannabe president of the US'. Last I heard, Tampoline was still on the campaign trail and behind in the race to win his party's nomination. But in Tampoline's world that probably means he's favourite.

Martyn is twenty years younger than me. An ex-member of Factor. He's also my fellow superhero. Dressed in a blue windcheater and denims he stands six feet. Cropped blonde hair has replaced the straggly locks he once favoured.

I look in the wing mirror, wondering why Martyn's in such a hurry, but I'll let him tell me in his own time. 'So your mom gave you the message?'

'And I said no.'

'Yet you're here.'

'Guess who appeared at moms?'

'Suits.'

'Bingo. Thanks for inviting them along.'

'It wasn't...'

He cuts me off. 'Artie, do me a favour. Get back on the main drag. Craig, do me a favour and don't pretend this has anything to do with my well-being. I'm back in the soup with the guys I least want to dip bread with. I've spent months trying to get my life into some sort of order and then you depth-charge me.'

I ignore the attack. 'How did you get to Toronto so quick?'

'Last-minute flight. I'd just landed in Newark when mom got a hold of me. Cost me a packet. That you care?'

I take the bait. 'Martyn, don't be so naïve. I've only kick-started what was already going to happen. Tampoline has us back in his sights. I've been well off the grid and he still found me. You were an easy find if he wanted. Easy to keep an eye on. Easy to pin down when they needed you. Now they've flushed me out, you're on their shopping list. It's that simple. They know we'll tie up at some point, and if they'd wanted you earlier you'd be in a padded cell waiting for God to set you free. What's happening was going to happen no matter how hard you stuck your head in the sand.'

'Bullshit.'

'Really? Think about it.'

'Fuck off.'

Artie joins in. 'Are you two always like this or is this a show you put on for strangers?' Artie's actually grinning. 'You do know I can just tell the two of you to fuck off as well, man.'

'And who are you?' Martyn turns to take in the Mystery Machine.

'Artie Woodstock.'

Well what else could his second name be?

Artie steers us back onto the highway. 'Where are we going by the way, man?'

'Good question.' I study Martyn's new buzz cut. 'Where *are* we going?'

Martyn rubs at the short hair on the back of his head. 'Screwed if I know. This will just be another ride in a boat of shit.'

'So why are you here if all I do is drag trouble? You could have stiffed me.'

'Yeah and that would help. Suits at my door, suits at my mom's place. Suits in the rear view mirror. The common denominator is you. And I've been doing some thinking.'

'About what?'

'What the hell do you think? The price of Outer Mongolian sheep.'

'Funny.'

'Well, while you've been hiding in the boondocks or wherever you got to, I came up with some information. Or rather, someone else did and I'm now the messenger.'

Artie is all ears and I'm uneasy with that. There's more to him than I can figure – or maybe he just likes hard-luck cases. I pretend to type on an imaginary keyboard. 'Wiki good for that stuff, Martyn?'

'Nothing is good for this stuff. I should know; I tried hard enough to find out what we are. But I drew a blank until Charlie called.'

My jaw hangs. 'You've been in touch with Charlie?'

'Not until just after you phoned mom the second time. He said you got separated.'

'We sort of lost touch.'

'Did he get away?'

'If you mean was he free to talk to me, then yes. He didn't say much about your divorce.'

'How did he get in touch with you?'

'Mom.'

'He didn't have her number.'

'He did. He phoned and asked for me.'

How or why? Both are valid questions. 'And you got in touch with him.'

'Sure.'

Something is out of the water here. 'Really?'

'What's the beef with this, Craig?'

'You don't know Charlie.'

'But I know of him. You made sure of that.'

'Even so. Why would he call you? You've never met.'

'We have you in common. He wanted to tell me a little story. And for me to pass it on to you.'

'And he couldn't do this himself?'

'It seems he has no transport, no idea where you are, no contact number. And he isn't psychic. Last he called he was in some ass-end town in western Canada.'

I hold my hand up to stop the conversation. The road outside takes over for a while. We sit. The Three Stooges. Well, one Stooge and two acquaintances. I want to quiz Martyn on what Charlie has dug up but I don't want Artie up to speed. The black velvet cloth of night unfurls outside the window, peppered with flashing lights as vehicles pass by.

An exit flashes by, followed by homes sitting squat with their fannies to the highway, as if blanking it – *we might use you but we don't like you*. I see a *For Sale* sign on one. Ten to a dollar that writ large in the flyer for the home are the words *No. You can hardly hear the noise of the traffic*. Triple glazing and a lifetime at AC/DC concerts will make that true for the new homeowner.

We've passed the downtown area and the conga line of commuters is thinning out. If Artie isn't careful there may be a gap between him and the car in front. I kind of wish there was. Artie doesn't drive fast but he drives close – so close to the car ahead that a single cylinder misfire from our prey and we'll rear-end it. The driver in front pulls over. Artie takes it as a cue to aim for the backside of the next truck.

I look at him. 'Artie, it's not compulsory to attach yourself to the nearest fender.'

'Well if they would move over I wouldn't have to. Anyway, if you let the speed dip on this thing it takes a month to get it back.'

Martyn is between us. Happy in his silence.

I iddn't like Martyn at first. Too young. Too brash. Too

much trouble. I dragged him from a gas-filled house when his friends tried to kill him. We took a while to warm to each other. The fact that we kidnapped a prospective presidential candidate a few days later showed we had moved a long way in a short time. Martyn was a pile of trouble to his mom. Still is. Having a son who is on the FBI's most-wanted list is never going to make for good dinner-table conversations. But Tampoline has, for his own survival and ambitions, ensured our involvement in his kidnap has been struck from the record. And, as far as I know, Martyn has been handed his life back. Until now.

What is niggling away at the corner of my head is the contact with Charlie. Martyn knows of him but hasn't met him. It all suggests something a little cozier than makes me feel comfortable. Then again, I owe my life to both. I just want to know the ins and outs.

Artie breaks the silence. 'Ok, man. Where are we heading?'

Artie saws the steering wheel to graze another road user. This one finds his horn. Artie does likewise and the world keeps revolving.

'Off here.' Martyn points to our right.

'Bit late for shore time,' says Artie.

'Never too late for a little lakeside action.'

Artie steers us off the main highway. 'A friend of mine used to have a forty-foot yacht. Holed it up near Socillido. We used to hit the bay in it. Alcatraz was cool. We used to play *Escape to Alcatraz* on the yacht's video player all the time. Ever seen it, Martyn?'

'I preferred *The Rock* with Cage and Connery.'

'Cool, man. Sean's the man.'

'Best Bond ever.'

'What about Daniel Craig?'

'Good, but forces the nonchalance.'

'Mischievous though.'

'Got that. *Skyfall* rebirthed the whole thing.'

'Mendes. Got to give him credit.'

I sigh. 'Oh, sorry, was that out loud? I didn't mean to interrupt your love-in.'

Artie plays tag with the next car.

Martyn sits back. 'Lakeside if you don't mind, Artie.'

'Certainly, sir.'

Instant friends. Just add water.

A large slab of industrial buildings rises around us, then bows out to be replaced by Lake Ontario.

Artie slows.

Martyn taps him on the shoulder. 'Artie, thank you. We can take it from here.'

Artie pulls the RV into the side of the road.

I turn to Martyn. 'Take what from where?'

Martyn looks at me. 'I'd say that we can thank Artie and let his life return to normal.'

Artie shakes his head. 'Well, man. All depends. I mean Craig here seems a little like a comet to me and I'm trailing the wake, free of this planet. I've cut the strings, I'm going with the flow. A little spice is good for me. Craig, my man, Martyn makes you sound like chilli powder. Makes me think. Makes me wonder what's next. I know where I'm off to and it's dullsville. With you? Maybe full of eastern promise.'

'Artie.' I open the door. 'You are so full of it.'

'Hey, man. That hurts.'

'I'm sure it cuts to the veins. You're better out of this.'

Martyn stretches and slides towards me. 'Don't knock it, soldier. When you hear Charlie's story you might be grateful of some extra help. You teamed up with me in less favourable circumstances.'

'Forced circumstances.'

'Still, we're all here because of you. I think Artie should have some say.'

I look at Artie. 'Artie, you don't want to get mixed up in this.'

'Seems you don't want me?'

'I've no idea what's next. Whatever it is, it won't be good for you.'

'And? I'm up for a good story. It sounds like Martyn has one.'

Martyn is still stretching. 'I'm not sure what I've got to say will help. It will entertain. But help? Not sure.'

'I'm always up for a good story.' Artie jumps out of the Mystery Machine.

We're all standing on the sidewalk. I look around. A giant set of metal gates seals the lake from the road. Around us is lifeless. I look at the gates. 'Nice place for a chat?'

'Not here, there. That will do.' Martyn points behind me.

A small neon sign blinks at the next corner. Ok, so not so lifeless.

'A bar?'

'Beats the cold, man.'

Artie's right.

I agree. 'Ok, but only if Martyn buys.'

# Chapter 27

*When Watson and Crick identified the famous double helix of DNA in 1953 they carved their names on the subject. The history of DNA, however, stretches further back. Back to the late 1860s. And, although not widely publicized, at the time, Deoxyribonucleic acid, the savior of CSI and a hundred thousand crime novels, registered a minor blimp in the PR man's diary in 1943 when Oswald Avery, and his associates Colin MacLeod and Maclyn McCarty, identified DNA as, what became known as, the transforming principle in the Avery–MacLeod–McCarty experiment.*

Artie and I are reading from a sheef of sheets that Martyn has laid on the table.

*And, with all things governmental focusing on the war back then, it would have stood out like a blade of grass in a football field had it not been for a curious chemist called Cirus Mandley.*

*Cirus was attached to a research facility in the backwater town of Coral Time in Kansas. He worked with colleagues to service the War Department's requirement for anti-inflammatory drugs. Mainly for the reduction in swelling and damage caused by gunshot wounds. His life, in 1943, was spent shooting pigs with bullets and then shooting them up with drugs. Bereft of the time afforded major drug companies for breakthrough science, Cirus was one of many given free rein to crack problems any way but slowly.*

*But Cirus still had one small goal. In his life, recognition had eluded him.*

*He was diligent and, after a fashion, hardworking. His chosen specialty was immunosuppressants. And therein lay the issue. It would be 1949 before Cortisone was shown to alleviate rheumatoid arthritis. Corticosteroids would then be recognised as a treatment for autoimmune disorders and, in the main, to prevent allograft rejection. Transplants were to be the driver behind immunosuppressants.*

*But during the war there was little call for transplants. Surviving was the best one hoped for.*

*The fact that Cirus was allowed to study in this field was down to the fug of war. His work on wounds was of use, but on the side he worked on transplants – a hobby that a small out-of-the-way office in Kansas could allow.*

*To facilitate his research he became an avid fan of the Russian dwarf hamster – an animal that suffered much in his attempts to successfully transplant limbs.*

*Cirus had taken on a breeding programme of sizeable proportions. His need for fresh hamsters was endless. With a relatively short gestation period the hamster was an ideal subject.*

'Where in the hell is this going?' I have finished my first pint. The bar is a graveyard. We are the only warm bodies, save the lone barman – and I'm not sure about him. His pallor is prison plus. The three of us are sitting near the bar, huddled in a circle around a small table.

'Charlie sent it by email. Told me that he talked to his boy in Italy who found this on the internet.'

'Isn't there an executive summary?' I drain the already drained pint.

Artie stands up. 'I'm quite enjoying this. My round.'

At least I won't die of thirst.

I shrug. Artie returns and I sip at the fresh beer. It helps.

We read on.

*Eighteen months into his studies, Cirus observed some extreme behaviour in some of his subjects. To avoid too many questions at work he kept the hamsters in cages in his garage. Up to forty at a time. His wife was none to happy about this. The smell was not conducive to good neighbor relations.*

*Cirus had learned long ago to keep the males separate from the females. However on the odd occasion a fight would break out amongst the females when a male was introduced. It took Cirus a while to realise that a certain male was to blame.*

On a hunch, he lifted out a few females at a time and put them in the cage next to the male. Most of the time nothing happened, but now and again the females would fight. Those fights would sometimes result in severe wounds or death. Cirus trialed other male and female combinations but nothing matched the guilty male's impact. He nicknamed the suspect Killer but could see nothing that the male was doing that would explain why such random violence was being induced. Female jealousy was his bet.

Killer was a lover of endless appetite and had already sired more than his fair share of Cirus's hamsters. Early one morning, Cirus dropped him in with a new batch of females and left for work. When he returned he found a scene of carnage so extensive that only a few females were left standing and even they were badly wounded. Killer was blood-spattered but untouched.

It soon became clear that Killer could indeed incite violence. His presence in certain situations was enough to set female on female. Cirus swapped out the females and experimented with introducing males to Killer, with the same result.

Things changed when Dr James Haggle visited to talk to Cirus about the opportunity to apply his work in the battlefield.

On the last day of his visit, Haggle, sent by the State Department, was about to leave when Cirus, to his own surprise, asked Haggle if he fancied a drink.

Twenty minutes later they were sitting in the Daisy Chain – the only watering hole within a fifty-mile radius.

It took Cirus three whiskies to unload on Haggle about his hamsters. Two hours later they were sitting in front of the hamster run in Cirus's garage as Cirus placed Killer in with the latest batch of females. Haggle smiled as the girls tore each other apart.

The next morning a dirt-green army truck rumbled into Cirus's life. A suited man, backed by a uniform, ordered Cirus into the truck. Killer and the other hamsters were placed in the back. A young *infantryman sat with a rifle across his chest. The soldier was unsure why he was guarding hamsters. But in the army you never asked why. Another uniform drove and neither the guard nor the suit would answer any of Cirus's hangover-laced questions.*

*Two days after the move, Cirus was introduced to Charles Troughton, who had stopped growing when he was ten years old.*

*Charles had cut his teeth as a doctor in the slums of London. At the turn of the century he had moved to America to study murderers. His specialty was serial killers, but, back then, the description had not been invented. His work had drawn the attention of the military. Killers could be useful. Charles's work was pushed in a new direction.*

I put my second empty glass down. 'I'm all one for stories but has this got a point?' I start reading again.

*Charles had stumbled upon a short paper by a Victorian scientist called Edward Mantleman. It had the catchy title* Man and Attraction. The Masked Connection: an examination of an ethereal assembly between minds.

*In less than eight pages, Edward postulated that the attraction people feel for some other people is not of their own making. People do not flock around those in power because they want to touch their greatness. He postulated that, along with the physical ability to touch, see, hear, smell and talk, there is another way that we are connected to each other – ESP, telekinesis, mind control, the sixth sense.*

*Edward also warranted that such ability was not in the control of the person who possessed it. Not in any overt manner.*

*For proof he simply listed, over four of his eight pages, the names of some of the most famous people in history and the names of some less so. People who could be said to possess an attraction that was above and beyond anything normal.*

*Some of the names were of good people and some were of bad. Genghis Khan sat below George Washington. Napoleon lay two names above Cardinal Woolsley. Many of the names were people with obscure footnotes in history.*

*Edward ascribed their position to their aura. An innate ability to draw others to them and to manipulate them to their own ends. He proposed that each one of them was aware of what they could do. Not that they could explain it but they knew. And, in some, it led to corruption in the extreme. He believed that within many was the ability to draw out the best but sometimes the worst in us.*

*Charles thought Killer had this aura.*

'You're kidding, right? Charlie sent you a cockeyed story with no reasonable ending and it's supposed to be some sort of revelation?'

Martyn pushes his chair back. 'Kind of makes sense to me.'

'How? Pray tell.'

'Seems that the hamster and both of us have some things in common. Seems that our man Cirus was studying a four-legged version of Craig McIntyre and it seems that the army became well interested in how they could use it all for their own ends. Seems to me that Charlie's email may have found the start of something that you and I are now part of. You've got to admit, Craig' – Martyn is shuffling the paper on the table – 'you, me – who else is out there? Who else has a little gift? A sixth sense. Both of us have been screwed around with by government surgeons. You? Well, you can release the bad in people. Me – I can drop you like a rag doll from fifty feet with nothing more than a thought.'

'Really?' Artie sits up at this. 'Pray tell more. A lot more. This is getting way more interesting than I ever thought it could.'

'Artie, you don't want to know.' But I know he does.

'Shit but I do, man. What have we got here? Superheroes?'

'Martyn, where is this going?' I'm not sure sharing this with Artie is a good call.

'I have a plan. Of sorts.'

I look at Artie. 'Artie, walk. You've known me less than twenty-four hours. Just walk.'

Artie smiles his smile. 'No way, man. I'm in. Whatever it is, I'm in.'

There are times when you should listen to your gut. Give it a voice and let it guide you. Ignore all else. And my gut says pay the bill and tell Artie to walk. But I don't and won't.

Martyn seems relaxed but I'm not in a happy place. 'Martyn, you don't even know Artie. Correction: *we* don't know him from a beggar in the street.'

Martyn pushes the papers away. 'I didn't know you 'til you pulled me from a gas-filled house.'

'But that was different.'

'Why?'

I have no answer. At least, not one that sounds strong enough. 'Artie, I have no idea what Martyn's plan is but if you want another beer then feel free to stay.'

Artie's smile goes supernova. 'Tell me all.'

I explain. Not all but all that is needed. I leave out Lorraine. I leave out a lot of the deaths, the TT and more, but I leave in enough.

'So, man.' Artie is looking around as if we are being spied on. 'You two really are superheroes.'

'Crap ones, Artie, crap ones.'

'So cool, man.'

I turn to Martyn. 'So give with the plan. And, while you're at it, why the rushed exit from the hotel. Agency?'

'Yes. When I booked the flight I got the last seat. Then two suits bounced an elderly couple. I heard them complain as I waited to board. The suits followed me from the airport but I managed to lose them. I didn't want to hang around as they wouldn't have taken long to find me again. Even in foreign countries Tampoline has clout.'

'And the plan?'

'How do fancy a trip to bonnie Scotland?'

# Chapter 28

'*Scotland*?' I say it a little too loud. The barman doesn't notice. Barmen never do. Not unless you want them to. 'Why Scotland?'

'Charlie thinks it all started there. He thinks the original experiments were carried out there. Charlie's Italian friend says that there's a rumored site that we ran during World War II; based on Scotland's west coast. A sort of Area 51 abroad. There are endless theories but, unlike Roswell, there's no agreement on location.'

'So we head for Scotland and what? Travel the land in search of a mythical US black ops site?'

Martyn leans back, and snaps a confident crack of his knuckles. 'Charlie thinks a note you have might just have handed the nutters their Area 51. Have you still got it?'

I nod and pull out my scribblings. I lay it on the table. Artie's eyes widen. He reads my redacted DNA memo.

'Cool, man. I used to love this stuff on thesmokinggun.com.'

I ignore him. 'But Martyn, what did it tell Charlie's continental cousin that no one knew before?'

'The location. Or at least Charlie hopes so. He's working on it now. It's all to do with Alfred Nobel and his dynamite factory.'

'He had one in Scotland.' Artie's eyes are still on stalks.

Martyn looks at him. 'I'm not sure.'

'It wasn't a question, man. It was a statement. He had a factory near the town of Irvine on the west coast of Scotland.'

I scratch my nose. 'Artie, you're full of surprises.'

'Not really. I have an album by a band called Stick. A little-known psychedelic rock band from Seattle. Made one album in the '60s; and it's not that good. It's called *Alfred's Place of Destruction* and the first song is *Irvine, I See You*. I don't know much more but it's about a dynamite factory near that Irvine, in

Scotland. You can probably get the track on iTunes.'

Martyn is excited. 'Charlie thinks that wherever this site is it might be the alpha particle to this whole nonsense. And I for one would love to know if it is.'

'Artie? Martyn? I hate to be the killjoy here. But let's say Charlie's man is right. Let's say that there *is* a secret base in Scotland. And let's say that it has some connection to us. They're not going to let us walk in, take photos, ask a few questions and leave.'

Martyn takes a moment to relax. Or, to be precise, relax more. He's at ease with this. Despite the frosty reception outside the hotel he has migrated the deep freeze of his welcome to a more chilled attitude.

'Craig, *you* may not want to know what they did to your head but I *really* want to know what they did to me. I've no idea what we'll find, whether we'll get further than the front door or even if there *is* a front door, but this is something I'm going to pursue. If for no other reason than I want these guys out of my life. I want them off my mom's back and I want to be able to walk the street without needing another dozen pairs of eyes. If Scotland has an answer – even if it's not a guaranteed answer – them I'm going. I'd rather we both went – as a dynamic duo we're hard to beat – but if you want to cut loose on this then it's cool with me. Artie here seems up for a bite at the adventure cake.'

There are times in your life when someone gives your sorry fanny a kick instead of pandering to your false self-deprecation and desire to burden others with the crap in your life. They take a hammer and a chisel and carve their own path, ignoring you completely. Martyn is happy with his call and I either put out a hand and shake on it or walk. No third way.

As Phil, Tony and Mike must have said when Peter left, '… and then there were three.'

★

'Airplane?' I utter the word with a crushing tone that infers, in spades, disbelief beyond discussion.

Artie tries on a small grin for size.

I take the bait. 'A plane? Are you serious? How the hell would we get on a plane? We'd be lucky to board a local bus without being picked up!'

Artie lets the smile linger.

I have a brief urge to step up to the plate and slug him. There's something about the smile – its smugness for one – that provides could be construed as justification for violence.

Artie catches the anger flaring in me. 'Calm, man. Calm. I'm being serious.'

Martyn, who's standing, staring at nothing, wants to add his own voice to my incredulity, but he barely knows Artie. It seems that if the impetuousness of his youth has taught him anything it is to count to ten before jumping in. He lets it run to see where Artie is going with this.

'It's the quickest way to Scotland.' Artie moves a little as he speaks. Keeps his joints rolling.

I want to vent in one go all the reasons why this is a shit idea. But I don't. Instead I join Martyn in counting. As I tick up to ten I reason that Artie will have some logic for suggesting the flight idea – even if I can't fathom it – but I still want to have my say. 'Ok,' I start. 'Let's roll with the basic flaws as I see them. Number one: we have no passports. Number two: we have a clandestine agency on our tail with substantial resources. Number three: airports are a bad idea – and let's not pretend that a Canadian airport is any safer than one in the States. Prey skipping over the border to escape their clutches will not be a new problem for our security boys. Canada will be on top of any US issues.'

Artie opens his mouth to speak. I raise my hand. 'Artie, let me finish, then you can tell me why I'm wrong.'

Artie backs down.

I pick up on my train of thought. 'To add to the above, airports are also some of the most secure places on the planet. Face recognition. ID checks. Well trained border guards. Resident police officers. Probably CIA and Canadian internal agencies. And then there's the little matter of the cost of three last-minute tickets across the Atlantic. And I haven't even got to British border checks. Or the fact the UK and the US are best buddies when it comes to sharing intel. Anything I've missed?'

Martyn clearly feels he's held his tongue long enough and piles in with his two cents' worth. 'Artie, we would also need to book the flights. Online isn't safe unless we find an old-style internet café – even then it's risky. A travel shop might work. But it could also give someone the heads up. Enough time to be ready for us at the airport. We could leave it late and pay at the airport but, as Craig says, that's going to be expensive. And who's to say that there are seats available for today? We can't spend a night in the airport if we can't travel. We'd also need a direct flight. Transiting through the US would be dumb. As would landing in any other country. That would only increase the checks and reduce the odds on us making it.'

Artie takes his turn to count to ten. 'Are you finished?'

Martyn and I shrug at each other before nodding to Artie.

Artie lets the smile overstay its welcome. 'Ok, passports I can get. I have a little black book of contacts from my past life. I don't like to use it but it can be helpful. The more difficult question is: what type of passport will work best – but let's come back to that later. Money next. Well, the RV is good for a quick sale and I've enough spare cash to make up the ticket price.'

I leap in. 'Artie, why the hell would you sell your RV and blow cash on two strangers?'

Artie keeps his voice low. 'You don't get me, do you? You really don't. This is an adventure, man. Pure and simple. The

182

RV and my money are the entry price. Cheap if you ask me. Real cheap.'

I can't think of a reply that doesn't imply he's mad.

Artie carries on. 'So, let's say we have the cash and passports covered. Let's talk security. If the passports are solid, we don't have to worry about that side of things. If they pass the checks at the airport then it's not Craig, Martyn and Artie on a plane, it's Dick, Van and Dyke. That leaves the other security issue – your chasing crew, Craig; who, if I'm honest, man, are not tearing up the trees in the effectiveness woods. It seems to me that you've got by just fine so far. Maybe your no longer on their dating site. You've been one step ahead this far.'

I want to interrupt again – to challenge Artie's thoughts – but I let him talk it out.

Artie keeps up the joint-easing shuffle as he speaks. 'So here's how I see it. We have limited choices for getting to Scotland. We can't walk. We can't drive. So, we can either fly or go by sea. Sea will take a week, minimum, even assuming we can find a boat going our way and hitch a lift.'

I open my mouth. 'Johnstone. His boat. The… What the hell was it called?'

'What are you on about?' says Martyn.

'The Canuck B,' I blurt. 'It's going to Scotland.'

Martyn screws up his face. 'The what?'

I realise that I haven't told them about Johnston and Honey 2 Honey. I bring them up to speed.

Artie is first to give my idea a punch. 'Who says the ship is going straight to Scotland? It could be going via Mexico for all we know.'

'We can Google it?' My voice tails off.

Artie points out the obvious. 'Sure. Do you want to log on?'

I rub my hand over my mouth. 'I thought you said my followers were useless.'

'I did – but so far that might just be luck. Plus, they may react if you look like you are bugging out of Canada. I'd forget the Canuck B – what the hell do we know about stowing away on a boat. Anyway, when was she due to sail?'

'Early tomorrow morning.'

'Even if we could make it, do you fancy a few weeks as a stowaway or would you rather a quick ride?'

'Ok,' Martyn interrupts. 'Let's assume I buy in to the how of going by plane. I still don't get the why.'

Artie is warming up to the task at hand. 'Ok, here's how I see the thing. Intelligence is always flawed. Always has been, always will be. It's all a matter of interpretation. You' – Artie points at me – 'are doing real well if this agency is so almighty, man. And now they've lost you altogether. Whatever intel they have is poor.'

I'm not so sure.

Artie spots my doubt. 'Well, if they haven't lost you, why don't they just roll in and take you down?'

Artie has a point. Back in the bar with Charlie we had played with the same thought. Why not just kill me and be done with it? Either they want something from me or they really are a few steps behind.

Artie keeps digging 'How high up the wanted list do you think you are?'

'I can't tell. At one point I thought I was up there with the stars. Now…well, now I'm not sure.'

'Have they had their chances to get their hands on you?'

'Yes.'

'But they haven't sealed the deal?'

'I'm talking to you, so clearly the answer is no.'

Artie turns to Martyn. 'And in Toronto did your followers have a chance to grab you?'

'Probably.'

'But they didn't. I'm guessing that at best this is watching-brief stuff. Observe but don't interfere.'

'And?'

'Craig, man. If we are quick we can skate right through the airport. It's so obvious, it's the last thing they'll expect us to do. And, if I'm right and you're being chased by low level guys – guys who need to report up for instructions – we're better flying. It won't give them time to make those calls.'

I throw in the obvious. 'But if you're wrong and they are able to make their own decisions, were all in for a spell in a cell.'

'Come on, man. If we hang around here we're dead meat. It might just take a little longer. Do you want to find out what's behind your party trick or not?'

'You can definitely get passports?'

'Just need your photos.'

*

The airport is the scariest place on earth. Our taxi passes under a blue sign – French and English – *Departe and Departures*. A modern, curved-roofed building hosts the departure gates. In the trunk of the car sit three new flight cases with some hastily purchased clothes to pad them out. In my pocket is a shiny new American passport in the name of Craig Raine.

Martyn and I spent a cold night in the RV while Artie vanished. He's sitting next to me now, sparked out. An hour after he left us he returned with a small digital camera and photographed us. He then left again and, early this morning, returned with our passports. I'm so sure this won't work I'm already wondering if I'll get a cell to myself or will be sharing with my new, tattooed live-in-lover.

We pull up at the building and I shake Artie awake.

I wait for the hand on my shoulder as Artie pays the driver. I try to look like anyone else – try not to look for a black SUV or men in suits.

Nothing happens.

We slide into the airport. Artie pulls out our three tickets. Air Canada to Glasgow, coach class. Courtesy of Artie's RV, sold to his passport buddy and dropped off at a parking lot near Mississauga before we picked up the cab.

Artie heads for the gates. We're already checked in. Just passport control to negotiate. So far so good, but I worry that it's been too easy to be true.

We get in line. Not as a trio, but not too far apart. Not too obvious, but close enough together that we can act should we need to.

I'm sweating.

I'm two places behind Artie, who is one back from a skateboard kid. Hoody, baggy jeans, oversized sneakers – the works.

The kid is called forward.

The guard takes his ticket and scans it.

Then the passport.

The kid is waved onto the scanner line.

Artie is next.

This can't work.

Ticket.

The machine bleeps.

Passport.

Artie's waved on.

My turn.

I smile.

Say hello.

Get nothing back.

My ticket is zapped.

The machine bleeps.

My passport.

I'm through.

Martyn follows suit.

Ten minutes later we are sitting in the waiting area next to the gate. Apart. Fearing that any conversation will be picked up by someone whose job is to overhear – to catch on to bogus identities like ours.

We are deliberately tight on time.

The flight is called. Being in cattle class puts us down the want list. I've swapped with Artie so that I have a seat on the aisle. Assuming this works, I need some space to stretch my legs. He has less of a requirement in that department because his legs are shorter. All of him is shorter.

We're called up. Our tickets are rechecked; as are our passports.

We're on.

We take our seats, me with one eye on the doors. Now would be the time for them to execute a last-minute rush and grab. I have a sudden feeling of claustrophobia. It's too easy for them to cover the exits. I eye up the emergency exit. Would that work?

Outwardly I'm portray calm – at least I'm trying to – but I've still got a sweat on. I pity the woman next to me whose nasal passages are being assaulted.

Nothing. So far.

Doors are closed, announcements are made, the safety dem-onstration is given, we push back, taxi, pause, then full throttle.

Up, up. And, more importantly, away.

# Chapter 29

The day is bright and dry. Rain lingers in the distance. Glasgow Airport is dozing in the early morning light. The three of us are standing at the pick up point in the main car park.

I am amazed that Artie's documentation got us out of Canada and in to Scotland. The border guards did their usual Q&A, then we were through. No hassle.

Around me is a new world. English-speaking but accents that sound like they are from another planet. Some are easy to decipher, others almost inpenetrable. The store in the airport was awash with brands I didn't recognize. All I wanted was a packet of gum.

Martyn points to a crowd of young men. 'Shit, it's got to be forty degrees and that lot are wearing t-shirts and shorts.'

Artie points out a pair of women. Both are in summer dresses. 'Maybe they have warmer blood over here.'

'What are we looking for?' I'm bone tired after the flight.

'Candice said she would pick us up.' Artie is rubbing his hands in the cool of the car park.

On cue, a Fiat 500 – an orginal, not one of the modern copies – whines up. A young woman, maybe in her late twenties, jumps out. 'Uncle Artie!'

We all squeeze into the car. Candice is dressed in a light-weight blouse and a pair of distressed jeans. Her only concession to the wind is a small woolen scarf – thrown round her neck more for fashion than protection. I put out my hand. 'Hi, I'm Craig. You're Artie's niece?'

She smiles. Almost as good a smile as the waitress at the mom and pop back in Canada.

'My mum came over to Scotland way back. Dad served in the Navy and got posted here. Mum was one of the few wives who came along. Dad left the navy and got a job with an engineering company, so they set up home and never went back.'

Her accent is soft; a gentle burr rounding off the consonants.

We all squeeze into the car. Four of us in it is so wrong. It's built for people who stopped growing when they were two. With four of us in it I expect the metal skin to explode at any moment. On the hills we would be better getting out and walking, it's that slow. The heater is busted and the steam from our breath has fogged up all the windows. Candice has to wipe the windshield with a cloth to keep it clear.

'Ardeer Point here we come?' She's smiling.

'Where the factory was,' Artie explains.

When Artie phoned Candice it transpired she knew exactly where the old dynamite factory stood. She lives less than five miles from it and promised to drive us to the site.

So why am I still a bag of nereves? We got into the UK didn't we? Well try the complete lack of a plan. Try the bookmaker-defying odds that we are even looking in the right place. Try the lack of suits chasing us.

Anything else? A teacher once told the class I was in that the less we knew the happier we'd be. I thought he was as mad as a brush. Why the hell would a teacher tell you that? And it's just plain wrong. I couldn't be more ignorant and I'm a country mile from being happy. But I need to go on. I need answers. They may not be the answers I want but I need to know. Not knowing isn't always freedom. My head hurts when I try and place order on the world of what might be, what is and what isn't.

After I came back from Iraq the first time, a mental wreck, I buried myself in Charlie's bar. Each night I would sit and work as much alcohol into my system as was possible. My bar bill grew but Charlie never called it in. A mixture of pity for me, love for my wife and the fact he had spent time in the same institution as I had – all mixed together was worth an unlimited credit account.

Life was simple back then. I would help around the house, prepare a meal for Lorraine, sit and watch TV and then, when her eyes closed from the strain of teaching seven years olds, I would slip down to Charlie's bar. At weekends I would shop, or walk in the park – or do a million other things and still be in the bar by nine o'clock. Lorraine never tried to stop me. Not at first. She saw it as part of the recovery process. But I knew it was a dangerous way to screw up your life.

When I got offered a security job out in Iraq I jumped at it. Lorraine wasn't so keen but I needed to do something useful. The fact I screwed it up was just the first step on the journey that has led me to sitting in a car with three people I barely know; driving to a place that is linked to a cryptic piece of paper that may not even be about me.

We bump along a road between strips of grass. I look up to see the sea rolling into view. We've been on the road for the best part of an hour and I'm still working my way through how far south my life seems to have gone.

Candice pulls the car into a rough-and-ready parking lot. All lumps and bumps – and no discernable difference between it and the surrounding sea front.

We vomit from the car, spewing out into the cold. On three sides of the lot the sea is taking a crack at the coast. A beach stretches out to the distance – narrow with an artificial sea-break less then twenty yards from the high water line. On top of the sea-break is a ragged line of fencing topped with barbed wire. A couple of hundred yards along the sea-break there's a mural of a man's face.

Candice catches me looking at it. 'Rabbie Burns. That's who you're looking at. There was a plan to cover the entire wall with art but funding ran dry.'

'What's behind the fence on top?'

'That's the old dynamite plant. The nearest bit is still active and well protected, but further along it's easy to get in as the fence is broken.'

A high-pitched whine cuts through the air. A motorbike snaps into view. Throttle open, it dashes along the shore beneath the sea break. The driver keeps the wheels just out of the sea as he winds up the speed.

Candice looks on. 'That's what I do of a weekend. It's trickier than it looks. You don't want to go driving through the water. The salt is a killer. And if you hit a hole you're mince.'

It's the first time I've really looked at Candice. There's a vague conencton to Artie in her nose and mouth. She has short, dark hair and darker eyes. I have no idea what mince is. 'Can you get past the fence up top?'

'Easily. The first bit is solid but, further along, the old area is abandoned. If you climb up next to Rabbie there's a break in the fence that the bikers use to access the ground beyond. They love it in there. The old bunkers make for a great place to fling the bikes around.'

'Bunkers?'

Candice waves her arm. 'When it was a dynamite factory they kept each building separate and built them as bunkers. That way if one exploded the rest didn't follow. They're little more than empty shells now.'

'How far along does the beach go?'

'About a mile and half. They built a visitor attraction called The Big Idea at the far end and bridged the river that cuts off the spit from the mainland. You used to be able to walk right into Irvine but the bridge closed years ago. Lack of visitors to The Big Idea. It never really worked. Some people call it The Bad Idea.'

'Ok, Candice, thanks for this; we'll take it from here.'

'Take it where?'

'Beyond the fence.'

'And do you know what lies there?'

'No.'

'I do. It's a maze. Do you know what you're looking for?'

'No.'

Candice brushes at her hair.

She turns away. 'How do you know I can't help?'

I feel like some out-of-this-world version of the Pied Piper. I spent a year on the other side of Charlie's bar and never made one friend. Now I seem to be collecting them with alacrity. 'I don't, but you've no idea what we are doing here.'

'It's her call.' Artie has walked round behind me. 'Not yours.'

'The hell it is. This whole journey starts with me.'

Martyn follows Artie. 'As I recall, it was my idea. I don't remember a vote making you captain.'

I stand, hands out. 'Are you serious? We have no idea what, if anything, is in there. If I had Arnie, Sly and Bruce with me I'd still be nervous. But with you three?'

'Not sure I like that, man.' Artie starts to walk away.

'I didn't mean it like that. All I'm saying is...'

Artie walks on. 'Man, all you are saying is you don't trust us. That seems a bit harsh.'

I stop talking. Artie is more right than wrong. He's here because he made the mistake of picking me up on the highway. By contacting Martyn's mother I've dragged Martyn in and Candice has ridden in on the back of Artie. I'm not trying to take control. I'm just worried about them. 'Look, I'm grateful as hell, but I don't want to expose any of you to any risk.'

Martyn catches up with Artie and turns his head. 'Not sure it's your call. What are you going to do if we ignore you?'

Candice jogs to catch up with them. The three start to wind their way down to the beach. I'm left in the parking lot.

With no car keys, no place to go and a mountain of questions,

I take a deep breath and walk after them. 'Ok, ok. Hell, I'm sure British prisons are more fun if you have people inside that know you. Except you, Candice – you'd need to make new friends as I doubt they bunk men and women together.'

We walk onto the beach as the motorbike returns. The rider pulls high on the beach to avoid us, spraying sand at the sea break. He waves at Candice. She waves back. Apart from the biker, and the four of us, the beach is deserted.

The sea bubbles next to our feet and a cold wind has picked up. Except for Candice, none of us are dressed for the weather.

As we approach the mural of Robert Burns, I'm looking forward to getting off the beach and into some shelter. The sea-break is steep. I try to climb it but fall back less than halfway up.

Candice catches my arm. 'Further along. The wall is broken.'

We walk a little further. Rubble lies around us. The break in the wall is the result of a collapse. With a bit of scrambling we all make it to the top.

A fence sits in front of us and a small sandy path runs between the fence and the top of the seawall. The path is rid- dled with bike tracks. Beyond the fence is what looks like a car park with rows of parallel white lines painted on dark concrete. But, on closer inspection, the painted white lines are too close together for a vehicle to fit. There are three such slabs, each a good hundred yards square, that contain the lines. The lines run from top to bottom and are numbered. Each marked slab is separated from the next by a six foot wall.

Candice leans on the fence. 'Took me a while to figure out what the lines are there for. It's for storing containers ready for shipment. Don't ask me how it works but sometimes the spaces between the lines are full of stuff. I reckon it has to be danger- ous; otherwise why have the fire lake?' She points.

Beyond the marked-out areas a large pond wraps itself around the southeast corner. The whole area is sunk about twenty feet below us. Candice lets go of the fence and points to my right.

She steps past me. 'Abandoned area. We can get in a little further along.'

I walk after her. 'Where does it lead?'

'If you walk far enough it leads to The Big Idea. If you walk inland you'll hit a business park. Do you know where it is you want to get to?'

I shake my head. 'The only clues we have are Nobel and Irvine.'

'It's easy enough to get into the abandoned area but the working area is fairly secure.'

'Let's have a look at the old area first.'

We squeeze through a broken section of link fencing. At first sight the scenery is a maze of small sand dunes, with tracks winding between them. But, on closer inspection, the dunes turn out to be long-since-deserted buildings. Or rather, the remnants.

I catch up with Candice. 'Who in the hell worked here?'

'Mostly local women. Especially during the war.'

'Making dynamite?'

'And bloody good at it.'

'Some job.'

'Took nerve and they knew the danger but, to them, it was just a way to earn cash and support the country.'

'So they don't make explosives here anymore?'

'Not in this bit. I've no idea if they still do in the operational section.'

Martyn and Artie split up to scour the locale. Half an hour in and there's little to be found. All signs of life are long gone.

I gather everyone together. 'Any ideas?'

Artie looks around. 'Has to be in the fenced off area, man. Ain't nothing here but sand and grass.'

'Martyn?'

'I'm with Artie.'

'Candice?'

'Maybe.'

'Only maybe?'

'If you're looking for some top secret base I don't think it'll be in the other bit.'

'Why not?'

'Because the business park is busy. How long did you say the place you are looking for has been here?'

'I didn't, but it has to have been fifty years or more.'

'There you go. The dynamite factory would have been here for that long, but the rest was wasteland. They built the original facrtory to be out of the way. So whatever you're looking for is either long since gone or hidden in the old area somewhere.'

'Not unreasonable. So where?'

'I have one thought.' She points down the peninsula. 'We ride the bikes all over this place. Most times we are left alone but every now and then we find a jeep on our tail. At first we thought it was the guards from the business park but after a while we realised the jeep would always come from the far end of the beach. Away from the business park. When we get too close to the far end it appears. We've learned that if we stay away from that end then no one cares.'

'What's down there?'

'That's the strange thing. Nothing. Just more of the same. If you go far enough you hit The Big Idea building. There was a wildlife sanctuary built as part of the attraction. Get too close to the sanctuary or the building and the jeep appears.'

'So what was The Big Idea?'

'It was for kids. The ground floor was full of machines they could play with and upstairs was an area to build kits.'

'Kits?' Artie shuffles in the cold.

'With your ticket you could choose a model to build. Each one was a scientific toy – a car, plane etc. You built them upstairs and could try them out. But it's been closed for years.'

I join in the Artie shuffle. 'And there's nothing else along there?'

'No, but there is one other odd thing. A couple of months ago we were ripping up the area in the bikes and got a bit too close to The Big Idea. It was lit up like Christmas was coming. We could see people moving around. I assumed they were stripping it out but one of my friends said that everything was removed years ago. We assumed that someone was moving in – there's been talk about the Chinese buying it, even turning it into a casino. Then the jeep appeared and we got chased.'

'And?'

'And no one ever moved in. Not that we ever saw. It looks sealed tight. Although every so often you see the odd light and once we saw a truck in the distance.'

Promising. 'Sounds like something we should take a closer look at. Does the jeep still appear?'

'I haven't been down here for a few weeks but I met a friend in the pub a couple of days ago and he said they had been chased. So I'm assuming that whoever "they" are still don't want visitors.'

I think a little. Why would someone be protecting an abandoned visitor attraction in the back end of nowhere? 'When did you first get chased? Was it when the center closed?'

'No. It was ages after. When it was open no one cared. For a long time we were free to roam and then, a couple of years ago, we started to get chased.'

'So whoever is doing this is new to the area? Has anyone ever enquired into what's going on?'

'One of my friend's dads asked once but he was told that there was nothing.'

'Ok then, let's take a look. Is it far?'

'Twenty minutes?'

I lead off with Candice at the front and Artie and Martyn taking up the rear.

The landscape around doesn't allow for much forward warning. The way the humps and lumps have been laid out means that you can see little beyond the next abandoned building.

Protected in the dip between the sea break and the land beyond, the cold still eats slowly through our too-light clothing. At least the lowered geography keeps the wind at bay. The sound from the sea is gone. Coarse grass has taken over much of the terrain. The pathways are sand and clear of the grass due to the bikes. Tire tracks are everywhere.

The winter sun is hidden. In this latitude we'll lose it in a few hours. I want to get some eyes on the prize as soon as possible. There could be an all-too-innocent explanation as to what Candice has seen. There's no real evidence to suggest that this has any connection to my condition. It's only a few years since they started to deter visitors. What I'm looking for has to be a lot older. The center could be occupied for a number of reasons. We're out on a limb here. Perhaps we're wasting our time after all.

Ten minutes later Candice puts up her hand. She doesn't speak. We all stop.

She turns her head. 'Listen.'

I open my ears but there's a little to hear. 'What?'

'Do you here it?'

'What?'

'Like an engine.'

'Car engine?'

'No. More like a generator.'

Artie cups his left ear with his hand. 'Got it. Faint but she's right. It does sound like a generator.'

I still can't hear anything but my hearing has never been the best. 'From the center?'

Candice shakes her head. 'Not sure.'

'Stay here.' I walk on.

I skirt a bump and catch the noise for the first time. Taking care to place the next building between me and the noise, I walk on. If I'm right the sound is coming from the middle of the next structure.

I reach the grass-covered wall and climb up. At the top I stick my head over and look down. Nothing. Just the same as all the rest; a sand-covered space where the floor would have been. But the sound of the generator is strong. I drop down into the dip. The noise is coming from beneath my feet. I fall to the ground and put my hand on the sand. I can feel the vibration of the engine. I scout around looking for an entrance but come up blank. Returning to the others I tell them what I've found.

Artie speaks. 'An underground generator, man. Sounds suspicious to me.'

I agree with him. This place was left to nature an eon ago. I turn to Candice. 'Do you know if there were any underground tunnels here?'

'I've no idea. But it would make sense. I assume they would want to keep as much of the explosives out of sight as possible.'

'Well, if they exist, someone is using them. There has to be an entrance around here somewhere. How far to the visitor center?'

Candice steps to the side. 'Not far.'

We walk on, but with a heightened sense of awareness. In the distance a large hillock of grass springs up.

Candice points to it. 'That's the back of The Big Idea. It's covered in grass. The front is sheet glass over two levels. The whole thing looks like a quarter of a football buried in the ground.'

'American or soccer ball?' Martyn smiles.

'Football.' She lays emphasis on the word. 'Not soccer. We call it football. Once we go past that last building we'll be exposed. The front of The Big Idea faces away from us but if anyone is looking they won't be able to miss us.'

I'm shivering now. The protection afforded by the land around us has been compromised by the opening in front. The wind is pulling at my jacket.

'I'm Alaskan cold.' Martyn wraps his arms around his body.

And some, I think. 'Let's get out of the wind.' I lead them up to the last building and we hunker down to gain some shelter. The generator is still humming. We sit with our back to the wall.

Artie taps me on the shoulder. 'We could wait until it's night and then make a move.'

I don't agree. 'We'd be frozen to the core. Plus we need some daylight to see what's what. We're not geared up for night.'

I shuffle to the edge of the last building. The visitor center sits in a world of plants and water. The back is a dome of wild grass. The front is not visible from where we are. There's an entrance at the base of the dome.

'I'm going to check it all out. Stay here until I get back.'

I keep hard to the collapsing walls of the old building until the last possible second. When I walk out I make straight for the rear of the visitor center. I keep my eyes and ears wide open but don't deviate from a straight line to the door. If anyone is looking I'll be spotted whatever I do. In a perverse way a shout or the appearance of someone would confirm that the building was occupied.

I stumble through long grass and onto a service road. The door in front of me is a large double shuttered affair with a smaller baby brother next to it. I try each. Both are locked solid. The only choice is to head for the front.

Keeping the wall to my left, I cross more wild grass. At the

next corner I stop and look out.

Once upon a time the front would have been a welcoming vista for visitors. Now it is a stretch of cracking cement. I lean round to get a full view.

Candice was right. The building has solid glass to the top of the dome. Flat fronted, there are two visible levels. The entrance is on the far side. If there's anyone inside I'll be seen as I walk over. The only option is to circle back round and try from the other end.

It takes me a couple of minutes to circumnavigate the building. I'm not expecting the front door to be open but you never know.

I reach the target.

Breathe. Slow the heart rate. Before I move out into the open I want as much calm as I can muster. There's no immediate danger. If someone sees me I'm a curious walker. Unless, of course, Tampoline's goons are around; then I'm dead meat whatever way I do this. I drop my eyes and focus on my lungs. Blue air in. Red air out. Cold for heat. Make it all look casual. I grab one more draft of the sea air.

No one screams, no one shouts, no one is visible. I make my way to the main entrance. No click of a gun being cocked. Even the ever-present seagulls seem to have taken a coffee break.

Show time.

I reach for the door handle and I'm less than surprised at the lack of give. It's as solid as the back door. I turn my attention to the interior. Cupping my hand I press my face to the glass. The light from outside doesn't help much. The floor is clear and some fixtures and fittings are hiding in the gloom. If the building is in use then it's either being used upstairs or in the back – the front is a desert.

I wasn't in the army long but some of the basic training stuck. *Small things matter.* It's often the small stuff that's important.

Something out of place. Something that should be insignificant but turns out to be a lifesaver or a life taker. A cough where no cough should be. A movement in the corner of your eye. A misplaced plastic bag. Or, in this case, the faintest smell of cigarette smoke.

As an ex-smoker it's unmistakable. Even the tiniest wisp and I am on it. Its appeal undiminished through the years. I could as easy light up and be back on twenty a day with but a tinge of regret. Smokers are never free of the beast.

I sniff at the door. The scent is there. Weak but fresh. I scan the ground. Someone has swept here recently. The debris of winter is missing but the sweeper was none too thorough. In the corner of the door a cigarette butt has wedged itself tight. Another sits a few yards away.

I look behind me, trying to get my eyes to focus in the gathering gloom. At the edge of the grass I can see two marks. Someone has brushed the grass back. Judging by the distance between the marks I would say that Candice's truck has been here. Generator, cigarette butts and tire tracks. Someone is home and someone is keen to keep it all private. I cup my hand over the glass again. The floor is dusty but on closer inspection it appears riddled with footprints and drag marks. I call it quits and return to my colleagues.

After I explain what I've found I ask for their thoughts on gaining entry. We brain-dump a lot of nonsense.

Martyn puts his hand up. 'Ther's only one option. We hang fire. With a bit of luck someone will come out.'

'And then what?'

I nod at Artie's question.

Martyn drops his hand. 'Well, Craig, have you any better ideas?'

I do. But it means one of us won't be going inside.

# Chapter 30

'Candice, I have no idea what we'll find inside. You have the car. You can get the hell out of here. I'm grateful for what you've done.'

I've spelt out my idea but Candice seems unwilling. 'We could do what Martyn said and all wait and see what happens?'

I disagree. 'It could be hours and I'm not getting any warmer.'

The sound of the motorbike is a distant thing. I look towards the sound and then back at Candice. 'Will *he* help?'

Candice nods. 'He used to fancy me at school. He'll help.'

If there are people inside maybe they will play chase with the biker. All Candice has to do is get him to agree to help.

The plan is simple. Candice will wave down the biker and ask for a ride. She will bring the bike in towards us and buzz around until the jeep appears. If my guess is right it has to come from the shuttered door. There isn't anywhere else it could be parked. When it rolls we go in.

'Ok,' she says. 'It's been fun. Uncle, when this – whatever this is – is finished, come up and see me.'

Artie walks over and gives her a hug. 'I'll see you before I go.'

She turns and leaves. I follow her until she vanishes behind a mound.

We wait.

*

The sound of the motorbike grows. It roars into view, throwing up a plume of sand as Candice, with her friend riding on the back, powerslides it to a halt. Candice leaves.

The bike cuts across the grass and rides out in front of the building. Candice winds up the throttle, making as much noise as possible. We break cover and run for the back door. As we slam into the wall the sound of the shutter starting up joins in the noise of the bike. The bike speeds into view as a jeep leaps from the doorway. Candice draws it away from us.

'Now!' I'm running. Artie and Martyn follow.

The shutter is already on its way back down. We all dive under, rolling into the area beyond. My eyes are wild as I try and recce the space. We're lucky. No one else is present. The room is small. When the jeep is parked it will take up most of the floor. A door leads out the rear. A pile of boxes hide one of the corners. The shutter snaps shut and we're plunged into darkness.

I let my eyes adjust. 'Artie, what do you think of staying here?'

'Why?'

'As our getaway man. When the jeep comes back I need someone to see how the door operates and a ready-and-waiting driver would be more than handy. You could hide behind the boxes. The jeep might be our only way out of here if things go wrong. We need an exit plan.'

Artie is little more than a shadow. 'Ok. But if you're not back in an half an hour I'm coming in after you.'

'If we're not back in half an hour get the hell out of here.'

'Not your choice, Craig. I'm happy to have your back but its my rules or I'm coming with you.'

'Ok.' There's not much else I can do.

I grab the door handle on the far wall and open it – just an inch. Enough light escapes to show Artie to his new home.

He waves. 'Good luck, man.'

'Thanks.'

Once Artie is secure, hidden by the boxes, I turn to Martyn. 'I'll take point.'

'No argument from me on that one.'

And now we are two.

I open the door a touch more. Listen. Nothing. I sniff. The smell of tobacco is stronger. I push my head in a little more. A wide zone opens out. It's lit by low lights on the wall. A mix of doors and glass reveal what look like classrooms along one side. I step in and check each one. They're empty. I signal to Martyn to come out.

A double door leads deeper into the building. The décor is bare minimal. Painted concrete. Very '90s.

Martyn stops me. 'Look.'

I follow his outstretched hand. A CCTV camera sits high on the wall. While checking the rooms I would have been in full view. We step back under it and wait. If someone is watching they'll be up soon. If we hear a noise we'll join Artie.

Then the clatter of the outside shutter beginning to roll up bounces off the walls. The timing couldn't be worse. If someone has spotted us on CCTV we're caught between a bad place and a bad place.

I look at Martyn. 'Go or stay?'

'Go. In the garage we're screwed. Let's hope the CCTV person is on a comfort break.'

'Agree.' We break cover.

I make a beeline for the far door. I open it slowly, fighting the urge to run in, as the sound of the outside shutter signals it's closing. The crew from the jeep will be in here in seconds.

The door opens onto the back of the area I saw through the front glass. Dust is thick but trails have been made that run from the door I'm standing at to a corridor to my right. I push my head into full view. The space is empty of people. I signal Martyn to follow me. He almost jogs in.

Martyn spots the dust trail. I grab him and shake my head. I point away from the corridor. A reception desk dominates the open area. A few footsteps lead up to it. A scattering of cigarette ends suggest that some people prefer indoor smoking. I walk to the desk before pulling Martyn down and out of sight.

I risk a whisper. 'Let's hope the people in the jeep go straight down the corridor.' We've also no idea what's down there. It could be a dead end. 'Let them go ahead and then we follow.'

He nods. 'Good thinking, Batman.'

We don't have long to wait. The door opens. 'Fucking kids. What's the point in chasing them? The fucker flicked me the bird every time we got close. What a waste of time.' The voice is deep, gravel for vocal chords.

'The boss says and we do.' Lighter, fruitier in tone.

'We're chasing ghosts. And they know it.'

'Feel free to take up your complaint with the boss. You know the procedure?'

'The fuck I will. I value my pulse.'

The voices fade as they walk down the corridor. Then they're gone.

I lift my head above the desk. 'Ok, we're clear.'

'This isn't agency we're dealing with.'

I agree with Martyn's observation. Tampoline's team might be bastards but they don't threaten death to the employees, as a rule of thumb. Whoever the 'Boss' is doesn't chime with the suits' world.

So these guys could be anything. Local criminals? The regional branch of a survivalist gang? A bunch of squatters? But I know it's none of the above. When the guy talked about 'valuing his pulse' he was serious. So, unless he's deluded, we're at the top of the class when it comes to dangerous people.

I scan the front as we walk down the corridor. I look for more cameras but if they're present they're well hidden. The more I think about this the more I think we are dealing with bad people. I was hoping it might be agency. I've dealt with them in the past and, although they're competent, they can be handled. Their rules might be thin at points but they have them. There's nothing to say that the people in here have any.

'Craig?' Martyn's voice is a whisper and still sounds too loud.

I stop. 'What?'

The corridor is dark. Little outside light stretches this far.

'Light under the door.'

Martyn's right. The corridor ends at yet another door. Light is leaking from beneath it. A shadow blocks out the light for a second. Live bodies are beyond.

I hug the wall. 'I'm betting this is the only way in and out. I didn't see any footsteps going anywhere else.' I'm trying to keep my voice as low as possible.

A shadow blocks out the light and an American accent comes from beyond the door. 'Going for a smoke.'

We move. Back the way we came. We reach the desk at a flat run, diving out of sight as the footsteps approach. They stop. Close. Both our heads are buried in our legs. There's a zip then a match flares. A drag. We have our indoor smoker.

I raise my head. Just an inch. A pair of feet are standing on the other side of the desk. If the smoker leans over, even a few inches, he can't miss us. There's nowhere for us to go. We're hard in under the desk, dust thick in our throats. Martyn is furthest from the feet. I watch as they shuffle. The smell of the smoke mixes with the smell of the dirt on the floor.

The feet walk away. I relax a little, then another voice rings out. 'Stay away from the window. New rules from the boss.'

'Shit, we just chased some kids all over the place. Who's to not know we are here?'

Gravel pipes up again. 'How long do you think we'll be here?'

Fruit answers. 'Not long. Most of the stuff was packed onto the truck. There ain't much left.'

So the truck Candice saw was picking up, not delivering.

Gravel. 'I'll be fucking glad to get out of here. That's some weird shit that the boss is into. Did you get a look at some of it?

Fruit. 'And the Boss will strip your heart out if he knows you've seen it.'

'Wasn't my fault the fucking forklift spilt its load. What a mess. Looked like the crash of a morgue van. And what do you think they were doing in that room?'

'Do you really want to end up dead? We were told not to talk about it.'

'Who the hell is listening? The boss is back in the room. We are it.'

'Shit, I just want paid and out of this.'

'Ditto. That arsehole has attitude. I don't ever want to see him again after this.'

'You've got me on your side on that one. That whine of a voice. I thought it was a joke at first.'

'Yeah, 'til he burst that young boy's nose with a shovel. Fuck, all the boy did was touch a few papers on the desk. Did you see what the papers were?'

'Come on Ted, shut up.'

'I'm only asking. I saw the title on one.'

'No you didn't.'

'I fucking did.'

'I'm telling you for your own good; you didn't.'

'Ah get you. Well I ain't going to tell anyone else.'

'You're telling me.'

'We're buddies.'

'If the Boss catches us chatting about this we'll be dead buddies.'

A little movement. This time two pairs of feet come into view. Both are wearing heavy-duty walking shoes. The CAT logo prominent.

Gravel takes another drag on the cigarette. 'Well, do you want to know what I saw?'

'No.'

'Dynamite.'

'What?'

'That's the word I saw. At the top of one of the sheets of papers. In bold letters.'

'And?'

'Funny thing to have written down. We ain't shifted any explosives.'

'Leave it alone.'

'Just saying. Strange word.'

'And none of our business. Now finish the cigarette and let's get back to work. We've to shift more crap to the jeep.'

'Give it a second. Let me enjoy the smoke. Fuck all point in smoking if you don't enjoy it.'

A drag later and the cigarette flies over the desk. It lands on my thigh. In a second it burns through my pants. I bite down to prevent myself shouting out. I daren't move to flick it away for fear of giving away our presence. I try to shift my leg a fraction to dislodge the butt, but it's stuck in the material. The lit end is lying on my skin. I bite even harder. Resisting the urge to move. I look to see if their feet have gone, but both are still there.

Gravel. 'When do we move out?'

'I told you, soon.'

'Not soon enough.'

My head is screaming at me to do something about the agony. I can see a twirl of smoke rising from my leg. The pain is excruciating. I'll need to move. The end is burning a hole in my leg. Then something flashes in my head. Not the usual full-blown explosion preceding an event. Just a flare. But with it comes a headache. Again, not the blinder of a usual event but enough to make me gasp.

Gravel. 'Did you hear that?'

'Someone else is in here.'

'Behind the desk.'

I feel Martyn move. We've been sussed. But the headache and the burn have all my attention. I roll over and paw at the cigarette. The relief from the action is dulled by the pain in my head.

Martyn is up. A face leans into view. Bearded and topped with thick curly hair. It looks down at me. 'Who the fuck are you?'

Good question. Except I'm in no shape to answer. I want to flick back a quip. 'Cleaner'. 'Doorman'. 'Failed rock-star'. I dribble instead.

'Are you fucking stupid?'

No. But I'm in fucking pain.

Then the inevitable tunes in. I get a front-row view this time. Right in my face. My headache is no supernova, just a small asteroid hitting earth, with me at the impact point.

The bearded man looks, to all my world, like he's leaning closer to inspect me. Only he does it with the sort of whiplash speed that suggests he's not in full control of the situation. Either that or he really enjoys head-butting solid granite. The 'oopmh' as his head connects with the stone surface above me is accompanied by a gob of spit splatting my cheek. His eyes roll back as his head is yanked out of sight. If I were a betting man I'd say his friend is having fun.

I roll over, waiting for the blue world, but it doesn't appear. My headache flashes, racks up a gear, and then with a blaze it lights up my head and is gone. I slump to the floor.

The next few seconds are lost to me, then Martyn arrives to see if I'm ok, while what sounds like a pub fight breaks out around us. A lot of huffing and puffing with the odd thump to emphasize a hit or two.

Martyn looks at me. 'Craig, is that you doing this shit?'

I blink. He takes this as a yes and helps me maneuver away. I wonder at the non-appearance of the blue world. A regular friend. The stop-start. The release from pain. The detachment. Absent.

Martyn reaches down. 'Craig, time to move.'

I can still hear the fight. I'm surprised. Usually we're at the end game seconds after the horn, but these two still seem to be at it. I try to stand up but I'm weak. Martyn takes the strain and lifts me.

Once, when I was eighteen or so, I got in a fight. Although I doubt Roget's thesaurus would agree with my definition. I had been in a local bar with a friend called Tim Collins, a man with the finesse of a cocaine-addicted hippopotamus. He had been a friend since fourth grade but had moved out from New Jersey to sunnier climes when sixteen. He was back in town for his stepfather's funeral. A man he despised but his mother loved. He was doing the son thing and didn't want to be there, but his mom was a gem and he knew when to back down. Not that his step-dad had been a bad man, he just wasn't Tim's real dad.

Tim, with me as his partner, had done the dutiful. It was no moment that his step-dad would have been proud of – or maybe he would. Six people turned up at the funeral, including Tim and I. If you add in Tim's mom, the step-dad's two brothers and the minister you had the number of bums on seats. The minister didn't know shit. Tim's step-dad wasn't the church-going type and I felt sorry as the minister cruised through the by-the-book ceremony. He even stumbled over the 'Callum was a good man' bit.

After a painful hour we hit a bar in a hotel that provided us with stale sandwiches and warm beer. I caught a businessman i in the restroom, pants down, sitting on the basin, enjoying the services delivered by a young man. It kind of summed up the day. The bar was loud. The Hard Rock Cafe but with no money, no burgers and cheap drink. Tim was on a mission to forget. To be truthful he was on a mission to forgive – himself.

We never made closing time. Tim decked a guy for brushing past him and we both left minus gravity. I landed first. Tim next. He got up and decided that the bouncer had been inconsiderate. He launched a doomed attack on a guy who could have doubled as Mike Tyson's big brother. Tim swung, missed and doubled up as the bouncer dropped him with one to the gut. In my less-than-sober state I went on the offensive. That went well.

Ten minutes later we were still both on the ground. Tim because he couldn't move and me through choice. I'd figured that getting up again was never going to end in a good place. Therein lay the quandary for the bouncers. Much as they wanted to close the door and leave us they knew this was off the cards. If the police turned up there would be questions to answer.

After a couple of minutes and no movement from us, Mike's brother came over. He talked a little. Enquired after our health. Got nowhere and felt it was only reasonable that he check we were both still breathing. Only his CPR routine involved kicking Tim in the gut. Tim moaned and I got mad. The bouncer reached down to grab me and I remember thinking that – somehow, somewhy – this wasn't the way that things should go down.

I have no punch. Not one that has any impact. But, as I would find out years later when I signed up for the Army, strength isn't everything.

I took a shot as Mike's sibling wrenched me from the floor. It connected. Mike's brother gasped and fell back. More from the surprise than as a result of the punch. I got up and grabbed Tim. Mike's brother's soul mate threw himself at me. I ducked. Mostly because I'd underestimated Tim's weight. The soul mate flew over us and introduced his skull to the alley wall. All in all I was two for zero.

We both walked away from the scene with no further intervention from the staff.

As Martyn lifts me I see the man with the beard approach. Bloodied. Eyes wild. And, knowing where this is going, I throw my eighteen year old punch. To my surprise he goes down.

Martyn looks at the fallen villain. 'Nice shot.'

I shrug. 'You know. Once you've got it you never lose it.'

After an event I'm usually dead to the world but this new shortened version is not as draining. The scene, when I rise from the reception desk, is two men down and neither are us. The man with the beard is lying at my feet and his colleague, a small man wearing double denim, has his head at the base of the large glass font window. The blood smear above him doesn't bode well.

'Can you walk?' Martyn is checking me out.

'Give me five.'

'I don't even know if we have one.'

I breathe, deep and long. I bend down and take more breaths. I stand up, and my world brightens. The lightheadedness takes me back to my knees. I push Martyn away. I grab the reception desk and use it as a crutch. I circle twice and, by the second time, I'm not using the granite as a third leg. 'Ok. Let's do this. It's time to find out what in the hell we are into.'

# Chapter 31

I totter forward. Martyn as my helper. I take stock of what has just gone down. New territory for me. Or just old territory with a new twist. The event was weak. Like a torch with batteries on their last legs. The residue is draining but not debilitating. The onset sudden and lacking in warning. The impact was the same though. Even the headache was vicious but not eleven on the dial. More an 8.5 with a severe aftershock.

I tap Martyn's shoulder. 'You could have dropped one of them.'

'Sure, but you were doing fine. We might need me in reserve. When the second guy went down I held back.'

'Spare bullet in the gun.'

'My thoughts. So are we going to do this?'

'I need five more.'

The door at the far side -the one the bearded man and his sidekick had come through – opens. We were dead to rights. A small man of excessive girth waddles through. Freezes as he catches sight of us. Then his hand flies to his pocket and a gun snakes into the air.

Martyn recognises him the same instant I do. Gaylord never gets the gun barrel level. His eyes blank out as he lets the weapon drop. It tumbles to the floor. Martyn follows him to the dust.

I know what's happened – our spare bullet has just been used. Martyn has pulled his party trick and Gaylord is out for the count. I'm now the last man standing. All the others around me are either dead or unconscious. I'm not doing that well but at least I'm vertical.

I look down at Martyn. He could be AWOL for a while. I pray he has a shorter pass than everyone else. I'm in no fit state to handle a domesticated rabbit never mind a couple of thugs and a psychopath like Gaylord.

Gaylord has put on weight – another thirty or forty pounds since I last saw him. He must be almost as broad as he is tall.

Gaylord was taped to his brother, Tampoline, when I last said goodbye. Tampoline is now back on the journey to the White House and Gaylord has…well I'm not sure what Gaylord has. Whatever it is, it's connected to me. His presence is all the proof I need.

I've been playing with the notion that the pot at the end of this rainbow might be bait, not reward. Ever since we hit the road I've the feeling we've been being toyed with, that Tampoline had us under close surveillance and has been leaving enough rope for me to play but not escape. But if that were true Gaylord would have been ready and his prostrate body is testament to his unpreparedness.

So now it's time to work. Figure the next move before circumstances overtake me again. I could do with Martyn back, but dropping people, the way he dropped Gaylord, has the same impact a full on event has on me. He could be down for a while.

More nonsense arrives in the form of a man with a semi-automatic machine gun. He arrives from the door that Gaylord walked out of. To say he's surprised is like saying that nailing your hand to the floor hurts. He has the sniff of agency about him. Thickset, muscled up and clean cut with a five o'clock shadow and clothes that are pure camouflage. Ex-agency?

His gun is pointing at the floor, indicating that the scene in front of him is not one he had been playing out in his head a few seconds before. At twenty yards there's no way of reaching him before he can level the barrel at me. In my state, twenty inches would be too much. I look around for something to use as a weapon. An old anglepoise lamp balances on the reception desk. It's plugless and thick with dust. My intent is clear as I move.

He speaks. 'Don't take a step.' US accent. Midwest.

I ignore the order and wrap my hand around the lamp. He raises the gun, flicking the safety to off. I have no time to raise the lamp to throw it. I go for a submarine pitch, swiping the lamp as hard as I can. It flies from the desk.

Midwest levels the gun.

But it's too late and the lamp clips him high on the shoulder, more by a historic bout of luck than by any Kent Tekulve-type skill. His gun spins to the right as a train of bullets rips through the ceiling. I throw myself forward. My legs work but they feel like lead wading through glue. The gunman is heading to the floor. Forced down by a combination of the lamp and the gun's recoil.

I set the slowest twenty yard time in athletic history. I collide with Midwest at half speed. We both end up on the floor. Me on top. I go for his gun and he slaps at my face. I roll with the blow. Claw at the barrel. He depresses the trigger again. My world is noise and death. The bullets keep flowing. The heat from the hot stream of lead burning skin.

I roll to one side. Midwest counters. The gun stops firing. He lashes out with his foot. I can't win this. I'm still too weak. This guy is no Stan Laurel. I focus all my energy on the gun. No matter the opponent, a gun levels all. I let myself fall onto my back, place both hands on the gun and pull. The gun is searing hot at the barrel. I yelp, let go and grab the butt, ripping it from Midwest's hands. He reaches to wrench it back. I swing it high and bring it down. I miss. It bounces off the floor. I raise it to try again.

He wraps his fingers around the barrel. He also yells at the heat, let's go and I connect head and gun – he grunts. I feel him go limp. He deadweights on my left leg. Lead adding to lead. He looks unconscious but might just be dazed. I may only have a few seconds before I'm back in fight land.

I raise the gun again and stop mid lift. Another blow and I could kill him. I haul at my leg to be free but he weighs in at north of two hundred pounds, with most of it resting on my calf. I twist my neck to see if help is coming from my colleague. Martyn is still sparked out. I twist once more on the off chance that Artie's curiosity has got the better of him. It hasn't.

A moan. Not from the gunman. The bearded goon I laid out is finding voice. I grab my leg with both hands and pull, dropping the gun to the floor. The gunman's gut moves, a ripple of fat allowing my leg to inch out from its trap. I pull again. Some more sub-gluttonous wobbles as my leg inches free.

I plant my free foot in Midwest's chest. I close my hands on my lower leg, rapidly count to three and kick out, pulling in one clean jerk. My leg pops free with the sound of a Wellington boot leaving heavy sludge. I lift the gun as I scramble away. I'm on my knees then I'm up. My head spins. I know I'll white out if I don't get down on my haunches. I've no choice. It's either that or go for a kip. My vision narrows and the white cloud closes in. I draw a deep one. My hearing fades, my world flows into a mist. I hold, waiting for it all to clear. I take another draft of air and the clouds part.

I force myself upright at a slower speed than I need to.

My sight gets back to as close to 20/20 as it will ever get. Midwest is still down but is moving. Martyn is showing signs of life. Gaylord is still face on the floor. Out for a while yet. The bearded man is moaning, whereas his friend beneath the window is not going to be moving this side of Judgment Day.

I check the gun. Despite the bullets now embedded in the ceiling and walls there are still enough left to give me a little control over the situation. Anyway, even an empty gun is better than no gun.

I slide over to Martyn and, keeping and eye on the prostrate crew around me, bend down. 'How are you doing, buddy?'

'Remind me not to do that again.'

'Can't do that. You saved the day.'

'Yeah, well I'm not happy about it.'

'Can you stand?'

'Give me a second.'

'You've got to the count of ten and then I need you on your feet. We have a hell of a mess to sort out.'

Martyn lifts himself onto one elbow. I help him. He shakes his head. 'What in the hell is Gaylord doing here?'

'Just the question I'm going to ask him.'

Martyn looks at the door that has spewed all our trouble. 'Do you think there are more?'

'No idea. If it were pure agency I'd say yes but this has the sniff of something less formal. Fat boy there is not on their payroll.'

'Yeah but he's Tampoline's brother and, last I knew, they were in thick with each other.'

'And, before you say it, I know it's my fault?'

'The thought never crossed my mind.'

And it is my fault. If Gaylord is here Tampoline knows about it. We needed to gain control.

I shake my head. Time for action not thought. 'Find something to tie them up with. We're in no fit state to hold them all without a little restraint.'

'There was a box of those plastic ties in one of the back rooms. It'll take a while to loop enough together, but that'll work.'

'Sounds good to me.'

As Martyn vanishes to get the ties, I keep the gun nice and easy. Ready to point in whatever direction trouble might come from. At the moment there are no red lights flashing. Gaylord and the ex-agency man are still down and out. The bearded man is moaning but more interested in where it hurts than in me.

In front of me the open areas lead to the massive front windows. Kids used to play in here. Families having fun – only not too much fun, otherwise the place would still be open. I scan my brood. All are still in the foetal position.

Seconds turn to minutes. Martyn must be having trouble finding the ties.

I walk towards the massive windows. The dust is thicker here, undisturbed save a few foot trails from the smoker I smelt earlier.

Beyond the glass the scene is one of controlled wilderness turning back to nature. It looks like it always was a wild landscape but nature has a way of reclaiming its own and making it look like man has never been there.

I keep an eye on my captives.

When I was a kid I was taken to a 'city garden' not far from my home. Some wasteland had been gutted and detoxified before the local green finger brigade had carved out a microcosm of a jungle, complete with vines and a few twisted and awkward-looking trees that may or may not have been Brazilian born. By judicious use of wire fencing and artificial green screening a mini jungle had been cut out from the rest of New Jersey. Some bright spark had installed outdoor speakers and recorded the soundtrack to the Amazon rainforest. A stuffed lion stood pride of place as you entered. The fact that lions lived in Africa was neither here nor there. Kids flocked in their hundreds to pretend they were in the heart of darkness.

It wasn't that large but, to a child, that 'city garden' was as big as it needed to be. I visited it again and again over one long hot summer. Me and a childhood friend Barry Cones. A small boy who coughed more than the Marlboro Man. We could lose ourself in the jungle for hours and the owners encouraged us to stay as long as we could.

Then we turned up one day, ready for another run at finding

Inca gold, only to find the place closed. A sign hung from the gate telling us to check back later. Later never came. We found out that some bad boys had come along with their version of Agent Orange and blasted the place. Most everything died.

By the end of that summer the jungle was ripped out and a developer claimed a stake. One day Barry and I found a crack in the security of the building site and were amazed to find that part of the jungle had grown back. Despite being zapped by weed killer, ripped up and dug out, the plants from a far off land had hung on in there. It was never the same again but it showed that beating nature ain't easy. Outside, in the cold wind of a Scottish winter, nature is playing the same trump card and will soon have the world back the way she wants it.

Martyn comes back, a chain of looped ties in each hand. He makes short work of the three on the floor. I look at the fourth, lying beneath the window in a pool of blood. I know it will be fruitless but I try to find a pulse. Nothing.

I don't want to move the body. This is now a crime scene and if or when the local police get involved I intend to be long gone. But if anyone walks by outside they will see the man. I signal to Martyn to come over. We start to shift the body out of sight – a trail like a snail following him – when I hear a voice.

'Craig McIntyre as a I live and breathe.'

# Chapter 32

The voice is high, southern and familiar. Gaylord is leaning on one arm, unable to rise because of the ties – a beached whale trying to return to the sea. He's so much fatter than when we last met and back then he was no terminal cancer case.

He looks at ease with the situation. 'Dead bodies and you have a habit of hanging out together,' he says. The together comes out as *togethaar.*

'Well Gaylord you're no stranger to the odd coffin yourself.'

'Sure ain't, son, but what brings you and your superhero cousin all the way to Scotland?'

'The weather.'

'And a tiny bit of detective work if I'm not mistaken. It seems a long shot that you're here for the property potential of this establishment.'

'Gaylord, don't you know that I'm now an investor of some note on the realtor front?'

'Would you be a good man and untie these shackles. My circulation has enough trouble getting round my body. These things are not helping.'

'Sorry, but that'll have to be a no. Not that I see you as a threat while I hold this gun, but I've underestimated you before therfore I think I'll risk a coronary thrombosis on your part.'

'So thoughtful.'

The bearded man is still moaning and has now been joined by Midwest.

'Well, Craig, I can't see how you plan to get out of this one.' Gaylord has rolled onto his back to ease the strain.

I walk up to him. 'Really. It seems easy to me. Leave you here and walk.'

'You think it'll be that easy?'

'Why? Are you expecting your hoards of thousands to pile through that door and rescue you?'

'And why not?'

'Because with all the racket that has gone down in here – the bullets and the like – there has been no mad rush other than by you and your friend with the gun.' I nod in Midwest's direction. 'If there were others I'm sure they would be here by now.'

'Astute but not necessarily accurate.'

'Well call on them. I promise I won't shoot.'

Gaylord thinks this over. 'There are miles of tunnels back there. Shouting would do no good.'

'How do you know? If I were you I'd try. Of course if you know there's no one then why bother?'

Gaylord surprises me and shouts out. 'Help! Anyone; we're under attack!'

I level the gun at the door and wait. The wait stretches and after a minute I ease the fun back down. Gaylord is no fool. Maybe there *are* others. That puts a premium on time.

I sit down next to him, far enough away that he can't get to me; he may be fat but he can still move if he wants to. 'Ok, Gaylord, let's start at the top and see how far we get. What is this place?'

'My good man, why would I even begin to share that with you?'

'Think on it. If no more of your friends are skulking in the shadows we have a lot of time to kill. I don't have to be any-where. Martyn, do you?'

'Could do with a coffee but other than that I'm good.'

I look at the door. 'Martyn, do a quick check see behind the door. You never know, there may just be a branch of Starbucks hiding away. Take the gun; I'll be ok here.'

Martyn takes just a few seconds to open the door, look, vanish and reappear. 'All clear as far as I can tell. There's a room with a few tables and chairs, oh and a coffee machine full of the hot stuff. Beyond that there's another heavyweight door that's locked tight. I've jammed a chair under the handle – just in case. It won't hold out an army but it'll slow anyone who's back there.'

'No sign of any keys for the other door?'

Martyn shakes his head.

I turn to Gaylord. 'Well, do you have keys?'

Gaylord whines. 'No. The door self locks. But I'm telling you – there are others.'

I pat him down but he could hide the keys to the Tower of London in his fat.

'Martyn, check the rest of the team.'

It takes him five minutes to confirm all are keyless.

I nod at the door. 'Do me a favour and have a once round the room again.'

He is back in less than two. 'Nothing.'

It would be strange if no one had the keys.

I bend down again. 'Ok, Gaylord, let's say that there are some more people coming to the party. You know what Martyn and I can do. We may not be that thrilled at using it but I'm happy to sit back and see what happens if there are more of your thugs on the way. So let's give it ten.'

Ten turns to fifteen and there is no sudden gas attack, no invasion of gun toting maniacs. Just the wind outside and the quiet moaning of the other two.

Martyn perches on the reception desk. Midwest rolls over. There is a sticky patch on his head where I caught him. He glares at me. 'You're fucking dead.'

I close my eyes for a second. 'Sure. I get that a lot. When you get free you're going to rip my head from my shoulders and piss in the void – or something even cornier.'

'Fuck you.'

I turn to Gaylord. 'You need to brush up your HR

departments' recruitment skills. The tone of some of your staff leaves a lot to be desired.'

The gunman tries to intensify his glare but only succeeds in making it look like he's in need of the bathroom.

I return my attention to Gaylord. 'Look, what's the downside of telling all? If I really am going nowhere then what's to lose? A chat might do us all some good. You never know. I might get generous and let you go if the story's a good one.'

The sound of the door breaking through Martyn's barrier gives me long enough to realise that long enough isn't long enough to do anything about anything. Three dark-jacketed men roll into the room. Each has a semi-automatic high and aimed. In the time it takes me to stand up they have a bead on me and Martyn.

# Chapter 33

'Gentlemen, could you untie me?' Gaylord's smugnes is gruesome.

I'm encouraged to back away and Gaylord is soon free.

Cookie cutter is an often-used phrase that means little. Except now. Either the three new arrivals are triplets or the hiring criteria is very specific. Each is five tenish. Each is thick across the chest and loaded around the upper arms. There are no five o'clock shadows on this lot. One is blonde, one is dark and the other is bald. Apart from that, their own mothers couldn't tell them apart. Each has dark glasses when they would seem to be more of a hindrance than a help.

Gaylord leans against the reception desk. It creaks in protest. 'Well that went better than I could have planned. Welcome back to the fold, Craig.'

I try to look calm but suspect I've failed.

'Well, you seem so interested in what we are doing that I'm going to indulge you a little. You may have arrived at a most opportune time. I'm afraid that our own Mr McIntyre over there looks somewhat incapacitated.' He points to the dead man we dragged from the window.

I'm looking confused. 'Your what?'

'Our own Craig McIntyre. He looks dead to me but, no mind, the good news is we have another and then we have you. An heir and a spare – isn't that what the royal family of this country say? Now, follow me.'

He points to Martyn and then to the blonde triplet, who unzips a pocket and jams a syringe into Martyn's arm before he realises what's happening. Martyn drops like a poleaxed bear.

Gaylord nods. 'And keep him out. If he wakes up he can do what you just did to him, only he doesn't need the syringe.' He points the bald triplet. 'Give me your gun and stay here.'

Gaylord pushes the gun into my back. 'Move, right now.'

I hesitate. He cracks the butt on the back of my head. I move. He knows what I can do. He wants me out of the room and on my own as soon as possible. We enter the room where the coffee machine sits. Another door is wide open. The chair that Martyn tried to block it with is up against the far wall.

'In there.' I'm directed through the door.

I find myself in a room about forty feet by forty. One wall is lined with shelves, each replete with glass and metal containers. The glass containers are filled with liquid and objects. The shelves are heavy duty. They are all snaked with wires, each running to an individual container. A row of high-energy arc bulbs sprays light on the shelves. Beneath each container is a tag. I'm too far away to read the writing.

Another door is half open. A cool wind blows in. It must be where the others came from. Probably the route to the tunnels and the generator.

To the left there is what looks like an operating theatre. A table sits center stage. It's attended by all the bells and whistles that I've ever seen in ER. A worrying, dark stain lies beneath the table.

Next to the mini theater, a series of chairs faces a screen on the wall. Coke cans, chip bags and assorted mugs lie around the feet of the chairs. At odds with the cleanliness of the theater less than five feet away. The screen is dead but an old DVD player supports a pile of silver discs. A small fridge is open and empty.

A computer and phone sit on a desk at the other side of the room, with a high-backed leather chair in attedance. Alongside them is a small bar. The optics are empty and the shelf behind is clear.

Gaylord flicks a switch and low-level lighting fights its cousins above the containers. 'Take a seat.'

I pull one of the chairs away from the screen, scattering an empty can of beer as I do so. It smacks against the operating table and comes to rest in the dark stain. Gaylord ignores it and places his hands on his non existent hips. Even though it's cool in here there are sweat stains beginning to form under the armpits of his light suit. Gaylord is never far from sweat.

I glance at the jars but my eyesight isn't good enough to make out detail. Some seem filled with nothing but water, some have lumps of something floating in them. A few are stuffed to the gills, but with what?

The bottom shelf is a sealed unit. A box as long as the shelf and a foot high. It's made of metal and has a row of small doors along the front, each stickered. Below the box there's a larger coil of cable; it looks like a mains quality.

I'm none the wiser as to what I'm looking at.

Gaylord seems happy to let me take it all in. He's easy with the gun although I doubt he'll use it. He won't be putting any holes in me if I've become useful due to the death of the man at the window. That doesn't mean I can make a break for it. In my experience, people with guns are liable to forget things in the heat of the moment. Things like not pressing the trigger.

Gaylord sways, using his enormous weight to roll his upper half around his midriff. He's easing the pain and he's only been on his feet a few minutes. Here's a man who lives to sit.

He crunches his shoulders. 'So we have time for a quick chat, then it's time we were going. You nearly missed us. Another hour and we would have been gone.'

'You own this place?'

'Not as such. A company that owns a company that owns a company owns this and we own the company that owns the company that owns that company. Passable deniability.'

I figure I may as well go for broke. 'Project Dynamite.'

He rotates his belly as far as sinew, tissue, muscle and fat will allow. 'Now where did you get that gem? I heard a rumour that a few of the Dark Web types got close to you up in the wild. I wonder? Did they have any documentation with them?'

I say nothing. His smile widens. 'Of course they did. That note. The redacted one. Careless really. None of the files were to be released but someone fucked up. Anyway it's next to useless. Although...' He pauses. 'Although it got you here. Pretty impressive given that I saw the document and decided it was harmless. Saying that... Dynamite, Nobel, Ardeer Point – maybe I'm the dumb one. What I'm also amazed at is that you've not fought a little harder to get this far before. You must know that you're part of something much bigger.'

'Dynamite?'

'Dynamite. A project that should have been another classic waste of time and money. Like so many nutcase projects. A lot of hokum and speculation. As bad as distant viewing or Project Bluebook or any of the other files that we tipped billions into only to come up with a fat zero. A stupid thought that turned out to be a long-term bet that, despite our best efforts to screw it up, came off – at least some of it came off.'

'Can we have the English version of the story? I don't speak bollocks.'

'Have you heard of Oswald Avery, and his associates Colin MacLeod and Maclyn McCarty?'

'Heard of them. And a man called Cirus Mandley.'

'You are now impressing the hell out of me. Cirus is not a well-known figure. Where did you come across his name?'

I realise I should have said nothing. I need to let Gaylord do the running but he's getting on a raw nerve that I have reserved for people I really don't like. 'They were on a file.'

'I never saw that file. Strange. So you know something about their work?'

I decide to play dumb. I shake my head. 'Nothing more than

the names.'

He tells me more or less what Charlie found out. He skips some of the story but when he gets to Cirus's recruitment I begin to learn new stuff.

'Cirus was no genius. He wasn't even that clued in. The whole hamster thing was on the right track but vague. His work stalled as he couldn't put Mandleman's work and his together. Then, as always happens, focus changed and the project was about to be iced until a senator from my hometown got wind of it. He wasn't as easily put of and managed to draw enough finance from the war effort – which by then was going our way – to keep it alive.

He brought in a few more experts. The upshot was that there was a clear and direct connection between DNA and what Mandleman called aura. Such a direct line that had we been smarter, or maybe braver, we could have made the breakthrough a few years earlier. As it was, the war was heading for Hiroshima and programmes that were once a matter of urgency were now ones of only mild interest.'

Gaylord was enjoing himself. All the better for me. He rattles on. 'The experts unpicked Cirus's work and what became clear was that certain individuals on this planet have a direct influence on others. But in a way that has nothing to with any of our understanding of how the world works. Like you, Craig, it seems that there is a subgenre of the human race with the sort of abilities that place them closer to the Fantastic Four than you would believe.'

I believe it alright. How else do I explain Martyn and me? 'So I'm a genetic next generation?'

Gaylord laughs. 'With a little help from some of the best minds in the world. Without a little intervention you would have just cruised through life wondering why you were always at the center of fights. It took a lot of scientists a lot of time and effort to get you to where you are today.'

'To where I am today? What...a freak?'

'An experiment that was needed to take us to where we wanted to be.'

'An experiment! I'm a fucking experiment?'

He places his hands out, plams up. 'Calm down. I'm telling it as it is. A grunt in the US army that happened to show the traits we wanted and was willing to participate in a few experiments for his country.'

'I signed off on nothing.'

'Not what my brother says. He has a document, official as hell, with your signature at the bottom.'

'I'm sure he does, but I didn't sign squat.'

'Are you sure on that?'

I sit back. And I'm not. At many points in the recent past I could have easily signed off on anything and remembered nothing. 'But it all failed.'

'No, it just didn't work the way we expected.'

'*We*? You didn't even know about this 'til a year ago.'

'True, but if you're ever wondering who *they* are then I am now one of *them*. And as one of *them* I can lay some claim to the work – given it's now my baby.'

'Tampoline put you in charge of this whole thing?'

'Of course. It was one of my conditions for not revealing a few of his darker secrets that could sink an otherwise-promising presidential candidacy.'

Putting the two brothers in a room together is perhaps my all-time number one screw-up. And that takes a little doing when you look at my history. 'Get to the meat.'

Gaylord checks the door and, satisfied that no one is about to rush in, collapses into the leather office chair. It groans as if it's going to expire. 'Better. So we have all the pieces of the puzzle but nowhere near the technology to put them together. For a start we needed to decode the human genome and that wasn't going to happen anytime soon. But we did know one thing. We knew that somewhere in the DNA of some very bad people – and some good ones – lay the secret to unlocking Mandleman's aura. So with little to do but wait for technology to catch up we did what was required.'

Replication possible but technology not available. Maybe ███████ years. Recommend annual revisit as tech unfolds.

The line from the file comes back to me. So they had the path but not the light to follow it. 'So what did our illustrious forefathers do?'

'This.' He waves a chubby arm at the shelves.

I follow his limb and look at the rows of containers. 'Ok, I give in. What in the hell are they?'

'You could say "*who* in the hell are they" and not be far from the truth.'

'Who?'

# Chapter 34

Gaylord makes no move to stop me as I approach the shelf to take a closer look. Things are a bit creepier than they first appear. The upper row of containers are mostly liquid – but not water. The occasional bubble rises and the slow speed of ascent suggests something more viscose. Floating in each jar are slivers of tissue. Some look like raw meat. Some like strings of badly cured bacon. The next row of containers down has more substantial content. Still meat but larger lumps. A few fill the jar and look like organs, but I'm no doctor and I can't tell what they might be.

It's the row below that freaks me. The jars are darker, the glass coloured brown, and I have to bend in close to see what's inside. I pick one and examine it. At first I can only make out shapes but no real structure, then my eyes adapt and I fly back.

Gaylord laughs.

There's a head in the jar. A full human head. 'What the fuck?'

'Much what I said when I first got here. Makes everyone jump.'

I stand back. It's now clear that the rest of the row is a parade of more heads. Flesh, eyes, hair – the works.

Gaylord is still laughing. 'Recognise anyone?'

I back off further. My first and only thought is Lorraine. The bastard would take pleasure in that. If Lorraine is there I don't want to know. I don't want to even go there. Then again, if she's there, preserved, hair still blonde will her eyes still be the magnet they once were? Her eyes could drown a man and her smile…well her smile was an illegal weapon in some states. I take a step, half an inch, no more and stop. Lorraine. My Lorraine. Her head. Here. God, please no. God, please yes. The last thought slips in. I waver. Gaylord just sits.

I so want to look. I so need to. I take another half inch off the distance between me and the jars. I don't do this voluntarily. I do it because somewhere, deep inside, I want to see her again. I want to touch her again. To be with her again. But this is wrong. Why would she be here? What has she to do with this other than being in the wrong place at the wrong time? She had no powers. She was not even a person of interest until I came along.

Charlie killed her. In front of me. When I was tied down. As I did what I do when I didn't want to do it. Throwing out the electric charge that sent Charlie into killer mode. Caused him to lift her head – the head that might be sitting in one of the jars. Took it in his hands and dropped it on the edge of a metal bed. Taking away the one thing I loved.

Not Charlie. Me. I did it. I did that awful thing. They were Charlie's hands but I was guilty. I can feel tears rising. Is she there? An inch this time. The heads are coming into focus. Now I know what lies within each container; it's easy to see the shape. I keep my eyes on the one I first saw. Because it didn't have blonde hair. It definitely didn't have blonde hair. Lorraine's blonde hair. Would it still be the gold that shone in the sun? Or a dim reminder of when stroking it was the only thing I wanted to do? Another inch and I stop.

'Go on.' Gaylord is enjoying this. 'I'm sure you might recognise a few.'

*A few*? Not one but a few. Who else could be here? If it's genetic – my mom? My dad? My grandparents? I stagger. Is this the McIntyre clan's final resting place? Did every cremation – every burial – proceed with no head. It's all to do with DNA, but there was no technology that could unravel it back then. So what better way to prepare for the future than to harvest the DNA of those who might have had Mandleman's aura?

'Gaylord.' I turn. 'Who are they?'

'I told you. Look for yourself.'

'And see who?'

'Who do you think you'll see?' He pauses and snooks his head to one side a little. 'Oh my dear boy. You have nothing to worry out. Your wife. Is that it?' He sees in my eyes that he's hit a homer. 'Oh no. Far from it. What would she have to do with this? I'm sorry about what happened to her. I truly am. I wasn't there but I heard. Awful but I assure you she is not amongst the rogues gallery in front of you.'

'Then who?'

'Look.'

So I do.

★

The arc lights above don't help. They cast shadows, obscuring the containers' contents. I return to the one I first looked at. Prepared to back off at the fist sign of recognition. Gaylord is not beyond lying. *So* not beyond it.

The face comes into focus. A man. Bearded. A thick moustache adorns his top lip. His hair is black, rich and curly. He has – had – acne and it still moon-craters his face, but he's not young. Fifties, maybe older. The eyes are hard to see. The darkness of the glass and the shadow hide them and they are little but pools of dark. I study the features but there is no instant recognition.

I move to the next one. Eastern features. Dark hair, neatly cut, almost a quiff. A bloated face with dropping jowls and bad teeth. I lean back a little. I've seen this face before. I study it more. The lips curl down at the edges. Something off about the upside down smile. A bubble rises through the liquid and ripples along the skin. I notice the eyebrows finish well before the edge of the eyes.

'Well?'

I ignore him.

I try the next one. And now I freeze. This face I know. Not

personally, but I've seen it enough times in pictures and on TV to recognise it. Another quiff – only tighter and neater. Another thick moustache but this time with no beard to balance it out. A single, heavy wrinkle in the skin under each side of the nostrils, leading out to the edges of the mouth. Still no detail in the eyes, but there is no need for eyes.

'Gaylord. That's fucking Stalin.'

'Well done.'

I look again. 'Either him or someone who looks a hell of a lot like him.'

Gaylord shifts some bulk. 'The real thing. Next to him is Pol Pot. Have a look at the others.'

I can't help myself. I go back one and...yes, it could be Pol Pot. I mean what the fuck?

There are maybe ten more. The face to the right of Stalin could be Eastern European but means nothing. The next is vaguely familiar and the next... Well, the next stops my lungs working. My heart leaps. A physical leap. A real Jesse Owens jump. It even considers stopping. I stare. I stare at the damage to the head. I look at the devastation. Most of the top half is missing. But none of that matters. Or maybe it does. What's left is more than enough.

I stagger back. 'Shit. That's John F Kennedy.'

'It is that. Told you that not all your fellow genetic partners were bad. We have more, but not all are here. Only the real candidates made it this far.'

'John F Kennedy. You have the head of John F Kennedy.'

'And some.'

I scan the rest. I recognise two more. Mao Tse Tung and an evangelist preacher from the southern states who used to be a regular on God TV.

I look at the locked box below. 'And who the fuck is in there? Jesus?'

'Now him we would have liked, but we didn't get started on the collection 'til way too late for that.'

'Gaylord, what's in the other jars?' I point to the ones above.

'Al Capone's kidney is in there. Top shelf, third from the right. Herbert Hoover's liver is on the second shelf and Marilyn Monroe's breast tissue. Just above JFK. Kind of appropriate.'

I can think of a lot of words for what sits in this room but *appropriate* is not one of them. 'Do you know what you have here?'

'My dear boy, let's forget the historic value of this collection. Dead people are dead people.'

'Elvis?'

'Second shelf, third from the right. His spleen.'

He's enjoying this. I touch the Elvis jar and can't help thinking what the world would think of just this jar. 'How in the hell did you get all this? I mean how do you get the head of the president of the United States of America? Who stole Elvis's spleen? I mean...how?'

'Amazing what can be achieved when you put your mind to it. It wasn't easy. I don't know a tenth of it. My grandfather was clued in.'

'Your grandfather?'

The senator was saved the project. Do you think my brother is the first politician in the family?'

'The first called Tampoline.'

'True, but my grandfather was on my mom's side. Aldus Trent.'

I've heard of him. 'Didn't he try for president?'

'Got rolled by the party. Back then, indiscretions were more accepted than today – easier to hide – but my grandfather had rather more than even the political establishment could keep under wraps.'

'Runs in the family.'

He doesn't rise to the bait. 'So what do you think?'

'Think? I think this is one of the sickest things I've ever seen. These are people. Ok, famous people. But people. People who had families.'

'Stalin, Pol Pot – are you serious? Who cares about their families? Ok, I'll give you JFK, Marilyn and Elvis – and a few others – but we lost a lot of good men and women fighting some of those other bastards. If they can help us in death, all the better. And if I were to go back and ask the others – the good guys – would they mind? I can bet the answer would be no. Why would they? You're looking at this the wrong way. If this all pans out, every one of them – and more – will help us take a giant leap forward.'

'By creating chaos.'

'By doing it before others do. I'd love to think we were the only ones on this trail. In our world secrets have a habit of leaking to the very people you want them kept from. This might be a collection to rival any but it sure as hell isn't the only one. We know of at least two other countries with an interest in this area. I don't want to be the one who loses in overtime. You know what you can do. What do you think an army of Craig McIntyres could do? It's my job to see that we're first.'

'And what's next? Why am I now part of the plan again? Haven't you worked out the kinks yet? Where's your army?'

Gaylord rises from the chair. It takes a few seconds for him to manipulate his bulk. The chair sighs a deep one as he vacates the leather. 'It takes time to work it all out. We're still on the starting line. And, if you were version 1.1, I'd say we were just about to launch the beta version of 2.0. Or we were until you terminated fifty percent of the output.'

'I love the way you talk about "output". We're people.'

'Sure. Anyway, your arrival is opportune. A little bit of surgery and you'll be good to go.'

# Chapter 36

I hear the word *surgery* and look at the mini operating theater without meaning to. 'Surgery?'

'Of course. We've improved the whole process a little since your drug days. Compare it to heart surgery when Barnard started. I'd rather go under the knife today.'

With his girth I'm not sure that day is too far away.

I look to the door. 'Sure. I'm all up for that. Could you fix my nose while you're at it? Always was a bit crooked.'

'Sure thing, old boy. Anything else?'

He's serious. 'Why? What in the hell could you need from me?'

'Proof of concept. It seems that my brother is having the devil's own time gaining traction for what we're doing. Oversight committees and a new eye on finance makes funding these projects a lot harder since the recession rolled over the country. But my brother has a view that if we can demonstrate real worth we can open a bottomless pit of cash. So I dipped into my own pocket. In the main it keeps him clean and allows me to pull the strings. I simply need a plausible, high-profile demonstration and away we go.'

'And this demonstration is?'

'Right here in Scotland. It kind of chose itself. Once you are immersed in a culture you tend to let your mind run free amongst the local issues. And…well, let's say an opportunity came along on a tartan plate.'

He leans on the table. 'Not far from here is Faslane and Coulport – the UK's bases for the its nuclear sub fleet. We used to have a base right next door at a place called the Holy Loch, but we let it go long ago. We thought we could do without, but got it a little wrong. The British public may think that only things

British slip in and out of the local waters, but that's not strictly true. On more than one occasion we've had to make use of their facilities as we're short on friendly sites on this side of the Atlantic. At least, short on friendly sites that are equipped to the standard needed to service a nuclear sub. So, with the permission of the UK government, we have availed ourselves of the local facilities. It suited both parties when there were only two on the dance floor. But now there are three.'

'The Scots.'

'Spot on. Even after their referendum said no to them going it alone, the powers passed more of the baton to Edinburgh anyway. Defense is off the table, but not for long. The current First Minister has a hard-on for getting the nukes off Scottish soil. He's on a mission and, to be fair, looks like winning. The British government want to keep the status quo. Moving the facilities would be expensive and finding another site almost impossible. You can't believe how good the River Clyde is for this stuff.

'But there's a ray of hope. The deputy minister of Scotland is of a different view to his boss. He sees the nuclear presence as against his principles, but it employs four thousand people and probably supports five times that. His view is simpler. Let sleeping dogs lie and if, in the future, Scotland gets independence, deal with it all then. That would suit us.'

'And where do I fit in?'

'We need you to kill the First Minister of Scotland.'

*

Some things pile up in you plate like too much beef in a Brazilian restaurant. Project Dynamite, the DNA of the good and the bad and now the assassination of a foreign leader. I asked where I fit in? Like a round peg in a round hole in a round world. I'm Gaylord Butterworth's new plan. A crude one. A late addition. A star pinch hitter.

'So you've created another monster and he or she's on the way to take out the First Minister of Scotland.'

'Crude but accurate. Already under way. I just need a back up. In case we have to go for take two.'

Gaylord has let the gun go. It's sitting on the desk and he's now walking round to the front. I could take him. I'm close enough to get the gun but I need to know more. I've no interest in Scottish politics but my mother is from here and killing a political leader to prove a point isn't something I'm happy living with. 'So you tighten up a few of my screws. And if your expected outcome becomes an unexpected outcome, I take one for the team.'

'Again, crude but accurate.'

'And you have a surgeon standing by for this.' I take another look at the intended operating theater.

'Not to hand but close enough. Anyway, you may not be needed; we'll know one way or the other soon enough.'

I gesture towards the gallery of people and their parts. 'And it took all these people to hone my clones?'

'Years of research. Every one of them had aura to spare. Whether for good or bad, it made no odds. They manipulated people. They could make the weak dance, the strong bow and the gullible die. They all had it. Maybe deep down they all knew. Somewhere deep inside they suspected what they could do. Think about what even this small crew achieved in their lives. And once we knew what we were after we just had to wait and work and hope.'

'And all that work comes down to killing a foreign leader to prove what?'

'We can't afford to be second. Imagine the power of JFK racked up to eleven. Stalin on steroids. Elvis on E?'

'So all is good in the house of Fuck You, We Are Doing This For America land.'

His face loses its easy shape in an instant. 'And what would you know about that? Eh?' His voice has cracked up half an octave. 'I have more red, white and blue through me than a half-breed like you.' He slams his hand on the table. 'Enough of this crap. Time's up. What will be will be.'

Talking over, I make my move. He has left six feet between himself and the gun. More than enough. I press Nike to blocks. Take the gun in hand while still in the air. Use the table as a slide, skidding across it. On the far side I twist hard and plant my feet on the ground. Gaylord turns, but too slow.

I slide the safety to off and level the weapon. 'Say a word and I fire. It makes no odds to me. Your guys can't get in here quick enough. So we keep talking and you keep walking or you go home in a body bag. Your call.'

Gaylord gives me the sort of look I suspect he reserves for the moments he places his thousand dollar John Lobbs in a puddle. He is neither flustered nor worried. My threat seems to be about as effective as Fatty Arbuckle trying to run down a cheetah.

He stands, hands still on his invisible hips, a smile a few seconds from appearing on his Vaseline-rich lips. He isn't looking at the gun. He isn't even looking at me. His eyes are middle-distancing on something beyond the walls of the room. Fixed, watery, empty.

His gaze deepens. 'Craig, put it down.'

I have no intention of doing so. I aim a little higher, trying to increase the threat level. Gaylord isn't playing my game. He keeps his eyes fixed on the midpoint. His sway is gentle, easing the discomfort that he suffers. A tiny bead of sweat forms above his hairline and rolls down the smooth forehead beneath. The room is cool but Gaylord is a heat sink. Three hundred pounds of a heat sink. The fat round his body would insulate an Arctic research station. There's no fear in the sweat drop. Just the open faucet that Gaylord Butterworth lives with every day of his life.

The stand off is uneven. I have the gun. I have the upper

hand. He has nothing. His trump cards outside are under instructions not to come in. I could pull the trigger and still be more than ready for the shitstorm that would follow.

Gaylord keeps the swaying going. 'Just drop it. It will be easier all round. You're not going anywhere and, even if you could, what would you do? I know a lot more about what's going on than you. I can even help you – or could if you weren't so damn dumb. Shoot me. What will that get you? A dead man who knows stuff you want to know. Who else can you turn to? My brother? That'll work well. Last I talked to him his interest in you had waned to that of a fly that might need swatting. Given where we've got to with the experiments, you are no first-draft pick anymore. You aren't even on the list. So put the gun down and we can talk.'

His talk of his brother, and his lack of interest in me, has me interested. If not Tampoline who in the hell have we been running from? Why the chopper on the border? The SUV when I played bank hero? Martyn screaming at us to get moving when we met at the hotel? None of that suggested my celebrity status was diminishing. With the resources that Tampoline seems to have on tap I could have been hogtied by now. But trying to become the president of America has a way of changing your priorities.

So I'm not in his Hot 100. Maybe bubbling under, but no danger to the established acts – fundraising, glad handing, schmoozing, baby kissing, shafting your opposition, shafting your friends, shafting the PA. Though the last on that list will be out in Tampoline's case, what with his downstairs equipment being on the Permanently Disabled list.

A sound like a wet bag of cement hitting a tiled floor comes from the next room. We both turn.

Seconds later, Artie arrives at full tilt, bouncing off Gaylord in an ill-advised attempt to tackle him. Gaylord's center of gravity is so low that a JCB would have trouble shifting him. But it's enough to distract him. Artie springs up, slightly confused at the outcome of his best William Perry. Gaylord glances at me with the gun and then back to Artie.

I'm no less surprised. 'Artie, what the hell is happening?'

'I got bored and did a little rummaging in the jeep. Came up with an iPad and settled in for a game of Tetris. Got bored and went surfing On the Web. Got bored and opened up the mail programme. Do you know that someone is planning to assassinate the First Minster of Scotland, man?'

'That was on the email?'

'Yip.'

I look at Gaylord. 'Boy do you need to review your security.'

He takes up the mid-world gaze again.

I return my attention to Artie. 'And what did you find out?'

'Some guy called Terrence Madden is, as we speak, heading for Edinburgh with as weird a plan as I've ever seen.'

'Are we secure next door?' Artie nods, his concentration firmly on Gaylord.

'Then tell me what else the email said,' I prompt.

'In front of him? And by the way who is he?' Artie points at Gaylord.

'Yes in front of him. He's the guy running the show. I doubt the email contains anything he doesn't know.'

'Seems dumb to lay it all out in an email. It was buried at the bottom of a long chain. Someone forgot to take it off is my best guess. Can't think of any other reason. Anyway, the plan is simple. There's a big do. At somewhere called Holyrood. A meet and greet with the First Minister of Scotland to launch some new investment initiative to do with renewable energy. Our man, Terrence, has to show up and somehow this will cause the First Minister to flake out and try and kill his deputy. Does any of that make sense?'

'Too much sense. Go on.'

'It seems there is a bit of history between the First Minister and his deputy. They went to college together and it would seem that the current Mrs First Minister used to be the deputy's girlfriend. At least short-term girlfriend. I gather it was all a bit messy. Political astuteness meant the two love rivals had to team up but the bad blood it caused is well known? Terrence is going to take advantage of this.'

'I thought you were trying to get rid of the First Minister.' I look at Gaylord. 'If he kills the deputy then your plan is shot; and if the deputy kills the First Minister I can hardly see them electing him as the next leader of the country.'

Gaylord keeps up the gaze.

Then it clicks. 'Ah but it doesn't matter. Not really. Either way you get rid of the current First Minster. Either way you prove your new Mark 2 model of me works. I assume the third in line for the throne is on your side as well.'

'She's married to the ex-Ambassador for the United States in London.'

'And when is all this supposed to happen?'

Artie pipes up again. 'That's why I moved. Today. Or rather, later tonight.'

'Artie, I've seen enough. Let's destroy this stuff and get the hell out of here.'

'What *is* this stuff?' He walks over to the shelves. There's just enough time for him to take one breath and then... 'Man, do you know who that is?'

He's at JFK's jar.

He spins round. 'Fuck. You can't destroy that. Is it really him? If it's really him... I mean, shit... I mean. Shit, I don't know what I mean.'

He starts to study the rest of the items. After a few more 'Fucks' and 'Mans' I realise he's right. God knows it's abhorrent and I don't give a shit about Stalin or Pol Pot or the other nutters. But who else is there? Is Marlyn's breast tissue or Elvis's spleen of value? Who knew they still existed? But if this lot went up in smoke who would know? Except me, Artie and Gaylord. I scan the shelves. I wave my hand at them. 'Gaylord, who else is there?'

'The who's who of recent history. There's even a bit of Hitler in there. Top shelf...' Gaylord has found his smile again.

'Stop. I don't care.'

Artie keeps scanning the macabre collection. 'Man, you can't trash this lot. I've no idea what in the hell you would do with it, but it's not our call.'

'Artie, no one knows they are here. Or at least no one who is going to say anything.'

'That's not the point. These are pieces of real people. They deserve respect. What would Fox News make of this being fire-bombed? Who else is here?'

Gaylord rhymes of a few others. All goodies. All designed to stop me trashing the joint.

Artie stares in disbelief. 'Elvis, a Pope, Charlie Chaplin – man you can't, you really can't.'

'And what do you suggest?'

'Leave it. Whatever it is they needed they've already got. This is now a museum piece. If they want to nuke it let them take the consequences, but I'm not going down in history as the guy who fried JFK's head. No way, man.'

And, of course, he's right. 'Ok, so we don't destroy it all. But we need to put this guy' – I nod towards Gaylord – 'and the others out of action.'

'And then what?'

'Well, if we are prepared to save the flesh of the dead I think it's our duty to try and save the living. We need to stop the assassination.'

# Chapter 38

Artie and I tie up Gaylord before moving all the crew into the Ripley's museum. We find water, a bucket and some food. They'll get free, at some point, but it will take a while. By then we will either have succeeded or failed.

Martyn is groggy but can stand. We exit. We'll take the jeep. It's not the warmest way to travel. Even after stripping the Ripley's visitors of warm-weather gear it will be a cold ride in an open top vehicle.

Artie shovels some heavyweight stuff from the garage up against the door but I stop him. 'They'll just smash their way out the front windows. Don't waste time.'

It takes us four attempts to find where we came in amongst the dunes. The way we walked is not wide enough for the Jeep so we need to backtrack. By the time we find our way down onto the beach the sun is already gone.

'What time is the reception?' I have to shout to be heard above the roar of the wind and engine. Artie is driving. Martyn is recovering in the back seat. I'm on map duty.

Artie shouts back. 'Eight o'clock. We have three hours.'

I flick the map to find Irvine. Then I find our goal. It looks doable but I don't know the local roads. A mile of time on a highway can be ten on a back road. I work out a route. I try and use the main roads but I'm conscious that an open-top Jeep on a highway in winter is nuts.

Artie is negotiating a traffic circle. The concept is alien to him and he draws a long blast of a horn from a small, blue compact.

I study the map some more. 'I think I know what they're trying to do but I can't believe that anyone will believe us. Hell I'm not even sure we'll get near the place.'

'And if we do stop it? What then?'

'That's such a good question that I'll leave it for another day.'

We hit a double-lane blacktop and Artie pushes the speed of the Jeep up a notch. The wind whips heat away like a blast freezer. I huddle down, playing with the heating controls in a vain attempt to overcome the Scottish weather.

What have I leaned? That I'm the result of some misguided attempt to harness a power that lingers in some really bad (and good) people. And this helps how? What was I expecting? A hell of a lot more than this. I'm little more than another attempt by a government to gain an edge on the opposition. What do I now know that helps me? What can I do with the information? Maybe crash the Internet and spread a little chaos? Then again, where's the proof, short of handing myself in.

I could take Martyn and myself and book a slot on prime time TV. Then what? Watch people kill each other? It would make for a hell of a ratings bonanza but then we'd be locked up. On what charge? I'm sure they would find one. Camp X-Ray might be a good option. I'm a threat to the security of the nation. A clear and present danger. And would it stop what's going on? Would Tampoline and Gaylord stop experimenting? Hell no! Not if they really believe other countries are on the same journey. If I went on TV they would probably have all the funding they've ever dreamed of!

We sling onto a highway. The cold takes another bite. The scenery is bare. Winter-drawn. Frost is hard on the fields. I drop down even lower to tamper with the non-existent heating again.

My focus is on the game at hand: keeping this guy Terrence away from Scottish politics. Fix that and then work out what comes next. Why? Because it saves a life and might set back Tampoline and Gaylord's plans. No proof of concept – no funding. That's the way to nail the bastard.

We aim for the main highways – blue on our map. It looks

as is we should be able to make it most of the way on those, at least after the first few miles. It seems the most straightforward route, even if it's not the most direct, and we don't have time to get lost along the way.

It's two lanes all the way to the outskirts of Glasgow, where the highway suddenly becomes the sort of twelve-lane monster that reminds me of LA. Somehow we negotiate the confusion and soon we join a necklace of slow-moving red lights – home birds seeking shelter – as we exit the built-up area.

'How far?' shouts Artie.

It's half an hour since we lost the lights of Glasgow. I'm amazed Artie can drive. He must be sub-zero.

I check the odometer, then the map. 'I'd say five miles. We are on the edge of Edinburgh but it looks like a maze to me from here on in.'

Martyn stirs. 'I hear they do a mean festival.'

He's still weak but I need him. In fact I'm counting on him.

My prediction on a maze is not short of the mark. Edinburgh seems designed to keep cars on another planet. It takes an hour of wrong turns and unexpected encounters with trams before we find a parking space. Even then, it's not only illegal but also dangerous. But who cares. It's not our car. I doubt a getaway is going to be needed.

We exit the jeep with a castle looking down on us. An imposing structure perched on dark gray rock high above our head. I check the map. We join the pedestrians to walk the last mile or so.

Edinburgh is history in your face. Every building seems older than my home state. The castle keeps up its dominance, only bowing to monuments and hotels when they hide it from view. We walk over a bridge that looks down on to a railway station. Then we head down, and away from the mases. The road we're on is loaded with mid-rise buildings that are separated by alleys straight out of Victorian mystery novels. Down any one of them you could murder six locals and no one would notice. Probably worth a visit, but we're not here as tourists.

When we hit some police barriers we know that we are close to our destination. People are being channeled away from a building if they don't have passes. But then, by a strange quirk of Scottish logic, you can circle the main entrance and come at it from the other side.

We are in no way dressed for what's going down. Worse still, we have no idea what Terence looks like.

I tap Artie on the shoulder. 'Artie, was there a description of this guy Terrence?'

'None.'

'I'm betting he's American.'

'Why?' Martyn is now fully in the land of the living.

'I'm wagering a silver dollar that this is all in-house. I'm betting Terrence is ex-military. Or at least in some form of militia. You and I are good examples. Gaylord and Tampoline are looking for control. They won't get that from non-nationals. This is a big ask. Even if you can do, what I can do you need to want to be here. They tried to force me to do something similar once and it went to hell in a handbasket. Why would a foreigner play ball? No, this guy is stars and stripes.'

'Renewables.' Artie's voice is a bit high. 'Your fat boy's email said renewables.'

'And?'

'That means there will be a few of the renewables companies along?'

'Like we are big on renewables,' Martyn adds.

Artie taps his head with his finger. 'We are, man. We are into it big time. Ok, so it's not Dallas, but we have a shitload of firms in this market. That will be his angle.'

'And this helps how?'

Artie scans the crowd and gives a thumbs up. He says nothing and leaves. A few policemen eye us but there are more than enough people to make us look normal.

Artie works his way back through the crowd a few moments later. 'Ok so we are now on the invite list for the do.'

I let my mouth open. A little. 'How?'

'In a previous life I used to work for a company that played in the renewables space. It was called Wave Away. A friend of a friend started it. He had some proprietary tech in turning wave action into power. It never really worked. The idea was good but the equipment has to be robust as hell and ours wasn't. Anyway he jacked it in and I was let go. But he's still into the scene. I had an idea. See the young lady across there with the clip board?' He points. 'She's with an Internet TV station called WhatsNextWhatsHot.com.'

'And you know her?'

'Seen her on TV. She doesn't know me but she knows my old boss. Ted Brace. I mentioned his name and said we were in the space, and looking to get in on the act.'

'And she gave you a pass for here?'

'No chance. Not for the political do. That's tight as a drum. She told me that no one is going inside who isn't political. But the after-show is in a place across the road called Dynamic Earth. That's where the announcement is being made. She can get us in there.'

'What's going down here?'

'The preliminaries.'

Martyn is not convinced. 'And if this guy Terrence is inside at the politics do we're screwed.'

Artie shrugs. 'Sure, but it won't matter. We're not getting in to the parliament building.'

'It won't happen there.'

They both raise eyebrows at me.

I explain. 'Gaylord will want maximum impact. That comes with TV cameras, and the TV cameras will be present for the announcement not the prelims.' I let my head do a wander. 'Artie, does your TV person know people in this world?'

'Sure.'

'If our man Terrence is a player would she know him?'

'Maybe.'

'Can you introduce me to her?'

*

'Hi, I'm Craig.'

'Hi Craig. Lucy.'

Lucy is small and looks like an old gym teacher I used to have. She's made up for TV – makeup too heavy. But under it she has the face for HD.

I start with flattery. 'Artie tells me that your channel is hot right now?'

'Nice of him to say, but there are a lot of us around. I used to know his old boss. Nice guy. Bit out of his depth but a nice guy. Artie says you're in the renewables business.'

'Wind power. I run a small outfit called Air To Charity, micro generation stuff, but with a social bent.'

'Tell more?'

'We work with charities to identify companies that could generate their own power. Large scale plants, manufacturing mostly. We sell them the idea of a wind turbine but on the premise that they give a percentage back to a local charity. It costs them a bit more but we're good at what we do, and the local charity angle helps with their CSR.'

'Sounds interesting? Where are you based?'

'New Jersey. We're only a couple of years old but things are going well.'

'Why have I never heard of you?'

'Private backer. He wants the company on its own feet before we court publicity.'

'Would you do an interview?'

'Sure, but after the gig. We didn't get much notice of this. We were in town for another meeting and just found out. Artie says you can help us get in later?'

'Sure.'

'Thanks for that. Look, we were also supposed to meet up with a potential customer. He said he would meet us at the hotel but we missed him. I think he might be here. I wonder if you might know him?'

'What's his name?'

'Terrence.'

'Terrence what?'

'There you have me. He left a message at the hotel. Said he was into renewables and had heard we were in town. He's from back home. Said he saw a blog I did on the long-term cost of wind power and would like to meet. He didn't leave a second name. But in our game any lead's worth following.'

'Sorry but I don't know any Terrence and I'm fairly sure I know all the main players, especially the ones from the States. If you know what he looks like I might be able to help.'

'A name. It's all I have.'

'I can ask around later but I need to get on with my job. See you at the do later.'

She taps the cameraman on the shoulder and trots off to the cordon. I watch as she flashes her pass.

I return to Martyn and Artie. 'Well that was a busted flush.'

We turn away. The security is too tight to contemplate trying to get in to the parliament. I can't warn anyone either. Not without sounding like a man with a day pass from the local sanatorium. The only option is to hope that Terrence is waiting it out in whatever Dynamic Earth is.

# Chapter 39

It doesn't take long. It's next to the parliament building and lords it up on top of a set of stairs; a glass and metal palace. It's lit up like Sunset Strip and there are plenty of people milling around.

'How do we get in?' I look at Artie for inspiration.

'Lucy texted someone.'

We mount the stairs to be greeted by a man with a cheap suit and scuffed shoes. He uses a tablet as a way to stop us going any further. 'Names.'

Artie steps up. 'Smith, Jones and Brown. We are with WhatsNextWhatsHot.'

He plays with the tablet. 'Lucy Corrigan?'

'That's her.'

'Ok. You need passes. On the left as you go in. You can drop your coats at the same time.'

With that we're through.

The space is bright and lively. A crowd of a hundred or more are already chowing down on snack food. Everyone seems to be guzzling the free wine as if the bar is closing in ten minutes. We pick up passes but keep our coats. A quick exit doesn't work if you have to stand in the hat-check line.

I ignore the free booze and encourage the others to copy me. Martyn looks disappointed.

I urge him on. 'Don't worry. If we can find our perp then we can all have one at the local when this is finished.'

I buttonhole a badged-up waiter, asking him when the festivities are due to begin. We have thirty minutes. I thought it would be longer. Now I just need to figure how to spot Terrence. With no description he could be anyone.

There's only one way to do this. I gather the other two in. 'Ok, I can't believe there are that many Americans in the room.

So we take a third of the room each and introduce ourselves to as many people as we can. We have thirty minutes and...' I look at the entrance where a line is beginning to form. '...I suspect that this number could double. Men only. Ignore the women. You are looking to meet a work colleague called Terrence. Listen out for the accent. If you land a compatriot and it's not Terrence, step away and raise a hand. We all do this. If we all find an American then the first one moves on but it's your job to remember where your first target is. We do this until we have covered as many people as we can in the time. If you happen to find Terrence tell him you have a friend who wants to meet him. Step away and lift both hands. Move a few yards and we rendezvous. Got it?'

With nods we set off. I start at the door, Artie at the free bar and Martyn at the far end of the room. It's far from perfect but it's the best we have.

Ten minutes in and Artie raises a hand. When he sees that we have both seen him he drops his hand and stands still. Martyn and I keep circling.

Another ten minutes and Artie is still the only one with a possible. I'm running out of people so I work my way back to the entrance to tag all the new arrivals. Then the line dries up, police move in and the front door is closed.

An entourage is making its way across the gap between the parliament building and our location. I check for Martyn. I spot him. He's still looking for Terrence but so far Artie has the only hit.

The entourage rises up the stairs. I ask a young man in a black suit, next to me, if any of them is the First Minister.

'The balding one at the front is the Deputy, the thin one with the goatee is the First Minister. The lady with the dress cut to kill is the First Minister's wife. Behind her are a few MSPs.'

'MSPs?'

'Members of the Scottish Parliament.'

'I hear there's history between the First Minister's wife and the deputy...or is that a scurrilous thing to say?'

The young man laughs. 'Talk of the steamie, as they say where I come from. Every time she comes out with her husband, and the deputy is there, the dresses seem to get tighter. She's lost a hell of a lot of weight lately. Rumor is that she is considering running for office at some point. The First Minister is losing on the popularity stakes a little. He's not on his way out but a recent poll put Helen, his wife, ten points ahead of him if she stood. She's bloody smart. She's got him where he is.'

I look at the deputy. His head is down, bald pate shining in the lights. His gut is folding over his waist band and his nose dominates his face in a way that makes him look like a Scottish version of WC Fields. 'He's no looker. What did she see in him?'

The man in the suit laughs again. 'He got her into the whole political scene in the first place. He introduced her to the First Minister and back then he wasn't as bald. Or as fat.'

I can see why she has dressed for show. To remind the First Minister that he is a lucky bastard and to let the deputy know what he is missing. I catch the deputy glancing at her legs. The look is brief but obvious. I'm not the only one who notices.

The young man nudges me. 'You can't blame him. She's a hell of a woman.'

The entrance by the entourage is low-key by US political standards.

I cross to Artie. Martyn joins us. 'So we have one possible. That makes life a bit easier. But I take it he isn't called Terrence.'

Artie has to speak loudly to be heard. The hubbub surrounding the arrival of the politicians has racked up the decibels. 'He's called Bill. I didn't get anything else.'

'I'll talk to him and try to distract him. Both of you keep an eye out. Martyn, if I signal...drop him.'

Bill is slim, with narrow shoulders that are struggling to keep his jacket up. His cheeks are sunken and his eyes are hooded by bushy eyebrows. He's standing in a crowd of three but he's playing gooseberry. The other two are in deep conversation. He seems to be showing little interest in the First Minister. At the moment he's eying up the bar; his glass is empty. He excuses himself and I move after him. He reaches the bar, gets a refill and is on his way back before I can step in. He's still showing no interest in the First Minister.

'Hi. Bill isn't it?'

'Sorry?'

I speak up. 'I said hi is your name Bill?'

'Yes, but I don't think we've met.'

'The name's Simon. I'm in the renewables game.'

'I'm not but my friend is. He said this would be fun. It's a new meaning for the word...'

His accent could be Midwest or mid anywhere. His eyes are fixed on me and not the First Minister. If he's our man he should be focused on the game and he isn't.

He steps a little closer. 'Been in the country long? Do I know you?'

'A friend pointed you out. Said he met you once.' I point at the congregation.

'Really. What's his name?'

'Douglas Ryder.'

'Doesn't ring a bell.'

'Do you live near by?'

'I live up north. I'm in the oil game. I'm a bit of a gatecrasher.'

'Douglas said you were an oil man.' It's an educated guess.

'Who does he work for?'

'He's self-employed. A consultant.'

'Maybe that's how I know him. We hire a lot of consultants. I'm the enemy to many in here but I don't care. There's room for anyone that can make energy. My company has a whole division on the case.'

'Have you always been in the oil business?'

He's still fixated on me. He actually seems glad to have found someone to talk to. The First Minister is mounting a small stage.

'Mostly. Went to college in Maryland but came over here twenty years ago. Can't dump the accent though. I married a local girl and we have a couple of kids. You?'

He's so not right for this. Married? Kids? Why in the hell would you give that in? You don't volunteer for Tampoline with a family and kids at risk. Then again, maybe he had no choice. Or he's lying.

I keep my eye on him and the First Minister. 'No kids and no wife. A loner. Did you come down just for is?'

'Hell no. I've been on vacation with my family. Just back from sunny Spain. I dropped the wife and kids off, turned right round and came down here. I'm less of a cuckoo than I let on. My firm wants me to look at a job in renewables. I came down to see if it's my world. So far, I'm bored.'

He has a tan, faint, and marks that suggest he's been wearing sunglasses all day. He could *still* be lying – it would be expected – but he has yet to look at the First Minster. Someone taps the microphone. Silence falls. Bill doesn't turn round. I think we have the wrong man. Terrence he's not. I tell him I have to go and he looks disappointed.

I rejoin the others. 'It could be him,' I whisper, 'but I doubt it. Martyn, keep an eye anyway.'

'What am I looking for?'

'No idea, but drop him if he makes any odd moves.'

'Are you sure? I'll be dead. And if it's not him – what then?'

I'm out of ideas. I examine the people nearest the stage. If I was doing this I'd want proximity. I take one last glance at Bill but he's more interested in his wine than the stage. What else would I do? If I just wanted to impact the First Minister I'm not sure I could. Then again, Terrence is second generation. Maybe he can do what I do but with the precision that Martyn can deploy.

'Ladies and gentlemen, the First Minister of Scotland.' The announcer stands down and the First Minister steps up to the microphone. He has a set of cards in his hands but ignores them as he takes in the audience. I decide to move closer.

The speech starts. 'Good evening and welcome to Dynamic Earth. An appropriate venue for tonight's event.'

I tune out. I'm looking for the unusual. People with too much interest in the ministers. But that isn't easy when everyone is looking at them. I put myself in Terence's shoes. I would want the First Minister and his deputy as close together as possible. At the moment the deputy is to the left and behind the First Minister's wife. I excuse myself forward a few more feet.

To my right, there's tall man with a feather cut. I didn't talk to him but Martyn or Artie probably did. He's flicking his eyes back and forth. First Minister, deputy and back. Or First Minister and First Minister's wife and back. It's hard to tell. A woman next to him says something and squeezes his hand. I ignore him. Couples are out.

I make my way to the edge of the stage, giving myself the best possible angle to watch the crowd. Martyn has Bill in his sights. Artie is making his way to the other side. I break from the bodies. I'm side on to the stage.

The First Minister is warming to the task. 'Our country is proud of its green credentials. We may be better known for our oil but this government has done more in the last five years to encourage renewable energy than previous governments have done in two decades.'

I zone out again. Eyes on the prize. I take in each man in the crowd, one at a time. The eyes have it. I'm looking for a look.

Any look.

'Donald and I...' The First Minister waves to his deputy to join him. '...Together we have worked to give our country an even greater focus, an even higher purpose, an even longer vision.'

Donald steps forward at the triplet.

Now. I'd go now.

My leg jackhammers forward as pain enters my life. I spin, clutching at my left thigh. My hand touches metal. I look down. Amazed. A handle sticks out of my thigh. A knife handle. A man is retreating. The angle at which he's caught me has sent me lurch towards the stage. I stumble and a security guard reacts.

The TV cameras catch the rest as my head explodes and the kernel shatters. I fall, electricity screaming from me. I feel the hate around me well up and then all I can do is collapse. My headache supernova begins to do its stuff. I catch sight of movement above me and then nothing.

# Chapter 40

I wake up. My leg is telegraphing pain but that pain is dulled by something else. I'm in a small room. It's bright and I'm lying on a sofa. I reach down and the knife wound has been bandaged. Two men sit on chairs next to me. Agency.

There's no sign of Martyn or Artie. One of the men sees me open my eyes. He leaves and the other man sits, me as his point of interest.

'What happened?' I croak.

The man says nothing. He's not here to talk. He's here to babysit.

The first guard returns. In one hand he has an iPad. In the other a glass of water. He hands me the glass. He then hands me the iPad, touches the screen and the two of them exit stage left. I stare at the tablet. I'm on Skype.

A familiar face slides into view. 'How do you feel?'

'The fuck do you care, Tampoline.' I spit the last word.

'To be expected. You may not know it but I owe you a vote of thanks and I thought I'd do it in person.'

'What happened to me?'

'Oh you performed like a star. Here have a look.'

The screen flickers as the iPad is given a new feed. The scene from Dynamic Earth appears. From the back. A long shot on a camera.

The First Minister is speaking. He has just invited his deputy forward to join him. I see myself stagger into the picture and go down. I vanish from view and the camera zooms in on the First Minister's wife. She has a stiletto in one hand. The First Minister is looking at the spot where I've fallen. Security guards swarm in to try and bundle him away. But, before they can, his wife, with balletic poetry, rises in the air and, hand in the stiletto like a glove, drives the point into her husband's neck. He jumps back. You can just make out a trail of blood misting into the air around him. A guard grabs the First Minister's wife. Chaos erupts as people run from the scene. Then the camera is knocked sideways and blacks out.

Tampoline reappears. A hand, not his, straightens the camera. He thanks the off-screen help.

His dark glasses hide some of his expression. 'I'm told the TV footage is excellent. Who knew the First Minister was playing away from home. His wife was more than loquacious on the point when asked. Of course, she has no idea what all the fuss is about. She can't remember a thing; even after seeing the film.'

I've been a dumb fuck of the first order. 'There was no Terrence – was there?'

'Never was. What gave it away?'

'Apart from being stabbed in the leg at the right moment?'

'Sorry about that but we needed your talents.'

'So give. I can tell you want to.'

'You can't guess?'

The bastard is loving this. I place my head on the arm of the sofa and angle the iPad to keep Tampoline in view. 'No Terrence probably means no next generation of me.'

'Go on.'

'So the facility at Ardeer Point is what. A fake? But why?'

Tampoline sits there.

'Am I right – the collection is a fake? No JFK? No Elvis.'

'Not quite true. We do have samples of them and more, but only small blood or tissue samples. It was Gaylord's idea to ham it all up a bit.'

'What for?'

'Guess?'

I think I can. 'For my benefit?'

'And for the visit of a few well chosen political heavyweights who needed to see where the money was going. JFK was the clincher. I gather their faces were a picture.'

'They all bought it?'

'With your file and Martyn's it was easy. We just needed to show we had moved on. Every black ops outfit needs cash and we were running thin.'

I adjust my leg. I'll need some painkillers soon. 'But if there's no Terrence then you're no further on.'

'Not quite true. Ok, so creating a new version of you and Martyn has been a lot tougher than we thought.'

'And all that bullshit about Mandleman's aura?'

'Not bullshit at all. It's where it all started. You are a product but a rare example. You, Martyn and a few others are the only ones that we have had any success with.'

Others? He can't see the surprise on my face and keeps going. 'We're on the right track but it's hard and damn expensive.'

'I thought your brother was bankrolling it all.'

'Even he's finding it a cash-eater. The science is all at the frontier of the frontier and we can't tap up the usual help. Colleges, universities the like. We've had to fund all the primary research. It's not been cheap. But we'll get there.'

'So you needed me to give your funding credentials a boost.'

'No one knows it was you. How could they? We got you out of there with speed.'

'Thanks. And I could have turned the whole thing into a bloodbath. So who stopped me? How did *you* stop me?'

'Martyn.'

'He's in on this?'

'Absolutely not. He just saw what was going down and acted. If he hadn't we would have. He did us a favour. Our men couldn't get to you quickly enough. A few moments more and maybe it would have been beyond their control.'

'So all of this was a set up.'

'What do you think?'

'Why not just lift me and fly me in? You've done it before.'

'And you would have cooperated?'

'No.'

'And we would have had to control the whole thing. Bodies on the ground. People talk. This way the only people who know are me, my brother and a few grunts.'

'So the guys from the Dark Web?'

'Patsies, designed to get that file to you.'

'And you figured I'd bite.'

'Was there ever any doubt?'

There wasn't. 'So we weren't being pursued?'

'Not as such. I had to keep an eye on you but this was all soft touch.'

'There was a helicopter up in the Canadian border?'

'Yes. A pain in the fanny. We lost you. I was sure you would turn up but I needed to know for certain. When they found you they were told to back off.'

And here was me thinking I had fooled them. I track back over the last few days. 'Your goons were at the hotel in Toronto?'

'For effect. We needed Martyn with you. I expected you to go on the treasure hunt, but not with Martyn. He was a bonus. We even ensured he got on the flight from New York to Toronto.'

'Why not just pick him up?'

'You still don't get this. There's an order to these things. Prove we have made progress, reignite the funding and then you and Martyn are fair game. Without the funding you are both interesting but useless. Once we – strike that – *you* had demonstrated that we had this thing under control then we could have picked Martyn up.'

'Where is he now?'

The silence tells all.

I have to smile. 'He's on the run.'

'Not for long.'

'And Artie?'

'With Martyn. By the way who is he?'

'You don't know?'

'He's not one of my team. In fact he's a bit below the radar. We have a photo but little else.'

'He's nothing. A man who wanted to help.'

'What? To cross the Atlantic and break into a top secret establishment?'

When put like that he had a point. Without Artie we would have been dead in the water long ago. His motivation is a mystery. Why go to such lengths for a complete stranger? For a moment, just when Tampoline was talking about the order of things, I had a suspicion that, just maybe, Artie was all part of his plan. I had danced to Tampoline's tune easily enough and Artie was an obvious plant, in retrospect. Although, with Tampoline in bragging mode, it's hard to fathom why he would lie about not knowing him.

I return to the iPad. 'So you had us tracked the whole way?'

'I knew you were on your way to Ardeer Point. It was just a matter of waiting.'

'And what if I had turned up well after the First Minister's event in Edinburgh?'

'It would have made no difference. There would have been other opportunities. His diary is – was – full. Plenty of other ways to get you in front of him.'

'We only got into Dynamic Earth by luck?'

'The Internet TV lady. I heard. Even if your friend hadn't known her you would have been let in.'

'And the email Artie found. Planted.'

'My brother is so dumb for someone so smart. There was no need. He would have told you what you wanted but he wanted to make you believe that you had found it all out yourself. I'd have thought an unlocked iPad with the details of an attempted assassination might have raised your antennae a little?'

It did and I am beginning to lose faith in my own judgment. When Artie ran into the room with the story I bought it without considering the source. An open iPad with an email laying out the whole plan? Really? What was I thinking?

'You said was?'

'Pardon?'

'You said the First Minister's diary *was* full.'

'He resigned. No choice really. It's hard to carry on when your wife has publically tried to murder you. And even harder when the press have found out you're having an affair. If things go well the deputy will get the job in the next few weeks.'

'So you got what you wanted?'

'I usually do. Funding, a friendly foreign politician in place and the opportunity to get to the root of the conundrum that is Craig McIntyre.'

'And that means what?'

'Well, back in the safety of home, we have a whole bunch of newly-salaried-up scientists eager to probe your secrets.'

'So I'm not walking out of here?'

'You're not walking anywhere. You'll take a nap and wake up in a new, comfortable bed.'

The connection is broken and my two guards return.

One is carrying a needle.

# Chapter 41

It's Tuesday or it could be Saturday. A light mist is damping the countryside. Wild and barren, the land around me is devoid of trees and heavy on rocks. Even on a clear day there are no hills or mountains to give depth to the world. Behind me a small stone-built farmhouse squats. A broken, shingled roof does its best to keep the weather out. Peeling window frames hold single panes of glass. A few are broken, but not too many.

I'm sitting on a crooked, wooden bench. It's where I sit when I'm allowed outside, which isn't often. I'm dressed in a pair of old 501s, oversized walking boots, a Jerseys tee and a thick Shetland knit pullover. When it's colder I have the use of a padded Helley Hansen jacket that smells of fish.

So far things have been slow. When I first came to my new home I feared major exploratory surgery. So far I've done little but watch scratched DVDs and read battered novels. I've been examined a billion times but noithing more. The farmhouse is a blind. The real gig is beneath the old building. I've only seen a fraction of the complex. I was told that the main entrance is over seven miles away – all seven miles being underground.

The compound is white on white, a sterile world, run on air conditioning and bleach. I have infrequent visitors. Tampoline called on a video link once but had little to say. My food is fed through a slot in the door. When I'm let out the door lock clicks and I can use a set of stairs at the end of the corridor to access the farmhouse. If I walk too far from the building a man appears with a rifle. I've yet to test how far he'll let me walk.

I've been here a few months. I kept a check on the time for a while, marking the days on the edge of a desk that sits in my room. I stopped one day and never started again. I'm sure that the room and the rest of the white world is under constant supervision but, even so, it just says a lot about what they want from me. I thought it would all be rush and dash. Get to the source of my power as quickly as possible. In reality the pace is more sedate than a home for the bewildered.

I'm keeping myself fit. There's no gym but I asked for a pair of sneakers one day. Just said the words out loud. The next morning a used pair of Nikes was lying outside my door when it clicked open. They're a size too large but extra socks take care of that. I can jog round the farmhouse or use the corridors around my room when the weather is bad, which it seems to be more often than not.

Water is on tap and there's a small shower in one corner of my room. The sheets and bedclothes are changed while I'm up top. I've never seen anyone do it though.

At first I tried a burst of screaming and shouting – threats and demands. Nothing happened. I began to realise that it helped if I was more specific about what I wanted. Hence the TV, DVD player, DVDs and books. I asked for a lot of other things but the responses seem random.

I have started an escape committee in my head, although the only route out is fairly obvious. With a rifle appearing when I test the limit, my options are narrow.

★

I was moved today. No great ceremony. I had just headed up for some air and found an old jeep sitting next to my bench. The driver pointed to the rear seat. A second jeep appeared from behind the farmhouse to trail us from a distance. I wondered if I could set off an event but both vehicles were driven solo. I'd give odds he drivers don't know each other.

We bumped across the landscape until we hit a gravel track. Then we skipped past a few old tin sheds. Some cattle dotted the horizon. So now I'm in a new home. It's much like the last only it isn't beneath the earth. This one is in a dilapidated factory, brick built with a tall chimney at one end. No one comes to see me in my new cell. The door still clicks and I still walk out. I explore a little but my friend with the rifle has come along for the ride.

I find a new spot to sit, next to a brick outhouse. The building keeps off the wind. With the noise at bay I can hear the distant sound of a fair-sized highway nearby.

My new home is different. Same white walls, but I've been in enough hospitals to recognize the smell of clinical disinfectant. I suspect my time under the knife has arrived.

This puts things back in perspective. The last few months have lulled me into a sense of depressed resignation. The lack of urgency, the solitude and relative calm have made me wonder if I really am of major interest. Even Tampoline's luke warm chat at the start indicated that whatever it was that they wanted from me could wait. Perhaps my day has passed.

Now, the smell alone makes me fear for the near future. I have to pull myself from this stupor and…and do what? Run.

Another jeep roars up. Only this one is occupied by two people. Suddenly taking chances? The man with the rifle appears. He isn't looking in my direction. He's much more interested in the jeep. I'm half hidden from the vehicle and, when the passenger jumps out, I have to grab my jaw to stop it mowing the grass. 'Charlie?'

A bullet smacks into the wall next to me.

Charlie is running back to the jeep. 'Get the fuck in!'

I don't need to be asked twice. I sprint for the vehicle and vault in. I try to sound casual as I greet the driver. 'Hi Martyn.' He places all his weight on the accelerator.

Charlie turns to me. 'We have one chance and this is it.'

Another bullet sparks the side of the jeep.

I have questions but they'll wait – hanging on for grim life is the order of the day. We bound across the ground. As far as I can tell, we're making for the highway. I look behind, expecting to see an emerging flotilla of pursuers but even the man with the rifle is gone.

The jeep hits a rise and, as we crest the summit, the highway comes into view. It's heavy with traffic and snakes towards a town. Martyn plunges us down the other side of the hill.

He slides us to a halt as we reach the edge of the blacktop. 'In there.'

Sitting on the side of the road is a powerful-looking Range Rover.

'Charlie, this isn't the same one we…?' Even before he shakes his head I realise he's sitting on the wrong side.

'Nope, just the best tool for this particular job.'

Martyn takes point and we bound onto the highway.

The End